PRAISE FOR

NEW YORKED
BY ROB HART

"Apparently an adept at the noir genre somehow created the literary version of *The Warriors*. I have never savored so many seeds in a 'seedy underbelly,' and when Hart finishes his next book, I am buying it instantly."
—Lyndsay Faye, author of *The Gods of Gotham*

"Now that even farthest Brooklyn has yuppie bankers up in its business, it's nice to be reminded this city still has places only the dead and Rob Hart know. The New York of *New Yorked* is a place of heartbreak and murder that I highly recommend you visit."
—Josh Bazell, author of *Beat the Reaper*

"One part Dennis Lehane, one part Lee Child, and one part pure Rob Hart, *New Yorked* is a dark, gritty love story to its eponymous city, and to one lost girl, which blends both mystery and romance while turning the two genres into something altogether new."
—Jenny Milchman, author of *Cover of Snow* and *Ruin Falls*

"In Rob Hart's urban picaresque, New York is a verb and the chase is on. You won't be able to turn the pages fast enough. Add an epic love story to the mix and an insider's cunning wit, and you'll be panting breathlessly, waiting for whatever Hart cooks up next."
—Suzy Vitello, author of *The Moment Before*

"Clever, witty, full of attitude—but never full of itself, Rob Hart's debut novel doesn't waste a syllable kick-starting its story then letting it rip off into the darker corners of the greatest metropolitan fever dream on earth."
—**David Corbett, author of** *The Devil's Redhead*

"With a deft eye for the dirt under its polished fingernails, Rob Hart finds the rotten core inside today's Big Apple—a city that many people think is too clean, too safe to be home for any modern crime fiction. In *New Yorked*, Hart proves them wrong in spectacular fashion. A debut that echoes Richard Price at his best."
—**Todd Robinson, Anthony Award-nominated author of** *The Hard Bounce* **and editor of** *Thuglit*

"*New Yorked*, Rob Hart's debut novel, brings New York to life with the skill of a seasoned author in full possession of his craft; the voice raw, the prose stripped down, and a story that hits you like a sucker punch to the guts before you turn the first page."
—**Matthew McBride, author of** *A Swollen Red Sun* **and** *Frank Sinatra in a Blender*

"Ash McKenna is a noir hero with a difference. He establishes his Hammett-Chandler bloodline at once...There are good action scenes, nice offbeat characters, but what lingers is the swoony dialogue...Noir with a tingle of doomed but sweet romance."
—*Booklist*

"Edgy...relentless pacing and strong sense of place"
—*Publishers Weekly*

To my grandmother, Anna.
Part of me thinks she wouldn't have liked this book.
But one of her favorite shows was HBO's Oz, *so who knows?*
Regardless, she would have been proud, and I'm sorry she isn't
here to read it.

"Most cities are nouns; New York's a verb."

—John F. Kennedy

ONE

SHARP CRACK AND I'm awake.

Whiskey-colored sunlight spills across my fingertips. There's a white wall and a crumpled blue bed sheet in front of me. A boot is pressing my face into the hardwood floor.

After a few moments, I realize that's just the hangover.

My blood weeps for nicotine. I need water and a cigarette. I need to go back to sleep and pretend this never happened. I need to reevaluate my decision-making process.

Somewhere in the room there's a hiss and a crackle. Through a veil of static a bored voice says, "10-36 Code 2, 10th and C." Automobile accident three blocks east, no injuries or wash down required.

Good. I'm in my apartment.

My cell phone shakes somewhere close. The vibrations rattle the floor and shoot nails into my skull. I work myself

1

into a sitting position, dry-heaving twice. Moving hurts. The phone is behind the nightstand. Probably buzzed itself across the surface, waking me up when it hit the floor. There are three voicemails waiting for me.

I need fresh air. After making sure I'm wearing pants, I crawl through the window and on to the fire escape. The bitter air clears me up a little. I'm no longer confused about being in my own apartment, which is a good start.

It's probably around four in the afternoon, from where the sun is and the look of the crowds on First Avenue. It's cold, and I want to go back inside for a hoodie, but the hangover wants me to not move ever again.

There's a half-empty bottle of water cradled in the rusted slats of the fire escape. I'm pretty sure it's mine, so I crack it open and swallow as I sit there and watch the city breathe in and out, comb through my memory for a clue about what happened last night.

It started in my office. For the past few weeks some degenerate has been running up behind women, groping them, and bolting. Always after last call, always women walking by themselves, always around or near Tompkins Square Park.

I organized a buddy system, so anyone who had to walk home alone could call a number and get an escort. There was also a decoy in place to draw him out. A pretty girl would walk around the park from 4 to 5 a.m., with a big angry bastard lingering in the shadows. The perp is a low-level coward. One beating would shut it down.

But more than a week had gone by and nada. No sign. I was frustrated I couldn't catch the guy, and I did what I always do when I am frustrated: Unspin some Jameson.

My memory gets fuzzy around the bottle's halfway mark.

Everything after that is jagged. Bar tops distorted through the bottoms of empty glasses. Bodies in a crowd smothering me. White subway tile. Then my bedroom floor.

At least I made it home.

I bring my hand up to rub the sleep off my face and find the words *you promised* written on my palm. It's my handwriting, but nothing else about it is familiar.

The phone vibrates again. I type my PIN, set it to speaker, and rest my head against the cold brick.

"Hey. It's Chell."

Chell. The harsh crack of her name makes it sound like a swear word.

May as well be.

Her voice is slow, guarded. Like what she's saying isn't exactly what she wants to be saying. "I'm still really pissed at you, but I need your help. I think someone is following me. There's this guy who's been… look, I'm scared. I'm at Fourth and B. Can you come meet me? I know that after what happened, we should talk. I'm going to walk toward your place. If you're home or you're close, I'll be walking up First. Can you come meet me? Please?"

There's a second message. Silence and a click.

The third message is from Bombay. "Dude, turn on your TV or call me back or something. It's Chell, man. Chell's dead."

THE STORY PLAYS in a loop on NY1. A helicopter looks down at a junkyard in the Jamaica section of Queens. People are standing on a brown expanse of dirt broken by tires and scrap metal. The helicopter is too high for the camera to make out any details besides the color of their clothing. An army of police cruisers dot the street, along with a single silent ambulance.

That scene shrinks into a little box that plays next to a sullen anchor, who says Chell was found mummified in packing tape. In a deep baritone that's subdued to signify grief, the anchor says there were positive signs of sexual assault, with no suspects at this time.

He calls her by her real name.

The coffeemaker beeps to let me know it's finished. I don't remember making coffee. I pour some into a mug, then put the mug in the freezer to cool. I close the door and lean forward, my palms resting against the smooth white plastic.

I can't think. I need a cigarette. I can't think without smoke in my lungs.

There's no pack next to the sink. If I had cigarettes, that's where they would be. The ashtray on the windowsill only has a few stray butts smoked to the filter. I could run to the bodega, but I can't open a door to a world where Chell being dead could be true.

My phone is quiet, but the message is spinning around my head like a bad song I can't shake.

How can I smoke two packs a day and there's nothing in this apartment for me to light on fire?

There are no cigarettes in the freezer or under the sink or in the medicine cabinet. There isn't a stray pack under the pile of clothes in the corner of my bedroom or behind the couch. I toss my sock drawer because I never really know what I'm capable of when I'm drinking.

And no, nothing except a small elastic hair tie. Threaded around it is a single red hair, long enough it would have fallen from the top of Chell's head down to her shoulder.

My fingernails cut into my palm, and I can't breathe. I wrap my arms around my sides, hold in the thing that's trying to split open my skin.

Chell is dead.

IT WAS AUGUST sometime, so hot you could smell the blacktop.

We were trying to find you a new pair of sunglasses. You had this thing about the glasses you wore. They had to match your hair, which was a shade of red somewhere between a fire truck and the blaze it was rushing to put out.

There are two places to find something like that. Canal Street or St. Mark's. We settled on the latter because it was closer. We were on that wild stretch between Second and Third that's jammed with street vendors and Asian tourists and karaoke bars and kids who hadn't heard Sid Vicious died.

I sought pools of shadow while you weaved between the racks, wearing dark-colored plaid shorts and a black tank top. Your skin so white it was like the sun never touched you. You modeled sunglasses, plucking them off the racks with your long, thin fingers. Every few pairs you would turn to me and contort your face. I would shrug, like my opinion on these things mattered.

You settled on a pair of cat-eye glasses with thick plastic frames. There were little glass diamonds in the upper corners where the arms met the lenses. You tapped them and smiled.

I didn't like them because I didn't like not being able to see your eyes, but I wasn't about to say that. Before I could say anything else, you pulled a fedora off another rack and put it on my head, then pushed it down until it pressed on the tops of my ears.

You said, *I want to buy this for you.*

I'm not a hat guy.

You're not an anything guy. You should accessorize more.

You handed me a mirror and the hat didn't look too bad. The guy told you it would be twenty dollars and you talked him down to fifteen. After you paid, you turned to me and smiled.

Happy birthday, you said.

I don't celebrate my birthday. Living long enough to take another trip around the sun doesn't strike me as much of an accomplishment. If someone hears about my birthday and offers to buy me a drink, I'm not going to turn it down. That's about it. I'm pretty sure I hadn't even told you when my birthday is.

We spent the rest of the day wandering around the city. There was nothing remarkable about it, but every detail is piling on me, so much and so hard I can barely stand.

We stopped at an ice cream truck for soft serve. I got a vanilla cone; you got chocolate with sprinkles. We ate them in Union Square Park while we watched a drum circle, then went to The Strand for air conditioning and discount books. When the sun dipped below the buildings, we headed to the bars, going from one to another, staying only as long as we could score free drinks. When we were too wasted to deal with the crowds, we went to my roof, where we ate tangerines and threw the rinds over the lip of the building. We laid on our backs and counted the twelve stars strong enough to shine through the light pollution that blots out the night sky. We fell asleep on a gentle slope of the roof and woke the next day, dehydrated and sunburned.

Even now I can hear the slap of your neon green flip-flops on the sidewalk, smell your perfume of lavender and cigarettes. I remember the way you would cock out one hip when you were standing still and how your laugh was the sharpest thing about you.

But in this moment, I can't even remember the last time I saw you.

MY COFFEE IS cold, but I drink it anyway. I sit on the couch and wait for NY1 to offer some new bit of information. Instead, the reporters ping-pong between the weather, teacher contracts, and a political sex scandal. The head anchor checks back in with the junkyard in Queens every twenty minutes or so, like he doesn't want anyone to forget how sad he is.

The coverage won't end anytime soon. Chell was pretty, white, and dressed provocatively enough so reporters could rend their clothing and slut-shame her in the same story. Primetime, front page stuff. Had she been black and murdered in Harlem, she would maybe get a mention in the weekend roundup.

The anchorman calls her by her real name again. I would never have known her real name if I hadn't seen her driver's license sticking out of her wallet. It didn't change anything. She was always Chell to me. I was always Ashley to her, because I made the mistake of telling her everyone always called me Ash.

The news report cuts to a commercial.

There's so much to process it's hard to focus on one thing. Still, I feel something scratching at the back of my head. I go back outside and find my phone, the plastic casing cold from being out on the fire escape. I listen to Chell's voicemail a few more times before I figure out what's bothering me.

She said: *there's this guy who's been.*

Past tense and historical.

Which means she recognized him.

Which means I can find him.

Which is good, because he and I need to have a frank discussion about the circumstances of her death.

My phone buzzes in my hand, and I nearly jump. My mom. I ignore the call and text Bombay: *Where can I find people?*

He comes back almost instantly: *Where else?*

I strip down and climb into the shower. The water is scalding. I stand underneath until it's lukewarm. That and a handful of ibuprofen begin to make a dent in my hangover. I consider wiping the condensation off the mirror, to see how I look, but I know how I look: I need a shave, and a haircut, and a few more hours of sleep. All those things will take too much effort. Anyway, it's not like I've got someone I need to impress.

As I'm getting dressed there's a knock on the door. I zip my jeans and wait. Someone on the other side says, "Mister McKenna, this is the police." The voice is thin but commanding.

I crouch down and then remember they can't see me, so I dress quickly. I dress even quicker when I hear the doorknob jiggle. They might be with the landlord, but I changed the locks after I moved in. He has yet to discover this.

Talking to the cops is not what I need to be doing right now. I have no idea where I was last night. I know I would never hurt Chell, but the cops don't know that. And if they've done their research on me, it's not going to be a fun conversation.

There's mumbling on the other side of the door. My cell

phone buzzes in my hand with a number I don't recognize. I ignore the call and turn off the phone, shove it into my pocket.

The November air is cold and tight so I pull on the gray pea coat with the thick collar. I find the fedora Chell bought for my birthday on top of my fridge and knock it against my leg to clean off the dust. I tie my umbrella onto a belt loop in my jeans and take one last look at the door.

"Mister McKenna, if you're home, it's very important that we speak to you."

The street is clear. I climb out onto the fire escape, lower the window, and make my way for the roof.

The dimming blue sky is streaked with clouds lit orange by the retreating sun. It's open and clean. I lean back, let it fill my vision. Breathe deep.

Then I cross down to the end of the block, to the last building on the row, check to make sure the stairwell is unlocked and the alarm isn't connected, and head down to the street. When I get to the sidewalk and know the cops aren't wise to my exit strategy, I pull out my iPod, stick the buds in my ears, and crank Iggy Pop.

"Search and Destroy."

Seems appropriate.

TwO

THE CROWD AT Apocalypse Lounge spills out onto the sidewalk. More crowded than usual, not that it's hard to fill the space. It's a tiny dive in Alphabet City, far enough from the trendy East Village bars that it never gets too busy. It doesn't even have a full liquor license, just serves wine and beer. Though there's always a bottle of Jay waiting for me behind the bar.

Most people who aren't regulars come in and turn right back around. The walls are covered in sloppy graffiti. The mismatched tables and chairs, scavenged from the curb, are scuffed and cracked. The name of the bar is cut into a piece of galvanized steel that hangs over the front door and swings in the breeze like the blade of a guillotine.

The name of the place isn't an accident.

The reason for the crowd is that the bar is hosting an

impromptu memorial service for Chell. In times of great loss or confusion, Apocalypse is where we turn. Not to our families. A lot of us are still pretending we don't have those.

No one notices me as I push my way through the front door. I linger by the dirty storefront-style windows. It's so crowded the air is humid. People stand shoulder-to-shoulder, hoisting glasses of wine and bottles of beer, trying to out-grief one another. Everyone knew Chell best, even the people who didn't seem to know much about her.

I want to stay out of sight and get to my office, but one person sees me and it ripples through the crowd until the place is nearly silent, save the melancholy Elliott Smith song playing on the loudspeakers. Probably selected to fit the mood because, of course it was. Most of the room is staring at me.

"Bunch of fucking assholes," I say.

The ones who hear it laugh, even though I'm not trying to be funny.

Bombay pushes his way through the crowd and throws his arms around me, so hard it almost sends us sprawling out the door. He holds onto me like I'm keeping him from falling. He's wearing khakis and a black button-down shirt, the opposite of his usual wardrobe: Parachute pants and a neon golf polo. His head is freshly shaven, and he smells like soap and red wine. When he pulls away from me, he's not smiling. The only time he doesn't smile is when I don't see him.

He tries to say something and stalls. I tell him, "Don't."

He nods and another pair of arms wrap around me. Tight and brief, like a handshake. Lunette's bleached white hair is matted to her head like she's just woken up. Her eyes are puffy and red behind black plastic-framed glasses. She pulls the collar of her flannel shirt to her nose and wipes. She can't think of anything to say either.

"Both of you, come down to the office in a few," I tell them.

The two of them look at me like I'm calculus. Maybe they're expecting me to be more broken up about this, but I have work to do.

Dave is shirtless behind the bar, bones sticking out of his emaciated frame at odd angles. He reaches to the ground and comes up with a bottle of Jay. I put my hand around the base, considering the forked tongue licking the back of my skull. I slide it back toward him.

"Need a clear head right now," I tell him. "Can you get some relief, come down to the office in a few?" He nods, doesn't judge. Like a good bartender should.

People stop me and try to talk. They want to know how I'm holding up. Which is bad enough. Worse are the looks. That 'I can't believe he lost someone else under horrific circumstances' look.

Before anyone can make the mistake of asking me how I'm doing, I head downstairs.

DESPITE THE CROWD upstairs, the concrete-walled basement is empty, the two unisex bathrooms under the stairs vacant. I slip into the one on the right, hang the 'out of order' sign on the knob, and close the door behind me.

The bathroom is wallpapered with band stickers, from the sink to the exposed piping. Everything except the empty wooden bookshelf set into the far corner opposite the toilet, which is scuffed but clean, holding a few spare rolls of toilet paper and some old issues of *Good Housekeeping*.

I slide my hand under the third shelf from the bottom and unhook the metal clasp and push the bookshelf into an unlit hallway. I step into the void and grope for the handle to open the reinforced steel door into my office.

I call it my office, even though it's not really mine. It's just where I work. It doesn't have a name, and truly it belongs to all of us who know about it.

The room isn't much, able to fit eight people comfortably. The floor is covered in a brown floral area rug that's flanked by two black leather couches. The eggplant-colored paint on the walls makes the room feel bigger and smaller at the same time. The frosted glass ashtray on the coffee table is empty. I pull it toward me, light a smoke, put my feet up, and wait.

Bombay, Lunette, and Dave come in together and sit on the couch across from me. No one wants to start, balancing on sharp edges and waiting for me to say something. They want some kind of assurance I'm still human.

I rub the palm of my hand, the words *you promised* cracked and faded but not completely washed away in the shower. I ask, "Did any of you see me after I left here last night?"

I'm met by a collection of blank stares. I tell them, "That's fine. Moving on. Chell disappeared from Fourth and B. Someone must have heard something. I need to know when each of you last saw Chell. If she said anything I should know about."

Dave rubs his thighs and looks at the floor saying, "She was in here two nights ago. I don't think she said anything interesting. I'm sorry, I have to get back to the bar. I can't trust Bess up there too long."

Dave leaves and Lunette nods up to my hat, her dwindling Russian accent twisting through her words like roots. "It suits you."

"Does it? I didn't know if I could pull it off. I thought you were going to give me shit for it."

"Not on a day like today." She looks away from me, and when she turns back, her face is pointed at the floor. "The body is still warm. Don't you want to take a few minutes to grieve?"

"Whoever did this is still out there. If he hurts someone else, it's on me."

"Let the cops handle it," says Bombay.

"I don't trust the cops to handle it. And this is our neighborhood."

Lunette nods, not agreeing but accepting my stance. She says, "Me and Chell did drunk brunch on Sunday. She seemed fine."

"What did she talk about? Anyone bothering her?"

"She didn't say anything like that."

I finish my cigarette and stamp it out in the ashtray. Bombay asks, "What are you going to do?"

"Not sure yet. I've been brushing up on the Old Testament for ideas."

"You're going to kill the guy?"

"If I'm fortunate enough to find him before the police do."

"You can't do that." I get to my feet. Bombay flinches. I would never hit him, but sometimes I'm not sure he knows that. I tell him, "This is America. I can do whatever the fuck I want."

Lunette says, "Ash, you need to talk about this. Can we please just talk?"

I shouldn't take this out on them. Besides my mom and Chell, Bombay and Lunette are the only two people who matter. And they mean well. I know they do. But I don't need to talk. Talking about dead people doesn't bring them back.

Neither would what I have planned, but it would make me feel a hell of a lot better.

"There's nothing to say right now," I tell them.

TIBO IS AT the bar's single booth, set back in an alcove across from the stairwell. He lives down the block from Fourth and B, so I march over. He's poring over nautical maps while Mikey talks at him. I stand in front of the table and Mikey looks up but Tibo doesn't, his face hidden behind a cascade of dreadlocks.

Mikey says, "Ash, I'm so sorry. I just can't believe it about Chell. Listen, if you want to talk man, I'm here for you, I really am."

"Shut the fuck up, Mikey." I rap my knuckles on the table and Tibo looks up, surprised to be in a bar. "You see Chell lately?"

He nods. "Last night."

"Outside. Conference."

We push through the crowd and step to the curb. Tibo produces a rolled cigarette from thin air and lights it. He doesn't wait for me to prompt him. "I was sitting by the window, saw her go walking down the block. Late, I don't remember what time. I was blazed, so, you know." He shrugs. "Definitely after midnight. I got home at midnight."

"Was she with anyone?"

"Couple of people."

"Did you recognize them?"

He eyes bounce back and forth like he's flipping through

a filing cabinet. "They're sort of familiar. A guy. I'd recognize him if I saw him. Older guy, handsome." Then he smacks his head. "Wait. There was another guy with them. But he had a bag over his head."

"What do you mean a bag?"

"Like a sack. A black sack."

"Did you see where they went?"

"East. I can only see so much from my window."

"Is there anything else you can tell me about it? Anything else that stood out?"

He cringes like it hurts to think. "Chell had on this old dress, like vintage. Some 1930s-type get-up, hat and everything."

That's not something I associate with her. She preferred bondage to vintage.

Tibo says, "If you want, I can ask around, see what the deal is. And listen man, something else. The cops were here asking about you."

I'm suddenly aware of everyone standing on the sidewalk, scanning faces for people who aren't familiar, or who just look too serious. "When?"

"Ten minutes ago. Everyone played dumb. They left cards with a few people. Do you want one?"

"Fuck no. But thanks for telling me."

As I'm turning to leave he asks, "Do you own scuba gear?"

My ability to deliver a witty retort is rendered powerless. "Why?"

"Long story. Don't worry about it."

With that, he walks down the block, back to his home planet.

Chell was in the neighborhood last night. I can work with that.

PEOPLE CALL ME a private investigator. That's not accurate. To become a private investigator in New York City, you need three years of experience. I don't know where to get that. Then you need to take a test administered by the state, which costs several hundred dollars. Then you have to renew the license every two years.

That's far more money and effort than I'm willing to commit to anything. And anyway, having a license means I'd have to play this game aboveboard, which would really cut into my business plan.

I prefer to think of myself as a blunt instrument. Point me at a job—find people, find things, transport stuff, look disagreeable—I get it done, and I accept money upon completion. Sometimes I accept alcohol or drugs because I'm comfortable operating on a barter system.

Bombay has joked that I should advertise, but I never really needed to. My number gets passed around by people who are happy with my work. Every now and again my phone rings and someone offers me a job. I take it or I don't.

It's not the job I dreamt about as a kid (archeologist), but it pays my bills often enough to indicate I'm pretty good at it.

MY STOMACH TWISTS on itself, reminding me I haven't eaten today. I stop into the pizza place on the corner and find Good Kelly seated at a white Formica tabletop in the back, digging into a spinach roll. She waves me over. Her neon green coat and jet black hair make her pale skin pop in the florescent light.

"Hey," she says. A shadow passes over her face and she

remembers we're supposed to be sad. "How are you holding up?"

"I don't know how to answer that without sounding like an asshole," I tell her.

"I'm so sorry. And I feel like a dick for having to ask this right now, but I was actually planning on calling you. I need a favor." She wipes her mouth and puts the napkin over the half-finished roll, says, "I'm moving in the next few days, and I need a hand loading stuff onto a truck."

"What neighborhood are you moving to?"

"I'm leaving."

"Soho?"

"New York."

"What now?"

She gets up and pushes in her chair. "I wish I could explain more, but I have to go meet Harley. I think I'm late. But if you could come give me a hand, I would appreciate it. Can I let you know when?"

"I'll help. But where are you moving to?"

"Austin, Texas."

"That's madness."

"I can rent a house down there for what it costs to rent bowling shoes up here. I'll tell you all about it when you come over." She puts her hand on my shoulder. "Can I count on you?"

"Always. But why the hell would you leave all this for Texas?"

"It's time."

"Before you go, did you see me or Chell last night?"

She frowns. "Neither."

She looks like she wants to say something, but settles for kissing me on the cheek. Her lips are warm and a little greasy

19

from the spinach roll.

Kelly is native. Her blood is made up of the same thing as mine: The limescale water that drips from the ceilings of the subway. I can't accept what she's saying as truth.

The guy behind the counter gives me a slice without me having to ask, and I pass two dollars across the glass to him. I step outside with it, balancing it on a white paper plate, and watch Kelly disappear into the crowd. The traffic is backed up on the streets and the lights and the sounds and the movement and I wonder how anyone could live without this. The silence must be deafening.

THE LAST NUMBER I had for Ginny doesn't work so I walk by Chanticleer and find a bored queen standing behind the velvet rope marking off the smoking area. I ask, "Ginny around?"

She exhales in my direction, the streetlight catching the glitter in her blonde wig. "Who?"

"Right then."

That'll be enough. Word will get back. That's not necessarily a bad thing. If you're going to talk to the Queen of the Lower East Side, it helps to have some time to work up the nerve.

After that I wander a bit, sorting through what I know about this.

I'm operating on a fair assumption Chell knew her killer. Probably someone with a car, or at least access to one. She called me at 4 a.m. and the news said she was found around 9 a.m. She was snatched and assaulted in the space of five hours. Which means the attack happened someplace in the neighborhood or in the car. If it happened in the car, it was probably a van. Something private, without windows.

The dress she was wearing, and the man with the sack on his head, that has me cold. But it happened before she called me, so if I can figure it out, I can pinpoint who was with her when she got killed.

I don't realize where I'm walking until I find myself at the corner of Fourth and B. Where Chell called me from. I stand there a long time, chain smoking cigarettes until my head hurts, even though there's not much to see.

There's a Korean deli that's closed more than its open. Probably would have been closed when she called last night. There's a bar across the street, one that's too trendy for me. No one is smoking outside so they must have a back patio, which means less of a chance someone saw something. Then there's a jumble of apartments and a building that's maybe a school.

There are a lot of windows looking down here. Most of them are dark now. A few are lit up and in one I see a figure sweep across beige blinds. It would take a year and a day to knock on all these doors.

The street is end-of-the-world deserted. Someone could throw me in the back of a van right now and no one would notice. There's no police tape. The cops must have combed through here. Maybe they didn't even check, considering it's not where she died.

I drop to my knees, run my fingers over the rough sidewalk. The pavement is cold and I know it's not possible, but I smell lavender in the sharp autumn air. The slice of pizza feels like a chunk of granite in my stomach, and I fight to keep it down.

She was right here less than twenty-four hours ago and then she was gone, like she phased out of existence. She reappeared dead in Queens, and I hope she took a chunk out of him during the time in between.

He can consider it a preview.

A bouncer comes out of the club across the street and stands guard outside the door. Big guy, with a neck the size of my thigh and a haircut like someone hacked at his head with a lawnmower. The kind of haircut that says 'I'm too big to care.'

"Hey," I call over to him as I cross the street. "You work last night?"

He doesn't budge. I stand in front of him and ask, "Incredible Hulk, how about a little courtesy?"

He whips off his sunglasses, moving faster than I would expect a guy his size could. His eyes are bloodshot and as wide as dinner plates. Juicer, probably. He says, "What do you think, talking to me like that?"

"I'm not sure that was a complete sentence, but fine." I point over my shoulder. "There was a girl across the street, on that corner, last night. She called me and then she got killed. I need to know if you were working last night so I can ask you if you saw anything."

"No."

"This is my fault for being unclear. I can't ask you, or you didn't see anything?"

"I didn't work last night."

"Should I even bother asking who was?"

"Why don't you get out of here?"

I take a step toward him and he flinches, but only because he's too big to be used to signs of aggression. "I know you're a tough guy, but you need to know I'm not smart enough to let that stop me. All I want is a name. If you can find it in your big teddy-bear heart to give it to me, I'll leave."

His eyes light up and he's wondering if he should drop me. I set my feet. If he comes at me, I'll go for his throat. Doesn't matter how much you can lift, your trachea doesn't get much out of that. But I'd rather not go down that road, so when the tension disappears from his shoulders and he puts his sunglasses back on, I'm pretty psyched.

"Guy named Steve," he says. "Not working again for a few days. Sunday, I think."

"Thanks, pal. I appreciate that." I extend my hand, but he goes back to statue mode. I take it as my cue to get the hell away from him.

THIS CITY. IT takes and takes and pieces of it fall away and we get lost trying to put it back together.

Christ, my thoughts are getting blurry. I need sleep. Real sleep, because blacking out after drinking too much whiskey is not nearly the same thing.

I pull out my cell phone to check the time, but I forgot to charge it so it's dead.

The siren of a fire truck echoes down the street, coming closer. As the rig passes, I take off my hat and hold it to my chest. One of the firefighters riding in the side cabin sees this and gives me a thumbs-up. I nod at him and when the truck is gone I put my hat back on and keep going.

When I hit the corner of Tenth, I light a smoke and consider my options. Which are sort of slim. I don't know what the hell I'm doing. I've found missing people before, but that's easy when you have a name and a picture.

I need newspapers. It's late, and the morning edition of the

Post will be released soon. The *Post* may have a bad rep in this town, but they leave the other tabs in the dust when it comes to crime coverage.

First, I need to charge my phone.

Then I remember Chell's apartment. I keep a spare charger there.

I should go to Chell's apartment.

The cops must have checked it, but it's not a crime scene so they can't still be there.

Cup of coffee and I'll be good to go. Maybe two, and my brain will fire back up and I can make the trip out to Brooklyn. It would be even nicer to blow a couple lines of coke because then I'll solve the case and build a house by sunup, but I keep thinking: Clear head.

First, bathroom break. I turn the corner to my block. There's a black, late-model Impala with tinted windows idling outside my building, which can only mean one thing. I consider running, but that'll look bad, and I really have to pee. So I hedge and hope they don't know what I look like.

Of course, they're in my back as I'm opening my front door.

There's two of them. A tall, cigarette-thin Latino and a shorter white guy carved out of an uneven block of sandstone. The tall one is the talker.

"Mister McKenna," he says, flipping out his wallet to show off his shield. "I'm Detective Medina, and this is Detective Grabowski. We've been looking for you."

THREE

MEDINA ASKS, "CAN we go inside?"

"Nope."

"Why not?"

"I don't know you."

Medina sighs. "We're the good guys."

"Did your buddies say that to Abner Louima before they gave him a prostate exam with a broom handle?"

He bristles when I say this. He's about to snap at me but takes a moment and says, "You can't judge all cops based on one guy's stupid decision."

"Sure I can. Now, what are we talking about?"

I'm stalling. I think they can tell. I'd rather give them the semblance of an answer about where I was last night, but I'm having a hard time coming up with something.

You promised.

Who promised?

More questions raised: How much did I drink? And what does that say about me as a person?

The way Medina is talking, it's like he wants to be my friend. But he's standing too far away, his body too tense. He's a bad actor. He says, "We want to know where you were last night."

I want to ask him if he checked with his wife. Instead I say, "I was here most of the night. Before that I was out at a bar."

"Which bar?"

"Most of them, apparently."

"How about some specifics?"

"What is this about?"

"You know what this is about."

I put up my hands in mock-surrender. "Actually I don't, so why don't you fill me in?"

He flips open a worn notebook the size of his palm and reads off Chell's real name, like he doesn't remember it. "She called you last night?"

"She did."

"About what?"

"Doesn't matter at this point, does it?"

Medina pulls out a cigarette and lights it. He holds the pack in my direction, and I wave him off. He says, "Any reason you're being so combative?"

The way he says it, it's pretty combative.

I say, "Could be that I'm emotionally distraught and exhausted and you're keeping me awake. Maybe you're wasting your time when you should be out catching the idiot who killed her. Maybe I just don't like cops all that much. I also really have to pee. It may be a combination of all those things."

"You're not the only one who's been up late. This can all be over in a couple of minutes. Just tell us what she said to you when she called you last night."

Grabowski jumps in. He crushes his words under his heel like a spent butt. "Just play along, kid. This doesn't have to be hard."

They can't have checked my background because they're being way too nice. I sit on the cold stone of the stoop and light a cigarette. Maybe if I cooperate a little, they'll leave me alone.

"She said she thought she was being followed," I say. "She called me and asked me to walk her home. As you can probably guess, I didn't get the message."

"Can we listen to it?"

"There wasn't anything helpful."

"We'll determine that. How about you play it for us?"

I think about it. I really do. They don't seem so bad. But none of them ever really do. If they want to listen, they'll have to work for it. It's not like they can't track it down on their own. Fucking Patriot Act.

"No," I tell them. "That you can't do."

"We could get a warrant," Medina says.

"Do it then."

"You know." Medina flicks his cigarette into the street. "We've interviewed a few people already, and they all say you knew her pretty well. If you cared about her so much, why don't you want us to find out who killed her?"

"That's not really the point, but rationalize it however you want."

Grabowski mutters loud enough for us all to hear. "You don't seem too upset."

I lean around Medina and look Grabowski in the eye. "We all deal with grief in our own way. I prefer to take my feelings and ball them up and push them down so that I explode in fits of rage."

He's stopped listening. "Was there anyone here with you last night who can vouch for you?"

"Nope." I reach my arms over my head to stretch. "Now why don't you guys go get yourself that warrant. Because lucky thing for me, being an asshole isn't an arrestable offense. Which means I don't need to keep talking to you right now."

"If you didn't do it, you have nothing to worry about," Medina says.

"I have nothing to worry about."

Grabowski asks, "What's your problem, kid?"

I'm out of clever things to say so I shrug.

They both stand there, tired and frustrated. Medina hands me a business card, doesn't even bother to say anything, and they turn to leave.

Over his shoulder Grabowski says, "Stay in touch."

Those guys might be on the level, but I'm not taking a chance. Not after the last time I tried to do the right thing. I wait until Medina glances back so he can see me toss the card onto the ground.

'LL NEVER UNDERSTAND why Chell insisted on living in Brooklyn.

I have a theory, that it was an easier transition coming from Ohio to New York City. The buildings in Brooklyn are tall, but not too tall.

Her apartment was bigger than mine but barely a day went by when she wasn't in my neighborhood. For what she was paying in MetroCards and cab rides, she could have bought the building next to mine.

Brooklyn is nice enough, and maybe it would be a good place to retire, but it's not even last call and already it feels like a ghost town. Only six people walked by in the time it took me to finish a cup of burnt coffee from the bodega down the street. And I still can't tell if the guy in the black car in front of her building is a cop or if he's waiting for someone.

He's been making a little pile of cigarettes outside his window. His car is a Ford Focus, not an Impala, but that doesn't mean he's not undercover. Which means using the spare key at the bottom of the potted basil plant outside her front door is not a good idea.

There's an apartment building at the end of the street, out of sight of the Ford. The building's door is locked so I ring bells. Angry voices crackle on the intercom until someone too lazy to care buzzes me through. I climb the five flights to the top floor and find the door to the roof isn't alarmed or locked, so I step outside.

It's a clear night, and I can see all twelve stars.

I turn away from the sinkhole in my stomach, climb across the connected roofs to Chell's, stepping over the knee-high walls that separate the buildings. I know I'm on the right one when I see a pile of discarded cigarette butts in the corner, gray and swollen from age and wet weather.

The fire escape leads down into the back courtyard. I take it slow and quiet, hoping no one looks out and sees me. At the bottom I've got a choice I don't love. I could lower the ladder but it would make too much noise and probably wake the neighbors.

The other option is: Drop and pray.

It doesn't look too far so I grab a solid section of the fire escape and lower myself down, until my arms are fully extended and my feet are hanging in the air. The rusted metal tears at my hands. I let go, land hard on my ankle, pain jetting through my leg. Bend at my knees, and roll onto my side to disperse the impact. Get up and shake it out.

Hurt, but nothing's broken. The force of landing knocked off my hat. I root around in the yard until I find it, then dust it off and put it back on.

There's another spare key back here, under the mat. Chell put it there the first time she went out for a smoke and the door locked behind her. It still works and, lucky for me, the chain isn't on the door so I don't have to kick it in. She never listened to me about keeping it fastened, but you'd have to be very clever or very dumb to make it down here in one piece.

Hence the shitty hiding place for the key.

Luckily, I'm a strong mix of clever and dumb.

The white venetian blinds are drawn, so the apartment is barely lit by the light sneaking in though the thin white slats. I stand in the corner, give my eyes a minute to adjust. When they do, I can see that not much has changed, not that it's been so long.

From the back door, the apartment is laid out like a cross. I'm in the bedroom, and the living room lies past it. Kitchen on the right, bathroom on the left. There's a rug, a bed, some paperbacks, wineglasses, and candles. Not much else. She never furnished her apartment. It's still nearly as bare as the first night I was here.

We were the same like that, both living Spartan lifestyles. Chell would say she did it because it encouraged her to go out more. I can't say I did it for the same reasons. I totally read

Fight Club.

I find my spare charger in the kitchen junk drawer. I plug in my phone and float through the bedroom and the kitchen, running my fingers over spotless, smooth surfaces, then think better about it and wipe down what I've touched. My fingerprints wouldn't be easy to explain postmortem.

In the bathroom I stop.

I can feel the warmth of the candles she lit the first night I was here.

WE MET IN a broken-down burlesque parlor in Coney Island. I don't remember the name of it. I wasn't even planning to be there. Coney is so far away it should require a passport. But it was summer and Adam was bartending so that meant free drinks. Enough to get me to the badlands of Brooklyn.

I was sitting there in the corner, nursing a bottomless glass of whiskey, the crowd crushing in on me in the slight space, weighing the pros and cons of the bar versus my couch. I might have been pushing my way toward the door when the music started.

It was a cover of the Divinyls' "I Touch Myself", a hardcore industrial mix pumped through a grinder and played on speakers drenched in blood.

The lights dimmed, and you took the stage. The way you looked made me want to find religion just so I could renounce it.

You wore a patchwork leather outfit that covered you from the neck down, carrying two pink candles in small glass jars.

You floated across the stage to a lone folding chair set in the middle. You lit the candles and put them on the floor and started a slow grind of a dance that stopped every conversation in the bar.

Your leather outfit was a jigsaw puzzle. You would reach up and rip, and a portion of your breast would be revealed.

Your forearm.

The flat expanse of your stomach.

Every piece of leather that disappeared revealed something about you.

The tiger outlined in black stripes on your right shoulder blade. The cat standing on the skull standing on the owl, on your left arm. The strand of DNA down your back. The stars mapped across the front of your hips. The small, barbell-shaped lumps in the black electrical tape covering your handful-sized breasts.

I like brunettes, and I like curves. You had the body of a swimmer, your legs narrow and deadly as poison darts. And then there was that red hair, done in a bob that wrapped around your head and splayed out across your right eye.

You were so far from what I consider my type. But I also can't get on the subway without falling in love.

After stripping off the leather outfit, you were barefoot, wearing the electrical tape and a black thong. You pulled a neon pink bandana from thin air and blindfolded yourself, then kept dancing. Falling backwards over the chair until just at the moment of impact, pulling yourself upright before you were about to smash your head on the floor. Every time your head snapped back, the crowd held its collective breath, until we knew you were safe.

Then you picked up those candles, blindfolded, and poured

the hot wax down your chest and onto your stomach. It dried into pink ribbons that hugged your skin like everyone in the room wished they could.

The song ended and the trance broke. You flinched a little and peeked out from under the bandana, like you were surprised by the audience being there. The crowd erupted.

You left the applause like it didn't matter and disappeared through a gray curtain. Ten minutes later you were standing at the bar, wearing leather pants and a white t-shirt, sipping a vodka soda and gazing up at the television playing *The Forbidden Zone* on mute. There was a line of guys behind you. You had short, tense conversations with them, and they left with their egos bleeding onto the floor.

I fought through the crowd and told you, *I'd like to buy you a drink.*

Why?

Because everyone likes free drinks.

You pointed to the television and said, *Tell me what movie that is.*

The Forbidden Zone.

You can buy me a drink.

That's your benchmark?

That's my benchmark.

I waved over Adam and got you another round, myself a Jay. You looked up and I saw tendrils of purple in the white part of your left eye, the eye that wasn't covered by the brush of red hair. It looked bruised but not damaged. Like your iris was a light bulb and someone blew smoke around it. Later on you told me it was a rare kind of birthmark. That night I was just trying not to stare too much.

Your lips wrapped around the thin red straw in your drink.

I said the first thing that came to my mind. I'm not even sure it was that good a line, but it seemed to work.

I said, *I'm sure a lot of guys would pretend they didn't just see you mostly naked, and it would come off as insincere. I came over because I think you're pretty, and I'm hoping you're smart enough to match.*

You smiled. It was the smile of a viper circling a field mouse. That's exactly what you saw when you looked at me, and I did nothing to correct you.

You asked, *Are you usually this bold?*

Not really. I'm prone to indifference but lately, I can't be bothered.

I'm just going to end up breaking your heart.

Do your worst.

I will, but only because I think you can take it.

You told me you had just arrived from Ohio and were living in Greenpoint. That made you a gent, not that I couldn't call it from across the room, but I liked you anyway. You told me you weren't sure what you wanted to do with your life so you were dancing and working odd jobs until you figured it out.

I raised my glass, toasted you, and said, *Join the club.*

You told me your name was Chell.

Like cello, minus the 'oh,' you said.

When I told you my name was Ashley, you giggled. I pointed out it was a good Irish name back when my great-grandfather was using it. Then Ashley Abbot on *The Young and the Restless* ruined it. I told you everyone called me Ash, and we both know how that turned out.

It got late. We didn't notice until chairs were getting flipped onto tables. Without making any kind of agreement, I walked you to the Stillwell subway station. Coney Island is a dangerous place, especially at night, especially more during the summer.

We rode the train north. You didn't invite me, but you expected me to follow. It was a warm night so we wandered through the squat caverns of Brooklyn. We wound up in front of your apartment, in the basement of a three-story townhouse. On the steps, you turned to me and your face went slack.

You said, *I'm not going to sleep with you. I'm not looking for that kind of thing right now.*

That's fine, I said, hoping you were lying, and followed you inside.

Your apartment was sparse. There was a rug in the living room and some old paperbacks piled in one corner. No furniture. You told me to sit on the rug and you disappeared, came back in wearing a baby blue Mickey Mouse t-shirt and plaid short-shorts, hoisting two mugs and a bottle of white wine.

We talked some more. You liked to talk and liked even more when someone listened. Half the bottle later you leaned back and exhaled.

You asked, *We're adults, correct?*

I believe so.

I'm dying for a bath. If we can be adults about me being naked then you can stay and we can talk more.

It was raining outside, but that's not why I wanted to stay.

You got up to fill the bathtub, and I still didn't think you were serious.

You walked out of the bathroom pulling your shirt over your head, came out bare and white. Nothing was shocking because I had seen most of it at the show. My mind had filled in the blanks.

But your whole attitude shifted. Up on that stage your

control over the crowd was complete and infinite. But here, alone, you looked down and away from me. Your stomach stuck out a little like your spine was curved. Your knees were bony and your feet pointed inward.

You climbed into the tub and lit lavender candles that lined the back wall. The way the amber light careened up the walls and down your skin, it was like seeing a sunrise for the first time.

You handed me a bottle of pills that had been resting on the edge of the tub. I sat in the doorway and popped the cap.

Klonopin, you said. *It's for anxiety. Take two at most. You'll be so screwed you won't be able to pee straight.*

I popped three and washed them down with a sip of wine. Sat in the doorway and listened to you talk while the drugs wrapped my brain in gauze and the sun stretched its blue eyes over the horizon.

THE GLOSSY PORCELAIN at the base of the tub is dry. There doesn't seem to be anything else in the apartment that might help me, but I can't leave with nothing, so I sit on the edge of the bed. Comb through my memory. There's got to be something in here I missed. I can feel it on the edge of my brain, dangling a foot in the air. Prodding me.

We were getting ready to go out. I had my coat on and was standing by the front door, checking my pockets to make sure I had my phone, wallet, and smokes. Chell was in the bedroom on her knees facing away from me. She called over her shoulder that she needed a second. There was a sound. A hollow knock.

In the corner of the bedroom there's a notch in one of the

floorboards, big enough for a finger to fit in. I pull it up, and there's an alcove underneath. Inside there's a wad of bills, a stack of racy polaroids, a half-full vial of coke, a thumb drive, and a business card.

The card reads *Noir York* with a URL, www.noir-york. com. Nothing else on it, front or back, but it's heavy stock, professionally printed.

The vial is from Snow White. Since it's not empty, and given the pace Chell kept, she must have gotten it recently.

The drive isn't the cheap plastic kind I've seen laying around Bombay's apartment. It's brushed aluminum, smooth and cold. Feels like it could take a bullet.

I put the cash and photos back under the floor, take the card, the drive, and the vial. Shove them deep in my pockets and plan my escape route.

My phone buzzes on the kitchen counter, and it keeps buzzing. Call, not a text, from a number I don't recognize. But as soon as I hear the voice I know exactly who it is.

"Darling." Ginny Tonic hangs on that word like a portrait. "I hear you're looking for me."

"That I am."

"I have a car waiting for you."

"I'm not at my apartment."

"I know. The car is waiting outside, and I have some appointments to keep. Do hurry."

Click.

That's the closest thing to an invitation I'll get from Ginny. Coming out of her mouth, it's probably an order.

FOUR

I DON'T EVEN BOTHER with the return trip across the roof. I leave Chell's apartment through the front door and the Ford is gone, replaced by a black Lincoln Town Car that looks like it was just driven off a showroom floor. Leaning against it is Samson. Ginny's driver, slash bodyguard, slash the only person I know who I'm pretty sure kills people for money.

I'm not a small guy. Six feet, broad shoulders, and solid enough that I can walk through a bad neighborhood at night without being worried. There are few people I have second thoughts about crossing. I know Samson would rip me clean in two, and that's coming from someone with an inflated ego.

He's massive like a childhood nightmare is massive. A doctor might call him obese, but if I bit him I'd chip a tooth. The streetlights make his shaved head gleam but cast shadows on his face, so he's just a blank object sucking up the light.

I smile wide and offer my hand.

"Brother," I tell him.

He looks at my hand like it's a rotten piece of meat. "Ride in back. If you even think of lighting a cigarette in this car, I will curb stomp you."

Also, Samson doesn't like me. I've never been able to figure out why.

I tell him, "Of course I'm going to ride in the back. Did you think I wanted to ride in your lap? Though I'm not opposed to it."

Samson takes a step forward, and I'd like to say that I don't take a step back in response. I would love very much to say that.

Satisfied with himself, he points at the back door. I climb in, and after he gets into the front, he puts up a glass divider, separating me from him and leaving me alone with my thoughts, which is a dangerous place to be.

The ride to the club is quiet. Brooklyn disappears and the city sparkles as we cross the Williamsburg Bridge. I crack open the window and let the cold air wash over me to wake me up.

SOMETIMES I WISH finding lost people and looking disagreeable was enough to pay my bills. Sometimes it's not, and that's when I take jobs from Ginny.

Ginny is a district leader. There are at least a dozen scattered around the city. The job description is as vague as the title, but it generally means anything that's fun and illegal, she gets a cut. At least, anything fun happening in her district, which is: 14th Street to the north, Delancey to the south, the Bowery to the west, and the FDR to the east.

Most of the time I carry things for Ginny. Things in briefcases. I don't ask what's inside because I don't want to know. Sometimes I track people down. Occasionally I hit people, but I always make sure they have it coming.

If not for Ginny, I probably wouldn't be able to sustain my lifestyle. I'd have to get a suit and sit in a cube and make somebody else rich. Not how I want to spend my life.

Anyway, working for Ginny is another way I can keep an eye on my neighborhood and contribute to the community. Make it a safer place to live. Do the right thing.

It even works, sometimes.

I'M DOZING OFF just as Samson pulls up to the front of Chanticleer.

He waits for me to exit the car and squeals away from the curb, without even checking to see if I get inside safe. But it's okay because after I push through the crowd of smokers packed around the front, the doorman waves me in without asking for ID.

It's just about last call but the club is packed shoulder to shoulder. The walls are painted black so the boundaries of the room are impossible to make out. Men in thongs dance on the bar while softcore gay porn plays on flat screen televisions mounted on the walls. Like *Girls Gone Wild*, but with frat guys, and penis. Some poppy European band is blaring from the speakers.

I'm a fan of gay bars. There's no pretense. The guys aren't itching for a fight, and the girls, the ones who aren't hunting for a fierce gay to go shopping with, they're in it for a good time. The music is better, too. Despite my love for Johnny Cash, I've always had a soft spot for Madonna.

I push my way through the crowd toward the back, where a monolith in a suit pushes on the wall and a door opens to a corrugated-metal staircase. I make my way to the door at the bottom and enter the second bar, which features a little less clothing. A couple of people look at me like I'm an intruder, which I am. I try to look nonchalant as I duck around the side of the bar and find the narrow door nestled in the corner. I turn sideways to get through it and make my way down the dark hallway to the final door, opening it onto what looks like the setting for a Turkish sex party.

The room could be huge or it could be small. I can't tell, because of the ivory curtains hanging from the ceiling, creating passageways and sheer partitions. Blood-red satin pillows dot the floor, which is covered with a patchwork of Oriental rugs. It smells like incense and cinnamon and sexual lubricant.

After catching myself in a curtain, I manage to work my way toward the center of the room, where I find Ginny stretched out on a chaise that's draped in brown suede, surrounded by half-naked servants. One of them is actually holding a giant feather and fanning her like this isn't completely fucking ridiculous. Everyone stops and looks at me like they were just talking about me.

Ginny is wearing a gold dress that clings to her body, and an elaborate headpiece in her blonde wig, which culminates in a sparkled piece of mesh that reaches across her face. Her Adam's apple looks like a boulder in her throat. She gestures with a long finger, tipped by a brown-painted nail, to the pillow and low table in front of her. Then she waves, and all the servants disappear through another door at the back of the room.

I point around the room. "Marrakesh-chic?"

Ginny nods. "You have a good eye."

"Not really. You did the Moroccan thing last year."

"Ah. Well, we repeat the things that give us comfort." Ginny sighs and leans back in the chaise. "Ash, darling. I'm so sorry to hear about Chell. I know this is a difficult time, and I don't wish to appear insensitive, but I'm going to have to ask you to remove that thing from your head."

I touch the brim of the fedora, having forgotten it was there. "You don't like it?"

"It's dreadful."

"It's not dreadful."

"You're right. It's a fashion abortion that was discarded on your head."

I take off the hat and hold it in front of me. Ginny's shoulders relax, and she takes the piece of mesh off her face, clipping it into her wig. She offers me a smoke from a jewel-encrusted case, but I shake my head as I sit on the pillow.

She pinches the end of a thin cigarette and puts it in her mouth. "I hear you've been poking around for me. I have a meeting, so if we could get down to it?"

I light my own smoke and put the business card on the table. "I heard you hooked Chell up with a new job. I figure it has something to do with this. Can you enlighten me?"

She takes the card and holds it up to the light, then tosses it back on the table like it's a piece of trash. "I'm sorry."

"Why?"

"I can't tell you."

"Can't or won't?"

"Either one works fine."

"Look," I tell her. "I remember when your name was Paul. And in fairness, you wouldn't have made it through high school without me standing behind you. Doesn't that count for anything?"

She frowns. "Don't use my straight name in this place."

"Ginny."

"Here's the problem, darling. Both of us want to get laid, but no one wants to get fucked. Where is there a dyke when you actually finally need one?"

"After all I've done for you."

"Jobs for which you've been handsomely paid. Last time I checked, I wasn't in debt to you."

I drop my voice to just above begging. "Ginny. This is bigger than that."

She sighs and her body sags. "Ash, there are things I can't discuss. You need to understand that if I help you on this, it will come at some cost."

"Name the price."

"A favor."

This is a bad place to be. I've always been happy to work with Ginny, but I've never owed her anything. People who have always ended up regretting it.

I ask, "What do you want me to do?"

"I'll let you know. But I have your word?"

"Yes."

The devil wouldn't make a deal with Ginny, but what choice do I have? We shake. Her hand nearly crushes mine. She stamps out her cigarette and picks the card up again. She studies it for a little while, sounding out the words like it's in a language she can't read. Then she looks me in the eye and says,

"LARP."

"Elaborate."

"Live action role playing. Think of it like Dungeons & Dragons, except instead of swords and sorcerers, it's dames and dicks. And you don't play in your mom's basement, you run around the city shaking people down for information."

"Where did Chell fit into this?"

"They need actors and actresses to play the parts. You pay some money and get to act out your hardboiled fantasy. But really, that's the extent of my knowledge on this."

"Why the secrecy?"

"Spoilers, honey. Even without press, it's a word of mouth sensation."

"Who runs it?"

"I don't know the man personally. I had the number, and I passed it along to our dear, departed Chell. The number doesn't even work anymore. I just know he's based in Brooklyn." She holds up a finger. "I'm telling you this on the condition that you do not hop on a train and go over there and start beating the shit out of people. I know it isn't your strong suit, but you must keep your feelings in check on this. And we never had this conversation."

"Fine. So you got her a job. What else has Chell been up to lately?"

"You mean you don't know?" She leans forward and rests her fist under her chin. "Now that's interesting."

"Why is that interesting?"

"Oh, darling. Please."

"Have you seen Chell lately?"

Ginny leans back, a wry smile on her face. "I have not. Not since I got her the job a few weeks back."

"Final question. Did you see me last night?"

"You are just full of fun questions tonight. I'll play along. No, I did not."

I stare at Ginny. Try to look past the mask she wears to her true face, but I don't know what it looks like anymore. It's amazing to me that we're the same age. Though, the upward mobility in New York's criminal community is staggering, if you're willing to work for it. I get up to leave. As I push the curtains aside, Ginny says, "Ash?"

The playful tone is gone from her voice. It sounds almost like I remember it.

"Forgive me for being so bold," she says. "But for all that Chell put you through, I'm left wondering what you think you owe to her."

I tell her the best answer I can come up with. "I loved her anyway."

She laughs a little under her breath and the veil goes back up. "Oh, straight people. Your social customs are so foreign to me."

I want to say something back, but it's generally best to let her have the last word.

I WALK NORTH UP Avenue A. The sidewalk is crowded with dumb kids who came here via bridge or tunnel. They're loud and obnoxious and more than once someone walks into me like I'm invisible. I hate being sober around drunk people. Partly because it makes me see what I'm missing, but also because it makes me see what I'm missing.

As I dodge out of the way of another gaggle of drunken

gents, my foot smacks into a bundle of copies of today's *Post* outside a bodega, still wrapped in twine. Chell's picture is on the cover next to the headline: GREENPOINT GOTH MURDER MYSTERY.

The picture of her is one I've never seen before. Someone else is in it with her, but that person is cropped out. It looks like the back patio of St. Dymphna's. Chell is smiling and holding up a beer, the birthmark in her left eye obscured by the dull gray ink.

I wave over one of the guys working at the bodega and ask him to cut the twine so I can take a copy, hand him some change that I don't bother to count, and flip to the inside cover.

A violent sicko killed a gorgeous goth from Greenpoint, wrapped her in packing tape, and dumped her naked corpse in Queens early yesterday morning, according to police.

The victim, a piercing and tattoo enthusiast who worked as a burlesque dancer and an actress, was strangled and raped by the heartless predator, sources said. Cops have questioned several people who knew the woman but don't currently have any leads.

The murder sent shockwaves through the downtown bar scene. Although she lived in Greenpoint, she was identified as a regular at a number of East Village bars, and patrons said they were terrified to hear that the young woman had been so brutally murdered.

The rest of the story is filler. A lot of vague nonsense to boost the word count, and more tripe about how it's terrorizing the nightlife. From the ridiculous amount of people out tonight, that doesn't seem true, but hey, whatever makes people afraid enough to buy papers.

I rip off the front page with Chell's photo, fold it up, and stick it in my back pocket.

SNOW WHITE IS sitting on the steps of her building, same place she always is when I'm looking for her.

Her gray hair is knotted together in greasy clumps, brushed back and out of her face. It's chilly, but she's wearing clothes that show off a lot of leg and cleavage for a lady her age.

She exhales a massive cloud of Newport smoke and smiles at me. In a leaden Bronx accent she says, "Babe, you lost some weight. Are you eating enough?"

I bend down and kiss her on the cheek. "Hey sweet pea."

She pats the stair next to her but winces a little when she stretches over. I ask, "What's the matter?"

"It's going to rain." She touches her thigh. "Steel hip."

"You've got a steel hip?"

"I never told you that story? I was a stock car racer." She pats the skin of her thigh and it jiggles. "All metal."

Snow White tells great stories. Like stock car racing, or how *Debbie Does Dallas* was based on her. I don't have the heart to call her out on her stories, because I'm not sure she's lying. Instead I tell her, "I had no idea."

"Well, you would know these things if you ever came around to visit. You missed my birthday party last week. I made ziti and special cookies."

"I'm trying to clean up my act."

"Are you telling me I'm about to lose my favorite customer?"

"I'll still be bringing people by. Don't worry about that. I need to ask you for a favor."

She doesn't say anything to that.

I tell her, "I know Chell bought from you, probably within the last week or two. I need to know if she said anything or did anything that stands out. Anything."

"Babe, you know I don't talk about other customers. I know you were friends with her, and I'm sorry as hell she's dead, but the only business I feel comfortable talking to you about is your business."

She extends her pack of cigarettes toward me. I nod her off and look for mine. I'd rather smoke ground-up fiberglass than a Newport, to see if I could tell the difference. After I get a cigarette in my mouth I fumble with my wallet like I'm looking for a book of matches, count off sixty dollars, stick it in the coin pocket of my jeans.

She shakes her head. "Because I know you so long. And if you tell anyone I did this, you're cut off. Worse than that."

"Deal."

Snow White pulls the money out of my pocket. From the sidewalk it wouldn't have looked like anything. She says, "Chell came by. Stocked up. Said she'd been stuck in Brooklyn working a job."

"What kind of job?"

"She didn't say. Just that she felt like Nellie Bly. 'Nellie fuckin' Bly' she said."

I take a long drag of my cigarette and flick it to the curb. I am tired. So tired. My brain is frayed at the edges. And sitting next to Snow White, it's killing me. I've got Chell's half-vial of coke pressed up against my leg, which I wish was burning a hole in my sinus cavity, but even that wouldn't be enough. I've got enough money left for another vial, which will keep me going for at least another six hours, if I'm conservative.

Which I won't be, but still.

As I'm about to form the words, I feel it. The cold hardwood against my cheek.

Stay in control.

I tell Snow White, "Thanks for that, sweetheart. I really do appreciate it."

We both get quiet, smoke our cigarettes, watch the people for a little bit. A woman walks by in a grotesque gorilla mask and an orange dress so tight I can see her DNA. A guy I'm pretty sure was the rapist cop in *Pulp Fiction* walks two enormous pit bulls past us. Three young Mormons attempt to hand us pamphlets, and we tell them to fuck off.

I like this neighborhood at night.

Snow White says, "You're wearing the hat she got you."

"How did you know she got me this hat?"

"She got it for your birthday. You told me that once."

"You have a good memory."

"Helps in this business. It's a nice hat, too."

"Thanks. How are the *niños*?"

She pulls a photo out of her pocket and shows me an apple-cheeked baby with a big smile and a pink bow in her wispy hair. "My new granddaughter."

"How old is she?"

"Three months. Her name is Isabelle."

"She's beautiful. This is your third?"

"Fourth. You would know that if you ever came around to see me."

"Either way, congrats." I toss my cigarette into the street. "I'm going to turn in."

"Remember, don't tell anyone I said anything."

I smile at her. "Can you look me in the eye and tell me you

don't trust me?"

She doesn't smile back. "I don't trust anyone."

NELLIE BLY. I don't know who that is. I should have paid more attention in school. I should upgrade and get a smartphone, but I like my flip phone. I break cheap plastic phones often enough—a big glass fancy phone isn't going to last long. Plus, I like that the receiver is in front of my mouth when I speak into it, even if it means I can't Google shit. I like to sit on my fire escape and look out at the city and not at a screen. I like to drink whiskey and I should stop in a bar to get some.

I need to go home. I need some real sleep. I can't do this if I'm exhausted. I'm going to make mistakes.

My stomach rumbles. It's lacking food. I haven't eaten in hours. There's a noodle shop on the way home. It stays open late for the drunks. I can get some noodles.

I try to calculate how much sleep I should have gotten versus how much sleep I've actually gotten but math doesn't work right now so I just walk, my head down, dodging people who stumble and weave into my path.

The door of the shop doesn't budge. I push it again before I realize the lights are off. I press my face up against the window and see the place is gutted like a turkey at the end of Thanksgiving. Even the fixtures are ripped out of the walls.

I can't remember the name of the place. The owner sort of recognized me and sometimes threw a free order of edamame in the bag.

On the door is a sign that says it'll be a bank.

FIGURES. I GET in bed and my head is too full up, and I can't sleep.

I throw off the covers and pace, trying to order my thoughts. I consider pants but the apartment is too hot for that. I need a downer. A downer wouldn't violate my no-drug policy. Prescription pills aren't bad for you. They give them to kids.

I toss my drawers looking for a Vicodin or a Klonopin or an Oxy or a Xanax. My pill supply is in serious need of replenishing. I'm glad I don't have guests, or else I'd be embarrassed.

The vial of coke is on the counter, standing upright, beckoning me. As much as it hurts, I open it in the sink and wash it out, watch the murky water disappear down the drain. Immediately I regret it, but know I made the right decision.

I pace until I get an idea. Something to focus on.

My kitchen is an odd shape, like a hexagon that's being crushed on one side. There's a big bare rectangle of wall between the window to the alley and the living room. Flat and white like a canvas.

Need some music first. I plug my iPod into the speakers in the living room, dig through it for Billie Holiday. She sings a couple of bars of "Long Gone Blues," but it doesn't sit right. Too romantic. I switch to Nina Simone.

Over the music I can just hear the static of the scanner. "10-31, south side, Washington Square Park." Assist civilian with a non-medical emergency.

In the very middle of the wall, I write Chell's name. Then at various points around that:

Ginny

Nellie Bly
Steve the bouncer
Man with bag on head
Other guy with Chell

I draw a question mark for the killer, then I draw a line connecting them to Chell's name. Then I make a list of all the places I know she went:

Snow White
Work
Alphabet City
Jamaica

I don't know what to do after that, but it feels good to see it all in front of me. I sit on my kitchen chair and stare at the wall for a long time. Wish the words would scatter and reform themselves into something that makes a little more sense, but it doesn't happen.

It would be nice to know about Nellie Bly. I could call Bombay and ask him to look it up, but he'll be sleeping. He has a grown-up job.

No matter how hard I try to look at the names on the wall, my eyes keep drifting back to the question mark.

How could someone hurt a person like that?

My dad drilled it into me early: Men don't hit women. More than that, you've got to stick up for people. The bad guys win only if the good guys let them. Those lessons are as simple to me as breathing.

Is it as simple as the right kind of upbringing? Kids who get abused grow up to abuse. To them the pain and the hate and the fear are a part of them. But if you've been hurt, knowing that pain, why would you want to inflict it on someone else?

Does it go deeper than that? Like bad wiring, one neuron is infected and over a lifetime it branches out like cancer?

There are 8.2 million people in this city.

How many people right now are dead?

Dying?

In the process?

Worse, how many are infected?

I stare at the map on the wall, like those questions aren't naïve. Like they actually have some kind of reasonable answer. But I think about them anyway, because otherwise, my mind wanders to an image I don't want to see: Chell's face, twisted in pain.

Nina Simone sings "Ne Me Quitte Pas," her voice like the bottom of the ocean. I pick up my cell. There's a message from my mom. I consider it. Instead I call Chell's phone. It goes to voicemail.

"I'm sorry, you dialed the wrong number."

Beep.

I play it again on speakerphone, close my eyes.

FIVE

AN INSISTENT KNOCK at the door wakes me up. Getting my head off the pillow is like moving a battleship. I check my phone and it indicates I've been out for four hours. If this is the cops again, I may punch one of them in the face.

I pull on jeans and a shirt, open the door a crack, and find Aziz. It's hard to read his eyes behind the coke-bottle glasses, but his face is pointed firmly south.

He says, "You changed the locks."

"I don't think I did," I tell him. "The key sticks sometimes."

"The police were looking for you."

"They're old friends. We straightened all that out."

Aziz leans around me to look into the apartment. "The woman downstairs says there's water leaking into her apartment. I need to come in with a plumber and have a look."

"Nothing in here is leaking. Sometimes I get water in the

sink and the toilet, but I figure that's normal, right?"

Aziz tries to move around me. I hold the door tight to my side and block him with my body. He asks, "Where's Miss Hudson?"

"Bingo."

"She's always out at bingo. Why does the apartment look like such a mess?"

"She had a party last night."

"You know if she doesn't live here anymore, then I don't have to honor your lease."

"I am fully aware it is not an issue."

He gives up trying to get around me and takes a step back into the hall. "Tell her she needs to come to my office. I have some paperwork she needs to sign."

"Have a heart, Aziz. She's an old lady. She's not doing great."

"Good enough to play bingo."

"Well, you can't expect her to sit around here all day. I'm not great company."

He looks into the apartment one more time, then stalks off down the hall. "Tell her to come by later."

Not an auspicious start to the day.

Rent-controlled apartments are like UFOs. You hear about them but you never actually see them. Lucky for me, I knew a guy who knew a guy. The first guy, the one I knew, owed me a favor.

There was a woman who lived here and she died. She probably moved in sometime around World War II and her rent was locked into place. The only good thing FDR ever did for me was sign the Emergency Price Control Act in the 1940s.

The guy I knew worked at a hospital, and the guy he knew worked in a morgue. They had a little system set up. If I wasn't owed a favor, I would have paid a finder's fee.

No one notified the landlord the woman died because it happened off-premises. So I moved in, up the fire escape and through the window in the middle of the night. For as much as Aziz knows, Miss Hudson does nothing but sleep and play bingo, and I'm her live-in caretaker.

The thing is, as soon as he finds out she's not alive, he'll junk her lease and charge market rate for the apartment. I can't afford market rate. And even though it's really tough to kick out tenants in New York City, what I'm doing is a lot less than legal.

Landlords will neglect repairs to force renters out. They keep champagne on ice so they're ready to celebrate when rent-controlled tenants die off. Aziz is fixated on me. I don't know how much longer I'll last.

I'm sure there are people around here who notice Miss Hudson is gone, but the neighbors don't give a damn, ultimately, and I don't give a damn about them. You'd think sticking so many people into such a small place would make them interact more. It just makes them angrier and more territorial. People outside New York think New Yorkers are rude. We're not. It's just that personal space is in very short supply, so we treasure every little bit we can get.

The people who live upstairs sound like they're always wearing high heels and the brick walls hold in the heat even during the winter so it's always sweltering, and what looks like a broom closet in the kitchen is actually the shower. The purple and blue and pink floral wallpaper makes me nauseous when I take too many prescription drugs, and the toilet never really flushes all the way on the first try.

But it's my apartment, and I love it and anything I could

ever need is right outside my door.

There's another knock. It's quieter, and I scream, "What Aziz?" but when I open the door he's not standing there. Instead, it's a pretty girl about my age, wearing a purple sweater, her black hair pulled into a tight bun. She's got the ragged look of someone who's been traveling.

She says, "Your mom wants to know why you don't answer your phone."

I don't know what to say to that. The girl looks familiar, but my brain is still foggy.

After a moment the girl shrugs. "C'mon cousin, are you going to invite me in or what?"

"Margo?"

"Correct."

"Fuck."

"I missed you, too."

She gives me a hug and I stand aside for her. She comes into the apartment dragging a black roller suitcase behind her. I suddenly remember the conversation I had with my mom a few weeks ago. Margo is from Pennsylvania and looking at NYU. She wanted to visit the city to feel it out, and my mom asked if she could stay with me. That must be why she was calling.

Margo asks, "It's still cool, right? Staying here?"

"Of course."

"Did you forget?"

"Yes."

Margo laughs. "You know, I can go get a hotel room or something if this is inconvenient."

"No, it's fine. Hotels around here are too fucking expensive." I lead her into the living room and put her on the couch, sit on the floor on the other side of the coffee table. She shrugs. "So, how've you been?"

"Alive." I reach for my cigarettes and pull one out, hold the pack up to her. She nods and I hand it to her. "So you might be coming here next year?"

"I hope so. I think I've got a really good chance of getting into Tisch." She pulls out her phone. "I'm going to text my mom and let her know I'm with you. You should do the same. Your mom says she never hears from you."

As Margo clicks away I send my mom a text: *Margo here. Sorry.* Then I turn off my phone. I take a long drag on my smoke. "Been a while, right?"

"I haven't seen you since the funeral. That was so long ago." She reaches for something in her bag but stops. "I'm sorry I didn't really get a chance to talk to you. There were so many people..."

"It got crowded."

"I know I should have called. Or, I don't know, been there. I'm so sorry about what happened to your dad."

"Most people are."

Margo looks away from me, her voice catching a little. "He was a hero. You know that, right?"

"Let's not talk about this."

"I'm sorry."

"You don't have to be sorry. The first thing anyone ever wants to do when they come to New York is talk about 9/11. What is there to talk about? It happened. It sucks. Talking about it is not going to bring him back."

She drops it there. Looks around my apartment, at the French Rococo walnut armoire in the corner, at the green painted Irish hutch. The plastic wrapped around the paisley-print couch creaks underneath her.

"You have an interesting taste in furniture," she says.

"I'm a fan of the classics. I still listen to vinyl too."

"Seriously, why does it look like an old lady lives here?"

"Well, that's sort of the point."

I explain my living arrangement and her eyes go wide when I tell her how much I pay in rent. She asks, "For this apartment?"

"Fact."

"That's insane. Student housing at NYU is nearly three grand a month, and that's with a roommate."

"Welcome to New York."

"It's a little weird though," she says, scrunching up her face. "Living in a dead lady's apartment?"

"New York real estate is a full contact sport. And it's pretty vanilla, compared to some of the things I've done." I finish off my cigarette and stamp it out in the overflowing ashtray. The scanner buzzes in the kitchen. "10-32, A and 3." Defective oil burner a few blocks away.

Margo looks toward the kitchen. "What was that?"

"Scanner. Listen, make yourself comfortable. I need to clean up."

I leave Margo on the couch, which is set back against the wall and behind a folding screen so I can use the shower when people are over without feeling like too much of an exhibitionist. She occupies herself while I manage a quick rinse. Just enough to make me feel human.

I pull on a shirt I feel confident was recently clean and head back to the living room. Margo has emptied the ashtray into the trash, and she's smoking another one of my cigarettes. She looks up at me. "What now?"

"Fuck if I know. You showed up on my doorstep. Tell me what you want to do."

"I don't want to keep you from anything. And I can go, really. I'm sure I can find a place to stay."

"No, you're staying here. Let's go get some food. I need eggs and coffee."

"Perfect. I saw a Starbucks on the way here."

"Starbucks?"

"They have breakfast sandwiches."

This is going to require attention. I tell her, "If you're going to live here, no Starbucks. The coffee tastes like crap and it's a chain. Chains are stupid. There are much better food options."

She arches her eyebrows and nods cautiously, like she thinks I might be scolding her. Maybe I am.

We hit the sidewalk and I stretch, breathe the crisp air. I turn in a circle, contemplate where we should go, and I catch Margo twisting a sterling ring off her right index finger. She places it in her purse.

I ask, "What are you doing?"

"I don't want anyone to take it."

And it's right here that I laugh so hard I pull a muscle in my rib cage.

Margo asks, "What?"

HERE'S THE THING about living in New York City: People from the outside are stuck on how things used to be in the seventies, when riding the subway meant you ran a 60/40 chance of getting stabbed.

The murder rate peaked in 1990 with twenty-two-hundred

deaths. Last year, it was a drop over five hundred. We're down in every major crime category, to the point where this is now the safest big city in America. We've gone from the urban hellscape of *Death Wish* to the whitewashed utopia of *Friends*.

And yet we just can't shake our rep.

Everyone has their own theories about what made things change. Gentrification, the Clinton economy. And they were factors, sure. But the big catalyst was Mayor Giuliani, a supreme asshole of titanic proportions. A craven, selfish fuck who stomped on civil liberty and, contrary to popular belief, didn't do jack shit after 9/11 besides trip over the first responders on his way to the television cameras.

Among his many "accomplishments" was appointing a commissioner for the NYPD who instituted a broken windows policy. The idea is that if you walk by an abandoned factory with broken windows, and there's a pile of rocks at your feet, you may be tempted to break more windows. But if none of the windows are broken, you might not think to do it.

In this instance, the idea was that clearing out lesser crimes would reduce major crimes. The NYPD went after the little things, like public drinking, fare beating, squeegee men. And it helped, a little.

The problem is Giuliani also turned the NYPD into a military-style unit of enforcement that could stop and frisk you for no reason, other than they feel like it. There were arrest quotas to make and CompStat reports to fill out, which were supposed to be about tracking crime, but turned into goals. Haven't written enough summonses this month? Then go out and snag someone for something. Doesn't matter if they're guilty of anything—as long as the numbers look good.

And crime did drop. The tourists flocked here in droves.

Kids with stars in their eyes moved to once-uninhabitable neighborhoods like Bushwick and the Lower East Side. Park Slope and Tribeca became suburbs tucked away between tall buildings.

Today's New York City is a luxury product to package and sell to tourists. In a hundred years, this entire city will be set behind glass and you'll only be allowed to live here if you earn a salary in the high six figures. Everyone else will be turfed to Jersey.

I explain this all to Margo and she listens very intently. When I'm done she asks, "Isn't being safe a good thing?"

"I know plenty of people who would take the bad old days back in a heartbeat."

"That's a little ridiculous."

"Maybe. But you live here your whole life, you understand a little better."

W E SETTLE ON a trattoria nearby that does good eggs and coffee. I don't like not working, but maybe some food will get the wheels spinning. Right now my head feels full of cotton.

The restaurant is empty and a bored waiter with neck tattoos leads us to a table near the front window. Lunette is sitting in the back, trying to keep her head aloft over a Bloody Mary. I tell the waiter we're moving and pull out a chair across from her. She barely stirs when I sit. She's wearing big sunglasses even though it's dark in the corner.

I knock on the table. "Rough night?"

She makes an affirmative noise with her mouth and looks at Margo. "Who are you?"

I flip through the menu even though I know what I want. "You'll have to forgive Lunette. She's part Russian. Lunette, this is my cousin, Margo."

Margo reaches her hand across the table and they shake. Lunette takes a long sip of her Bloody Mary while the waiter takes our order. I tell him to bring me sunny-side eggs and toast and hash browns and a pot of coffee. He laughs even though it's not a joke and goes back to the kitchen.

"So," Margo says to Lunette. "What do you do?"

"What do I do?"

"For a living."

"Is it important for you to know?"

"Just… making conversation."

Lunette makes another noise with her mouth and digs through her purse, then reaches her hand up to her mouth. I grab her wrist. "Don't be mean."

"She's a gent."

"And she's blood."

Lunette shakes me off and dry-swallows whatever pill it is she's taking. To Margo she says, "I'm sorry dear. My hangovers make me into a different kind of person."

"I know the feeling," Margo says. "But what's a gent?"

Fearing Lunette will give her the unkind version, I jump in. "It's a nickname for people who move here but weren't born here. Gent is short for gentrification."

"Why?"

The waiter puts down my coffee and a glass of ice water. I drop three cubes into the mug and tell Margo, "Because when some trust-fund baby is willing to shell out three grand a month for an apartment, it drives up the surrounding property values and prices people out. Places like CBGB closed because of people like that."

Lunette nods her head. "Dreadful."

I take a swig of my coffee. "My landlord is pretty close to getting me out, I think. He could get four, five times what I'm paying, easy."

Margo pokes at her light-and-sweet mug. "Where will you go if you have to leave your apartment?"

"I can afford a bench in the subway, but it would have to be on one of the crappier lines, like the G train."

"What about moving to a borough? You could go back to Staten Island."

"That would be like admitting defeat," I tell her.

"What about Brooklyn?"

Lunette cringes. I laugh.

Margo scrunches her brow. "I thought Brooklyn was supposed to be cool. I know a lot of people back home who talk about Williamsburg like it's Shangri-La."

"Williamsburg is where you go when you're afraid to be an adult. I wouldn't last a week."

"If I move here, you could stay with me. We could figure it out."

I smile at her. "Thanks, but you don't need that kind of trouble."

"So," Margo asks both of us. "How do you two know each other?"

Lunette laughs at the memory. "Some guy whipped his dick out on the subway and waved it in my face. Ash leveled him."

Margo purses her lips. "Does that kind of thing happen often?"

"The penis on the subway or Ash hitting people? Both are surprisingly frequent. Don't worry though. The city is safer than it seems."

I'm gearing to defend myself when the food arrives. The eggs are salty and scrambled, but I don't care. I wave to the busboy for more coffee and Margo asks, "It's not, like, that safe, is it? Did you hear about that girl? The one who got killed near here two nights ago? The one the papers called the Greenpoint Goth?"

Lunette looks up at me. I keep looking at the plate. I don't want to have this conversation. It would be rude to get up and go. I'm tired of talking about dead people. It seems like I can't avoid it. I shrug my shoulders. "She was a friend."

"Oh Christ Ash, I'm so sorry," Margo says.

"Please don't apologize. You didn't kill her."

"My mom almost didn't let me come here because of that. She didn't want to drive me to the train station."

"It's not dangerous," I tell her. "Sometimes it can be. You just need to be smart."

Lunette says, "Chell was smart."

"She was. How about we all back the fuck off this topic of conversation?"

"We can't actually," says Lunette.

"Why?"

"Because there's something I need to tell you."

"About?"

"About Chell."

I put down my knife and fork and fold my hands in front of me. I don't look at Margo when I tell her, "This is terribly rude of me, but could you give us a second."

Margo nods. "I'm going to go out front and smoke."

I wait until she's out on the sidewalk, then ask Lunette. "What have you got?"

"I asked around a little bit because you're too angry to have rational conversations with people. I found out on the day she died, she went to go meet with the head of her burlesque troupe. They're doing a show tonight at Skidmore. At night, she was out at whatever mystery job she was working that nobody seems to know anything about."

"Good. All things I didn't know."

"Yes, but there's more. Do you know what she was doing in the morning?" Lunette pauses for effect. "Brunch with Ginny."

I let that glance off my chin, then nod and push myself out from the table. Margo is standing just outside, finishing her cigarette. She offers me one, but I take out my own. She asks, "Do you want me to leave?"

"No. It's fine. We'll take you out tonight. I just have no idea what to do until then. It's still early."

Margo tosses her cigarette to the street and says, "I need to be at NYU for a meeting pretty soon with one of the advisors from the film department. Maybe you and Lunette could come up with me and show me around the neighborhood a bit."

"Sure. Why don't you go back inside to finish eating with Lunette. I need to make a call."

Margo heads inside. I walk down the block and my hands are shaking.

Ginny lied to me.

She said she hadn't seen Chell in what, weeks? I should kick in her door and punch her in the face before her guards take me down, and it's fine to because she's really a guy. But the only way she'll tell me the truth is if I confront her with it.

I toss the half-spent smoke into the street and head back to the restaurant. Lunette is sitting by herself. She cocks her head to the side. "In the bathroom." I sit across from her. She frowns, says, "I didn't mean to upset you."

"Not much to say right now that won't upset me."

"We're going up to NYU?"

"Yes. And it would be a big help if you came. She's supposed to be staying with me, and she can, but it'll be good if she has some other people to hang out with. Keep an eye on her. Can you do this for me?"

"She's sweet." Lunette picks up a spent sugar packet and tears the pieces in half. "Is she my type?"

"I didn't ask."

"So, Ash." She puts down the sugar packet and takes my hand. "I know this is hard. I hope you're being smart. Please promise me you'll be smart?"

"I love you too much to make you promises."

"Well, at least you seem... calmer than normal."

"I'm off booze until I see this through."

"You're not drinking?"

"Clean and sober."

Lunette's face registers a level of shock that makes me uncomfortable. She says, "I don't know that I've ever seen you this serious."

WE STOP AT the northeast end of Washington Square Park to get our bearings and so Margo can look up the address on her phone. Her meeting is in a building around the corner, and I tell the girls to head over because I need to run an errand.

After they disappear, I head diagonally across the park to the chess tables. Most of them are full up with players, except for the one at the end of the line where Craig is sitting by himself, pondering the carefully-aligned pieces on the stone playing surface.

His hair is wrapped into a sloppy ponytail, done with his hands and not a comb. His skin's cracked from living outside and eating a diet that consists mostly of booze. But his gray eyes are sharp, and when I sit across from him, they probe me in a way that makes the muscles in my back tighten.

I start the game the same way I always do. Clearing some pawns, a bishop, and a knight into the middle so I can castle my king behind the rook. Craig chips away at the sides of the boards, looking for an opening. I think I'm holding him back when he manages to snatch one of my pawns.

And then another.

And then my bishop.

I panic and push into the middle. Put my spare rook onto a square I think will cost him his queen. I don't even see the bishop that takes it out. It's not long before I'm down to a knight and the three pawns guarding the king. Craig still has a lot of his pieces.

The game is over, but I keep playing out of respect. Within a few moves he's backed my king into a corner with a bishop and a rook. I knock over the king and he smiles for the first time since I sat down.

"Chell died two nights ago," I tell him as he resets the board. "Hear anything about it?"

He shakes his head.

I pull a twenty dollar bill out of my pocket and slide it across the table. "Ask around, see what you can find out. I was black-out, so if anyone saw me stumbling around, that would help too."

He looks around to make sure no one is watching us, then

crumples the money in his hand and pushes it into the pocket of his tattered Bomber jacket.

Craig doesn't say much, but when he does, it's worth the money.

We play two more games and both times I hang on a little longer, until he decides to stop toying with me and gouges my defenses. When I'm tired of getting my ass kicked, I thank him for his help, then walk over to Mamoun's to grab a shawarma, wait for the girls to finish.

I WANT TO WORK the case, but I don't want to abandon Margo. I'm glad Lunette is sticking with us because that makes it easier. The two of them talk on an endless loop and I only have to weigh in occasionally.

We grab dinner at Milon so I can introduce Margo to the joys of cheap Indian food. Then it's time to drink. Margo wants to go down to the bars on MacDougal because that's where her friends have told her to go. I tell her MacDougal is a great place to get puked on or date-raped by a frat guy.

Instead we go to Stillwater. Lunette disappears for the juke box and fills it up with Faith No More even though we won't be here long. The bartender slams down a glass of whiskey for me, but I pass it off and ask him if he saw me or Chell the night she died, but he didn't.

After a bit, we head across the street to KGB, where the red lights make everyone look like a junkie. The bartender offers me his condolences and I stop him from pouring me a vodka. Chell was a regular here, and I ask him if she'd been around and he says no. I can smell the alcohol and I want a drop, just a tiny little drop. Lunette and Margo are tipsy and that makes it worse.

Bombay and Romer show up and they order drinks but say they want to knock off to Coyote Ugly. Drunken idiots drooling over tits isn't really my scene, but Bad Kelly might be working, and last I heard she was dating a cop. That might be useful.

I introduce Bombay and Romer to Margo and head for the bathroom where a guy I sort of recognize is ducking into the stall. He offers me a line of coke and I wave him off with a heavy heart.

We leave and find Coyote Ugly is packed out the door and that annoys me. We push our way in and Bad Kelly is dancing on the bar in a black bra and skintight jeans. Her red hair hangs in sweaty ropes in front of her eyes. She's pouring tequila down guys' throats and they're reaching up, trying to grope her, but she's kneeing and elbowing their hands away.

Lunette pulls rank on some guys at a booth in the back, making them get up for her and Margo. They think she's hitting on them, so they try to squeeze back in after the girls sit. It's fun to watch their crestfallen expressions when they realize they've been had. Bombay appears at my side with a glass of Jay on the rocks, but when I don't take it he shrugs, throws it back, and proceeds onto his beer.

I want to talk to Bad Kelly but she's on the bar, and I don't know what else to do with myself because it's too loud inside for a conversation. Some guy grabs me and yells into my ear that he needs to hire me to find someone. He rattles off some details, his face way too close to mine, but I'm not listening, and when he's done, I tell him I'm booked. I consider exit strategies when I notice Bad Kelly waving at me.

She rubs her fists at her eyes like she's mock-crying.

Sorry about Chell being dead, is what she's trying to say.

Most other people would do something like that and set me off, but Bad Kelly has a stunning inability to understand what's appropriate in polite society. We're a little similar like that so I give her a pass. I point at her and then at the door of the bar. She holds up five fingers, spread out, so I go outside and wait.

The crowd makes me anxious. Too many guys flailing their arms because they drank too much and there are woman nearby. Just as I'm finishing my first cigarette, Bad Kelly comes out wearing a heavy fleece. A guy's fleece. Probably demanded it from someone standing at the bar. She meets me at the curb and takes out her own cigarette, the pack ragged and wet from being crammed in her sweat-soaked jeans. She leans toward me for a light and asks, "You okay, sweetie?"

"Not even close."

"I'm sorry."

"Nothing to be sorry for."

"What do you need?" I light another cigarette for myself. "Information. Anything you can tell me about Chell. What she'd been up to."

Some guy with a popped collar and a backwards baseball cap comes up to Bad Kelly and gets two inches closer than appropriate. "Hey gorgeous. Taking a break?"

She wraps herself around my arm, her body warm and small against mine. "Boyfriend."

I tell him, "Fuck off."

He takes a step toward me, but when I don't take my eyes away from his, he retreats. When he's out of earshot Kelly says, "Thanks."

"My job. So, anything?"

"Haven't seen her around lately. She's been off in Brooklyn, working on something for Ginny."

"What kind of something?"

"She didn't tell me. I mean, I didn't ask her. But she said something about the 'fucking hipsters.'"

"That's good. One other thing. Are you still dating that cop?"

"We don't date. We fuck."

"Want to do me a solid? And if you pull this off, I'll owe you big time?"

She speaks slowly, drawing out the word. "Depends."

"When there's a high profile murder like this, the cops withhold details so they can separate the real suspects from the cranks. I need to find out what they're holding back from the press. Can you poke around?"

"How am I supposed to do that?"

"You'll think of something."

"Me and this guy have been on the skids."

"And?"

"You're essentially asking me to let him fuck me so you can get an inside track."

"First off, that's not what I'm asking you. And I wouldn't even ask you this if it wasn't important."

Bad Kelly turns away from me and crosses her arms. She says, "I'm not a whore, Ash."

"I didn't say you were. I'm not saying you have to fuck him. But are you never going to see this guy again?"

She drops her cigarette and shakes her head. "You're an asshole."

"Kelly. How many times have you called me on the tail end

of a bad relationship to keep things clean? I have always been there for you."

She shakes her head, still refusing to look at me. "You are such an asshole."

"I'll owe you."

"Yes, you will." She heads back for the bar.

For a very fleeting moment, I feel guilty. The feeling passes.

Margo and Lunette are sharing a cigarette outside the front door. They're deep in conversation so I don't try and break in. Some guy comes up to me and asks if he can have a cigarette. I tell him a pack costs eleven bucks and to go buy one if he wants one so bad. Inside I find Bombay drinking a new beer. He sees me and puts two fingers up to his mouth.

Good, because I don't smoke enough anyway.

By the time we fight our way back outside, Margo and Lunette have disappeared. Bombay lights himself a cigarette, then lights mine. I take out the card for Noir York and the thumb drive.

He asks, "What do you need?"

"Anything and everything. Whatever you can tell me."

He nods, sticks them in his pocket.

"Another thing," I tell him. "Find out everything you can about Nellie Bly."

"The journalist?"

"You know who she is?"

"Sure. She was a journalist back in the 1900s. She was famous for infiltrating a mental hospital to uncover abuse of the patients."

"How do you know that?"

"I read books."

"Thanks dick. Find out what you can about the rest and I'll

swing by tomorrow."

I head back into the bar and find Lunette and Margo back at their table. Lunette looks at her watch and says, "You should head to Skidmore. That burlesque show is starting soon."

"Thanks, kid. Can you take care of Margo?"

She curls her lips up in a very drunken, very suggestive smile. "Oh, I'll take care of her."

"Stop that." I turn to Margo, hand her the key to my apartment. "Hang out with Lunette. If you get tired, she'll take you back to my place. Sleep in the bed and I'll take the couch."

Margo is drunk and doesn't appear to be used to being drunk. "But we're having fun!"

"Then keep on having fun. I'll see you in a bit."

She calls something after me but I don't hear her.

THERE'S A LINE to get into Skidmore. There's also a door with a bouncer stationed outside that no one is lined up at. I recognize him, and he recognizes me from around. I ask him, "Girls back there?"

He shifts on his stool. "Why?"

"I need to talk to Cinnamon West."

"Sorry man. You need to go in like everyone else."

I consider passing the guy some cash, but my wallet feels light. I can't keep paying people for information. I nod to him, thank him for his time, and get in the line. It doesn't move, so I light a cigarette and a girl standing near me grumbles and waves a hand in front of her face, even though the smoke isn't going anywhere near her. "Welcome to New York," I tell her.

Suddenly the line moves forward and I'm at the door. A

pretty girl asks for ten dollars. I give it to her and my wallet is now empty.

The place is simple. A bar along one wall, a stage across from it, and tables and chairs sized for toddlers. Lots of wood and amber lighting, so the place has a previous-century feel. There's a makeshift stage at the back of the restaurant, which doesn't look like much more than wooden pallets and plywood.

The show hasn't started yet, so I work my way toward the curtained-off area in the back. Cinnamon peeks out, probably looking for someone else, because when she sees me she rolls her eyes. I wave to her and she points me to another doorway across the bar.

It's a storeroom, white tile walls and shelves with cleaning supplies. Cinnamon sweeps in. She's holding a robe tight around her body. Her afro is comically big. I wonder if it's a wig but am too afraid to ask.

She looks at me like she's waiting for a punch line. "What?"

"Nice to see you too."

"Ash, this isn't a good time."

"Then I won't keep you. I knew Chell met with the troupe the day she died. I just need to know if she said anything or did anything that might point me to who killed her."

"I saw her, but I don't even know what you mean."

"Anything. Anything you can think of that stood out?"

"So you're a private detective now?"

"I'm a friend who wants to rip the throat out of the guy who killed her. Especially before he hurts someone else."

Cinnamon shakes her head. "You know Chell hasn't danced with us in a while. She wasn't even looking to get back in. It was a social call."

"That's fine. I just need to know if she said anything."

She nods, slowly. "I think so. Maybe. You didn't hear this from me?"

"Of course."

"She's in something. Some kind of game kind of thing. It's an acting gig."

"I knew that already."

"There's a girl, she's another dancer. She went for the same part and didn't get it. She was pissed, saying Chell only got the job because she knew somebody. Something like that."

"What's the girl's name?"

"Her stage name is Fanny Fatale. I don't know her real name."

"You think one of the other girls might know her?"

"You're not coming back stage."

"That's fine. I'll wait."

Her face takes on the edge of a straight razor. "I shouldn't even be talking to you."

"Why?"

"You know why."

"Clearly not."

She shakes her head. "Because you loved that girl too hard, and she carried it like a burden."

"What's that supposed to mean?"

She turns to leave. "We have to start the show."

"Cinnamon, c'mon, don't be like this." She doesn't say anything. I yell after her, "You know what? Don't comment on shit you don't understand."

When I duck out from behind the curtain, people are staring at me. I stick my middle finger in the air as I head for the door.

DO YOU REMEMBER that night we went to the Brooklyn Bridge?

You complained that I never wanted to do anything touristy with you. When you first moved here, you had designs on seeing the big attractions. The Statue of Liberty, Ellis Island, the Empire State Building. You were shocked to learn I had never visited any of them. Locals don't do tourist shit, I told you.

After some begging, I agreed to walk across the Brooklyn Bridge. I wasn't going to be caught doing anything else. At least I could explain that away if someone saw me. Plus, it was on the East Side. I still wasn't comfortable being within ten blocks of the trade center.

You were okay with the bridge. In fact, after I told you, you became fixated. Within days you were spouting off history and facts. If it weren't for you, I would never have known it's the oldest suspension bridge in the United States, or that it's a bad spot for suicides because it's too low to the water.

The night we walked up there it was in the middle of the summer, and it was warm, but it wasn't hot. It was early evening and we decided that the best time to go would be at dusk when the sun was dipping behind the horizon and the lights in all the office buildings were clicking on.

We scoped a park bench on the Manhattan side of the span and stood by it for twenty minutes, waiting for the couple sitting there to vacate. Then we pounced, barely beating out a European family. They looked amenable to sharing the space so we spread out and took it all.

We sat there watching the city twinkle and you nestled your head into my shoulder. You were wearing a sundress and no bra and heavy combat boots. We traded a flask of whiskey

ROB HART

between us until it was empty. Eventually you leaned back and made a noise and it sounded sad. I asked you what was wrong.

You said, *I can only see a couple of stars. Maybe, like, twelve?*

Light pollution.

That's sad.

It's no big deal.

Have you ever even seen *the stars?*

When I was a kid. I was camping with my dad up in Bear Mountain.

What did you think?

It looked pretty amazing. But it looks pretty amazing here too.

Can we go up to Bear Mountain?

We'll borrow a car from someone.

Can we do it soon?

Are you okay?

Just a little homesick.

You're homesick?

Just a little.

We sat there for most of the night. The whole time I was working up the nerve to ask you a question. After that first night in your apartment and the bathtub I guessed something would happen between us and I was wrong. Things stayed platonic, and I didn't want to scare you off so I didn't push it.

But I spent a lot of time wondering whether I should kiss you.

I didn't want to just do it and have it come off the wrong way. Being as big as I am has always made me skittish about how my advances would be interpreted.

When I had drank enough whiskey that I had some nerve and figured you'd be a little more relaxed, I asked, *Can I kiss*

79

you?

You didn't say anything. I didn't want to look at your face. When I did look at you, the way your mouth was set told me I shouldn't have asked.

You said, *Ashley, you're a good person and a great friend. Please let's not ruin that?*

I know, it's just, I thought...

I'd like to break the cycle. I don't want to hurt you.

You don't scare me.

You looked at me, the smoke in your eye billowing, and you wrapped your arms around me. I considered vaulting myself over the railing of the bridge. Not that I wanted to die, but I wanted to get away from the shame digging a finger into my neck.

You said, *What we have is perfect. And I just don't want to be with anyone right now. Can't we just stick with this?*

Sure. Forget I asked.

We never went up to Bear Mountain.

I SHOOT A TEXT to Lunette to find out where her and Margo are, and she responds almost immediately: *She's staying with me tonight. Will call tomorrow.*

And there's that.

I consider walking by Chanticleer. But I'm still fitting the pieces together. A full night's sleep to think this all over would be nice and I'm free of other responsibilities, so I head for home. Margo still has my key, but I have a spare hidden in the hallway of my building.

As I turn the corner to my block I think I see something in

the corner of my vision, darting away. Probably a cat. I pat my jacket for my smokes when I hear a shuffle behind me.

There are two of them, both in tight jeans and dinner jackets, with ski masks over their faces. They're wearing thick Buddy Holly glasses over the ski masks, the arms slid through eye-holes. They're the same height. One is thin and one is heavy.

The thin one pulls out a knife.

SiX

NOD TOWARD THE knife, ask, "What do you think you're going to do with that?"

They pause and look at each other, then back at me. The thin one asks, "Where is it?"

"Where's what?"

They stare at me like they're trying to light me on fire. I can't believe no one is seeing this but it's late and the block is empty. I shrug at them. "Are you new at this? What are you looking for, you fucking morons?"

The thin one steps forward, holding the knife up. "The jump drive."

"You mean the thumb drive?"

He pauses. "I call it a jump drive."

"You know what? I don't have the patience for this." I pull the umbrella from my belt and click the button on the side.

The canopy stays wrapped but the stick snaps out to full length.

The thin one steps toward me and asks, "What are you going to do with that?"

I guess it is pretty funny, the sight of me standing there holding it out at my side like a broadsword. It'd be even funnier if it were a regular umbrella, and not a steel rod with a Kevlar top.

The thin one stops laughing when I swing it at the knife. It flies from his hand and lands on the steps to my building. He reels back with a fist full of broken fingers.

The shock is greater than the pain so I drive my fist into his stomach to even the two out. He leans forward and I'm about to bring my fists down onto his back and put him on the ground when I see the heavy one scrambling for the knife. He gets it and comes at me, swinging it in the air but leaning away from it like he's afraid of it.

I sidestep, but the thin one is falling forward and gets in my way. He shoves me into the path of the heavy one. I'm off balance, so I put my forearm up and the blade clicks off bone. A floodlight explodes under my skin.

I grab the wound and back up to the parked cars lining the block. I roll over a hood and into the street to put something between me and them. But by the time I'm steady on my feet the two of them are turning the corner at high speed.

And still, there's no one around to see what happened.

I take some deep breaths of cold air, try to tamp down the adrenaline screaming through my blood. After a few moments, the pain shows up.

BOMBAY OPENS THE door and looks at the arm of my jacket, at the charcoal cotton now deep black and shiny. He shakes his head and says, "You're lucky I don't have to work tomorrow." He steps aside and lets me in.

His apartment is in the same state it's always in: Covered with the corpses of pizza boxes, tortilla chip bags, bottles of diet soda, and more laptops than I can count. Comic book posters clutter the walls wherever there aren't bookshelves loaded with graphic novels.

As I make my way to the table near the kitchen he says, "You are a walking oxymoron."

"Because?"

"You are the most brilliant stupid person I know."

"Emphasis on the stupid. Am I right?"

"I'm glad you're enjoying this."

"You have to laugh. Better than the alternative."

Bombay sets down a first-aid kit and puts a towel under my arm. This is the second time I've been slashed and he's had to sew me up. The previous occasion was actually completely unrelated to my job—a girl I was seeing thought I was flirting with her friend. She was also mixing meds with Riesling. The broken stem of a wine glass can cut pretty damn deep. I don't like hospitals, and Bombay likes to be prepared. It's a good combination.

He douses the cut in cheap vodka from a plastic jug and it feels like fingernails scraping out the raw skin. Once the excess blood washes away, it doesn't really look that bad. A three-inch gash on the back of my forearm, midway between elbow and wrist. It's deep and a little ugly but manageable.

Bombay sets down a shot glass and fills it to the brim with vodka. Next to it he places a large white pill. "Oxy with a vodka back."

"No drugs, no booze. Not right now."

"You're really doing the sober thing?"

"For the time being."

"I never thought I'd see the day."

"Fuck you."

"This is going to hurt."

"I'll take my chances."

Bombay roots around in the kit and pulls out a spool of heavy purple thread.

"C'mon man," I tell him. "Really?"

"If you're going to make me sew up the hole in your arm, you damn well better believe I'm going to have some fun with this." He nods toward the shot. "Last chance."

I hold the base of the glass and consider it. But then I remember the hardwood floor and I push it back toward him. "No dice."

"You sure you don't want to go to the hospital?"

"What if they report it to the cops? I'd rather not deal with that bullshit."

Bombay nods. "Can't believe you're sober." He pounds the shot, leaves the pill.

"I am full of surprises."

"Didn't know you were so stupid, either."

"Then you don't know me at all."

TRUTHFULLY, NO ONE knows me better than Bombay. And no one knows him better than I do. For example, his name isn't Bombay. It's Acaryatanaya, even though that name is so far in his past, most people don't know it.

Bombay isn't a devout Muslim, but he was raised in the religion and occasionally dabbles in things like not eating pork. It never lasts long, but it's enough he occasionally catches shit for it.

We started junior high at the same time, and while it's never been totally safe to be a Muslim in America, it was especially dangerous in the years following 9/11. Because even though New York has a reputation for being progressive, it's often not. On the second day of school I came across a bunch of kids calling him a terrorist and shoving him into a locker.

I made them stop. I don't like bullies. I didn't like how I got picked on for having a girl's name, I don't like other people getting picked on for anything else. Especially for things they didn't do.

Anyway, it got bloody. I got suspended for a week and by the time I came back to school, Bombay and I were inseparable.

When I told him my name was Ashley but everyone called me Ash, he said he wanted a nickname too. I asked him where he was from. He said Bombay. Technically Mumbai, but that didn't have a nice enough ring to it.

We work well as a unit, because his first response to a problem is to think through it instead of hit it. Pretty much the opposite of me.

BOMBAY GRIPS MY arm as best he can without slipping on the blood and makes the first pierce. In cuts through the jumble of pain like a hot beam of light. I grit my teeth, think about cupcakes and bunnies.

The blood is making his fingers slick. They slide off the needle so he takes a moment and resets his grip. "So what did you do to deserve this?"

"This wasn't even my fault. It was two random guys."

"What did they want?"

"Who knows?"

He moves fast. I don't like the feeling of the thread worming its way through my skin. By the time Bombay is halfway done the pain has faded into a gentle buzz. A thing I can live with.

He says, "You can't bring her back, man."

"I never said it would."

"Then why?"

"There are other things to be gained."

He stops mid-stitch and looks up at me. "Like what?"

"What if this guy hurts someone else?"

"And what are you going to do if you manage to find him before the cops do?"

He pulls through the last stitch and ties the loose ends of thread. I pour a little more vodka over the wound and it's suddenly much less scary to look at. As he's placing a bandage over it I tell him, "There's a certain way a man's supposed to act."

"Like this, you mean."

"You know what I mean."

Bombay pats tape onto the bandage and leans back in his chair. "Are you really going to kill him?"

"Why do you need me to say it?"

"If you want to toss him a beating, fine. It's deserved. I'll even help if you want. But you can't go killing people. And I know you have a reason, but just because you have a reason doesn't mean you should do it."

"I don't know what you want to hear," I tell him, checking to make sure the bandage is tight.

"It's not about telling me the right thing. Don't make this sound like a hang-up for me. You can't just kill someone, man. Blood doesn't wash away blood."

"I'm not trying to fix this. I know I can't fix it. But someone has to stop him."

"I know you must be a mess right now, but please, for me, ask yourself who you're doing this for."

"What are you saying?"

"You know what I'm saying."

It happens without me thinking about it. The muscles in my fist ball up. And my instinct is to throw it at him. He doesn't see my hand in my lap because his view is blocked by the table, but he sees something in my eyes and that makes him slide his chair back to put some space between us.

Breathe deep. I tell him, "Regardless of how things were between me and Chell, this is our home. This is where we live. And I will not tolerate this."

Bombay pours himself a shot and throws it back. He pours another but lets it sit on the table. He reaches for it, but instead of taking it he says, "Then go catch all the rapists. Go stop every murder. Why don't you go be a cop, if this is how you feel?"

"Cops are sanctioned bullies. They get their badge and their gun and then they're more concerned with what the job can do for them, not what they can do for the city. All we have is each other. There are good guys and there are bad guys, and the good guys need to stand up for one another."

"You're Spider-Man now? With great power comes great responsibility? Do you even hear yourself?"

"My hearing is fine."

Bombay takes the bloody towels and the vodka into the kitchen. He says, "I only say this because I love you. You do understand that, right?"

"Say that to my face, you pussy."

He doesn't say anything back.

My conscience tells me to go into the kitchen, hug him, thank him for being a good friend. I ignore it, ask him, "Make any headway on the crap I gave you?"

He comes out drying his hands on a dish towel and carries a laptop over to the table, pulls up a browser, and types in the URL from the business card.

It leads to an all-black screen with Noir York in big, white lettering. Underneath that it reads: *New York is the brightest city in the world, but if you look close enough, you see the dark underbelly festering below the surface.*

There's nothing else on the screen. No buttons, no links.

Bombay says, "Now watch." He clicks a couple of buttons, opening a small white screen of messy text. He pulls over a pad and a pen and writes down a phone number.

I ask, "How did you do that?"

"I pulled up the source code for the page."

"Talk to me like I'm not a nerd."

"The source code is what the site is built out of. The programming language. Sometimes people hide clues in it. It says you have to look 'below the surface.' It's not fancy, but it's decently clever."

"What does it say?"

"Just a phone number."

"How do you know it's a phone number?"

"Because it's ten digits long with a six-four-six area code."

"You are such a nerd."

He shakes his head. "You are really bad at saying 'thanks.'"

"Fact."

He hands me the sheet of paper. I fold it up and put it in my pocket and ask, "Can you tell me anything else about the site?"

He clicks at the keyboard for a little bit and calls up another website. "There's this thing called a 'whois' search, which is how you figure out who owns a URL. When you buy a domain, you have the option of blocking it as a privacy setting. This person blocked it."

"Can you get around it?"

"Maybe. Might take a few days. If I do it, do you promise to not kill anyone?"

"I love you too much to promise you anything."

He stares at me for a moment, then his shoulders sag. "I'll figure it out."

Next he takes out the thumb drive. He doesn't put it in the computer, just leans forward holding it in his hands. "Do you know what this is?"

I don't want to tell him it's what I almost got stabbed over. I say, "Of course I don't."

"It's a Steel Drive."

"Elaborate."

"It's military-grade. You could run this over with a tank. The encryption is impossible to crack. If you enter the wrong password ten times it self-destructs."

"For real?"

"For *real* real. I mean, it doesn't explode like a bomb, just the chip inside burns out."

"Can you break in?"

"Dude, if you actually manage to crack this open there's an epoxy that snaps the chip. I'm pretty good, but even if you took this to an elite hacker, they wouldn't be able to do anything with it. Where did you get this?"

"Chell's apartment."

"You stole it?"

"She's not using it. Any idea where she got it?"

"They're available to the general public. About a hundred bucks. I actually wanted to get one. They're pretty cool."

"Any idea why Chell would have one?"

He shrugs.

It doesn't sit right. Military-style indestructible hard drive. I wasn't even going to take it. Now I'm glad I did. Bombay plugs it in the side of the laptop and a prompt screen appears.

I ask, "Any ideas?"

"A few." He types and hits enter. The screen shakes like it's angry and the number six appears in the corner.

Bombay says, "Huh."

"What?"

"Someone has already tried to get into this thing. Three bad attempts."

He types two more, and both times it comes back wrong. The number drops to four. Bombay says, "The three most common passwords are 'password,' 'sex,' and the person's birthday." He takes the drive out and hands it to me. "You have four more tries before it's useless."

"I'm glad there's no pressure."

He closes the laptop and cracks the top of a diet soda. "You look like you need some sleep."

"That is probably correct."

"You can crash here if you want."

"Need a little fresh air." I get up and walk to the door, turn. "Thanks, man."

"Any time. Please don't come back here bleeding anymore. I'm not sure if you realize this, but people have a finite supply."

"I'm getting a lot of reminders about that lately."

A T THE ATM I'm very tempted to check my balance, but the fear holds me back. I ask for twenty dollars and the machine spits it out. Enough for a pack of smokes and a granola bar.

What I didn't tell Bombay, what I can't tell him because I don't want to hear the words out loud, is I don't know exactly what I'm going to do when I find this guy. I do know it's going to be long, and it's going to be bloody, and it's going to end up with him dead.

Just the thought of Chell screaming, helpless. Thrashing. It hurts so bad to think about, but then I realize that's just the charred skin from where I've wrapped my hand into a bloodless fist around my cigarette. I drop it to the pavement, brush the loose tobacco off on my jeans. There's a little scorch mark on the fat pad under my thumb.

Breathe deep.

T HE DOOR TO my apartment is kicked in, splintered around the lock. My muscles deflate. This is fucking ridiculous.

The place is a wreck. Everything has been tossed. Drawers are pulled out. Clothes scattered everywhere. The cushions have been sliced open. The plates have been smashed on the floor. Which is just mean.

I panic, run for the scanner. It lives on a little table by the outlet in the kitchen. It's been knocked over and unplugged. I plug is back in and a calm, tired voice says, "10-27, 221 5th Street." Incinerator fire, a few blocks away.

Small wonders.

I check the apartment. Nothing seems to be missing, not that I have anything worth stealing. The scanner is the only thing with sentimental value. I can buy more clothes. My television is smashed too, but I hardly ever watch it.

Probably the two assholes who tried to mug me for the drive did this. They must have been coming out and seen me.

If they were in here, they saw my murder map on the wall. I get a little sensitive about the information I've written down, so I stand in the kitchen and stare at the wall and wonder if there's anything there I should worry about. I can't think of anything, so I fall onto the couch and pull the drive out of my pocket. It can't have a tracking chip in it or else they would have gone to Bombay's apartment.

Someone knows I have it.

The door. I need to fix the door. If Aziz stops by and sees it, he'll come in and then I'm out of here.

My phone buzzes with a text from Dave: *Groper struck again.*

I wing my phone against the exposed brick wall and it shatters into pieces, then I curl into the couch and prepare to pass out. If someone wants to break in and kill me, so fucking be it.

SEVEN

THE GUY AT the cell phone store tries to talk me up to a smartphone. But since I haven't gotten a new phone in two years, I can get a plastic flip phone for free. I tell him I want that.

He grumbles and tells me I should at least buy a protection plan and a case. I call him an asshole and tell him to sell me the phone. He complies and activates it, treating me like I have the plague.

I walk out of the store and immediately get a text: *Apocalypse*. But I don't have any phone numbers programed so I have no idea who it's from. It was my next stop so I head there anyway. Maybe it's a trap. At least I'll know who's after me.

Instead I find Lunette and Margo sitting at the bar drinking mimosas. Since Dave is working alone and the bar is otherwise empty, he's playing Bach's cello suites over the speakers. He's also playing an invisible cello behind the bar.

I sit and ask for a bottle of water. Dave passes it over and when I reach for it, my sleeve pulls back and reveals the fresh bandage I wrapped around my arm when I woke up. Lunette grabs my shoulder. "What happened?"

"I got mugged last night. Well, I almost got mugged last night. They didn't get anything off me."

The two of them look at me, mouths agape. Dave asks, "Did you show them your umbrella?"

"I did." To the girls I say, "It's fine. They came out of it worse. Listen, what are your numbers?"

I pull out my new phone and they rattle them off. Margo asks, "I thought you said they didn't take anything?"

"No, I broke my other phone."

"Why?"

"I was angry."

They both have looks on their faces like they want to sit me down in a corner and lecture me. I take another swig of water. Lunette excuses herself to go to the bathroom. Dave tells me he needs to run down the block to get smokes and asks if I can watch the bar.

I walk around to the other side and pick up the iPod plugged into the speakers and switch over to Cock Sparrer. Dave is good for two things: Classical music and British punk.

Margo asks, "Does your arm hurt?"

"It's fine. What's your deal?"

"With what?"

"With Lunette?"

Margo pauses. "You're not going to tell my mom?"

"I don't give a damn what you do."

"Thanks. I just don't know how she'd take it. She's a little…

conservative."

"As I recall. Still, I didn't realize you were on the muffin squad."

Margo narrows her eyes. "Are you kidding me?"

"What?"

She shakes her head, takes a sip of her drink. "So the thing last night. Did you call the cops?"

"No need. It was two guys who wanted my wallet and ended up embarrassing themselves. I'm not going to waste a day filling out reports and looking at mug shots."

"You're surprisingly nonchalant about this."

"Not the first time this kind of thing has happened."

Lunette comes back and takes her stool, holds her open palms above her empty drink and shrugs. I root around under the bar for the champagne and orange juice. She says, "We're going to the walk around Central Park."

Margo jumps in. "I'd really like to see Times Square, too."

Lunette shakes her head. "God fuck no."

"I'd rather kill myself than go to Times Square," I tell her.

Margo gives me an inquisitive look. I tell her, "It's the same reason I would never want to go to Disney."

Margo shakes her head. "Liking Disney doesn't make you a bad person. Do you want to come with us on our adventures?"

Check with Bombay.

Fix my door.

Address the groping issue.

Find Chell's killer.

"I've got a packed day," I tell her. "Will you two be okay without me?"

Margo nods. She doesn't seem upset. That's good. She heads for the bathroom. Lunette leans forward and holds up her hand for a high-five. "Dude, I fucked your cousin."

"Fuck you. I'm not high-fiving you for that."

"Don't leave me hanging." She pushes her open hand toward me, practically in my face. I roll my eyes and give it a smack. Satisfied, she sits back with her drink. Dave leans in the front door, holding a lit cigarette outside, and asks, "Talk?"

I leave Lunette in charge, tell her to say goodbye to Margo for me, and head out to meet him. He hands me a sheet of folded-up paper, ripped from a yellow legal pad.

"The location of last night's grope attack," he says. "Plus, a bonus. One of my guys heard about a trend of purse-snatchings and muggings. He did a little research and found a lot of incidents, all within the last two weeks. Could be a random spike, I don't know."

I check the page. There's a dozen dates, times, and locations as well as other details on perps. Four of them include a note about ski masks, and two about glasses. It sounds a little like my friends from last night.

Which doesn't make any sense. These are random, scattered around the East Village. Those two were after me for a reason.

More shit to figure out.

"Thanks for this," I tell him. "Listen, can we get a few other people out on rotation tonight? I really want to get this asshole."

"You think he might be the guy?"

"That got Chell? No, these attacks are too small. Takes a special kind of monster to do that to someone."

"I'll send a few people out. Will you be around tonight?"

"I'll try, but no promises."

I BANG ON BOMBAY'S door for nearly two straight minutes before he yanks it open. He's bleary-eyed, wearing a tank top and plaid pajama pants. He sees me and goes to shut the door, but I stick my foot in it. He lets me in and heads into the kitchen.

"Got anything for me?" I ask.

He comes back out, the coffeemaker hissing behind him, and sits across from me at the table. He slides a sheet of paper over. "I stayed up late. Couldn't resist. It took a little doing but I found the name of the guy. Joel Cairo. Do you know who that is?" He waits for me to answer. When I don't, he says, "A character from *The Maltese Falcon*."

"So whoever registered the site did it under a dummy name?"

"Yes. But." He taps the page. "There were some financials I may or may not have stumbled across, and if I did, which is only allegedly, I might have cross-referenced an address. Not that any of this is actually possible to accomplish. But if I did, this is where the bills for the site would be sent. It's a bar called Slaughterhouse Six in Bushwick."

"Are you kidding me with this nonsense?"

"Sorry." He goes back into the kitchen and comes out with two steaming mugs, sets one in front of me. I put my hands around it to warm them up. He says, "There's something else. You're not going to like it."

"Because I'm in a peachy fucking mood already."

He hesitates. "Last night after you left, I went to the bodega. I ran into Tommy. Tommy had just seen Quinn." He pauses to take a sip. "Tommy said Quinn was pretty broken up about Chell."

"He would be."

"Quinn told Tommy the night before Chell died, he proposed to her."

"What?"

"And apparently she said yes."

WHAT WAS IT, Chell, that attracted you to Quinn? He's handsome like a model in a Sears catalogue. Forgettable. He has a fat bank account from his fancy Wall Street job, but you weren't a gold digger. He's sweet in a dumb way. Other than that, I don't know what he has going for him.

I remember that night I first saw the two of you together. We were in my office at Apocalypse. There were a couple of us. Lunette and Bombay, one of the Kellys, a few other people. We were passing around a magnum bottle of wine and doing bumps off a little pile of coke in the middle of the coffee table. We were slung low on the couches and talking about music, or politics, or something equally as pointless.

You were sitting on the opposite side of the room. This was a couple of months after the Brooklyn Bridge. After I shifted the tectonic plates of our relationship. We were still talking, but less. The space between us felt like a vacuum. I kept a candle lit in the window in case you came around.

Quinn walked in and greeted us each in turn, and sat on the arm of the couch next to you. You crossed your legs toward him and the two of you talked like old friends. Something sharp and cold slid between my ribs.

Lunette held a rolled-up twenty in front of my face and had to smack me on the side of the head to make me focus, because I couldn't see anything besides his hand on your arm as you laughed at a joke he made.

After a little while, he whispered in your ear. You smiled and nodded. He got up to leave and said his goodbyes and walked out. You waited two minutes and checked your watch and left without saying anything to anyone.

I followed you into the bathroom, caught you just as you were swinging the bookcase back into place. You looked at me like you were expecting something. Like you knew what was coming.

So, I said. *Quinn.*

He's a friend.

When did you meet him?

A few weeks ago. Bombay introduced us.

Okay.

Are you upset?

I thought you weren't interested in that kind of thing.

The bathroom was small and we were standing close and I could smell you. Cigarettes and lavender. You looked away from me, readjusted your purse on your shoulder and asked, *What?*

Quinn is a friend, I said.

I know.

It would be weird. Do you know what I mean?

What are you trying to say?

Promise me it won't turn into a thing.

The muscles in your face went slack. You asked, *Promise you?*

It would just be a weird thing.

You nodded your head, slowly, like some long fought-for realization had dawned on you. And you left me standing in the bathroom. I locked the door and sat on the edge of the toilet and stared at the wall, studying the collage of band stickers, holding my guts in place. I sat there until Lunette left the back room and saw me and thought I was actually using the toilet and she freaked out and ran back inside. Then I sat there a little longer.

After I left Apocalypse that night, I stumbled the five miles north to Quinn's apartment. I stood across the street and wanted more than anything to knock on his door and see if you were in there.

Quinn and I grew up on the same block. He was taken by the gilded edges of the Upper West Side while I heard my siren song in the punk rock clubs on the Lower East Side.

Some friendships fade because it's better if they do.

By that point, where the three of us intersected, me and him had nothing in common. Nothing now, except you.

THE DOORMAN AT Quinn's apartment building is way too trustworthy. He doesn't know my name but I've been here a couple of times for parties and he recognizes me a little bit. It's on the tip of his brain, and when I toss out Quinn's name, he slaps his forehead and nods. We chat for a couple of minutes, enough to make him think my intentions are pure, and he lets me inside. Which makes me think that he's not actually a very good doorman. I certainly wouldn't trust me.

There's a small fountain in the middle of the marble lobby. It gurgles over the elevator music streaming through hidden speakers. The air is clean and cool, like it's coming off the ocean. There's a security guard at the desk, but he doesn't bother me. If I got past the doorman I must be cool.

When I get to Quinn's floor, I knock on the door but no one answers. I would call him but I don't have his number and I can't ask Bombay, because he'll assume I'm going to murder him. I check under the mat and find a spare key. Another example of poor key management. Though, Quinn has a habit of losing his belongings when he's been drinking, so it makes sense, a little. And it's not like theft is a problem in a building like this.

The apartment hasn't changed much since I was here last for his birthday party, when I stayed for ten minutes and left without saying goodbye.

Everything is pristine and white, futuristic edges that make me feel like I'm on a sci-fi movie set. A green swath of Central Park stretches out from the bottom of the floor-to-ceiling windows. The living room is sunken into the black hardwood floor. There's a small fireplace in the corner that's built for show, not warmth.

I feel like I'm going to ruin everything I touch, which makes me want to touch everything. The least inviting surface is the sofa, so I plop down, put my feet up, and wait. I find a remote control on the glass coffee table and fiddle with it until a flat screen television lowers from the ceiling, making the whole apartment that much more fucking absurd. There's nothing on television worth watching. After clicking through a few hundred channels, most of them infomercials and cable news, I turn it off and put my hands behind my head. Focus on my breathing.

A key scraping in the lock jostles me from the edge of sleep.

Quinn comes in and crosses the apartment. His hairline is starting to recede, the only sign he's getting older. His tie is undone, hanging off a crisp white shirt, and he looks like he's been at it for a couple of days. It's not until he's at the bedroom door that he sees me sitting on the couch, and he does a very exaggerated double take.

"Ash," he says, tossing down his briefcase. "How did you get in?"

"I am very clever."

He rests against the wall, like he needs it to hold him up. "Man, give me a second. I've been stuck at work since this morning."

"It's only three."

"It's Saturday."

"Ah. Well then."

Ten minutes later he comes back into the living room, wearing a hoodie, a tank top, and basketball shorts. His dark hair is freshly spiked, and he smells like a French hooker. He sits on a chair across from me, leans forward and puts his elbows on his knees. I stay where I am, sunken into the couch. He doesn't offer me his hand. I don't offer him mine. This sets a bad tone.

"So," he says. "To what do I owe the honor of you breaking into my apartment?"

"I didn't break anything."

"Don't play games with me. Why are you here?"

"You know why."

He looks away from me. "Chell."

"Little odd, you being at work. She died two days ago. And considering you were headed to the altar, I would have assumed you'd be a bit more broken up."

He drops his head. "You heard?"

"That I did."

He rubs his face hard, to hide tears or produce them, I can't really tell. "First, with the way things are at work right now, if I don't show up, I lose my job. I don't have a choice. We can't all make our own hours."

"You have a life to maintain. But if she was your fiancée, you'd figure they'd give you some time off."

Quinn says something under his breath. I ask him to repeat it.

"She didn't say yes." As he's finishing the sentence he jumps off the chair and heads into the kitchen. Over his shoulder he asks, "Beer?"

I decline. He reappears with a freshly-popped Heineken. I'm glad I didn't take him up on his offer. That's a beer I'll never understand. He returns to his seat, sitting with his back a little more straight. He takes a sip, and he doesn't look at me as he talks. "I saw Tommy and told him she said yes. I guess that's how you heard. I shouldn't have said that."

"You shouldn't have proposed to her."

"Are we still on this? I loved her Ash. I'm sorry, but I did."

"But you knew how I felt about her. You broke all kinds of codes when you went and tried to get her away from me."

"If she were alive she'd be disgusted to hear you say that."

"She'd be even more disgusted to find out you're going around playing the widower-to-be."

Quinn takes a long gulp of beer, the kind of gulp when you're looking for something to say. When he's done, he places the mostly-empty bottle on the coffee table and holds it for second, before letting go and looking up at me. "Fine. So what? Why are you here?"

"Where were you the night she died?"

As I'm saying this he's about to pick up the bottle, then he stops and slams it on the table. A little fountain of beer shoots out of the top. "If you're going to ask me questions like that you can get the fuck out of here."

"Or what?"

"I'll call the police."

"Just like you, not man enough to stand up for yourself. Go ahead and call them. Ask for Detective Medina, I'm sure he'll be happy to see me."

"Get out."

"She knew she was being followed. Did she call you?"

"When?"

"The night she died. Did she call you?"

He pauses. "No."

"She called me. You couldn't protect her, and she knew that."

"It's because you live nearby."

"Tell yourself that."

"Well, two nights before she died she was in my bed. Rationalize that."

My hands are shaking so hard I can hardly hold them back. He sees this and says, "I think you should go. Neither of us is in the right frame of mind to be having this conversation."

I get up and ask, "What did she say to you, when she said no?"

"Chell is dead, Ash. Can't we just let this go?"

I stand up. He gets up too. We stare at each other, eyes level, close enough I can see his nostrils flaring as he breathes. We search for things we used to know about each other, finding nothing.

"I know she's dead," I tell him. "But you're still an asshole."

He fumes in his beautiful apartment and I walk outside and let my feet carry me through unfamiliar blocks, past people walking purebred dogs and yelling into cell phones and looking at me like I'm going to mug them. Which is probably my fault for not putting on clean clothes.

I consider the subway but settle on looping around to First Avenue. I head south. I need to think, and that means I need to walk. I turn on the autopilot, weave through the pockets of people on the sidewalk, dash across the street to beat the cabs bearing down on intersections. Try to think about anything other than Chell and Quinn together, which is exceedingly difficult. The image forces itself into my head like it's got a grudge.

As I get closer to Times Square, the crowds of tourists get thicker. I keep getting stuck behind people who aren't walking fast enough or who stop in their tracks in the middle of the street to consult maps or take photos. I come to regret my decision to walk.

Worse is, I want to lash out at them. Tell them to move, to walk quicker, to get the fuck out of the way, to treat the sidewalks like a highway, where rules about constant speeds and merges apply.

I'm shaking. I duck into a doorway and light a cigarette, close my eyes.

Deep breath.

I don't think Quinn could have killed Chell. He would have been upset when she said no. Anyone would be. But he doesn't own a car, so he'd have to plan to get one. Not enough time to get his hands on one. I don't think so, at least. Anyway, Quinn needs three drinks in him before he'll take a side in an argument.

He's not a killer. As much as I'd like him to be, so I can put a beating on him.

I take out the sheet of paper Bombay gave me with the website's phone number and consider it, just to give me something to do with my hands that's not smoking or hitting, but figure it might be best to solve the problem of my apartment first. I was able to close the door just right so it didn't look broken, but it certainly wasn't going to lock.

If I could get Miss Hudson to pay a visit to Aziz I could probably get him off my back.

I EXPLAIN THE SITUATION with my landlord to Snow White. She listens silently, sucking on a Newport. I ask her to play pretend and sign some paperwork. I never knew the lady who lived there before me, but I'm banking on Aziz not remembering what she looked like, or not caring much.

Snow White asks, "How much?"

"What do you mean, how much? Can't you just do me a solid on this one?"

"Look cutie, that's time I'm not working. This is my office. You ask me to leave my office, I'm going to lose on sales. You have to compensate me for my time. It's simple economics."

This is why you should never assume your drug dealer is your friend.

I ask the ATM in the bodega across the street for one hundred dollars. It spits out five twenties. I walk back and hand them to her. She gives me back two. I write down all the information she needs, where to go, the name to sign. I tell her to wear a scarf and sunglasses, say she's moving down to Florida for the winter because the cold is too hard on her, and she'll be back by summer. That'll give me time to figure things out.

Snow White takes it and doesn't ask any questions, she just stuffs the paper into her bra, flashing a brown areola to the whole street as she does it.

CHANTICLEER LOOKS SAD in the daylight. So quiet. No one inside but a bartender, and he barely looks at me as I make my way toward the back.

Ginny's private room is stripped down to the studs. She's standing in the center of the room wearing a bright pink pantsuit, a brunette wig tied into a tight ponytail at the back of her head. She's barefoot, dangling a pair of tortoise-shell glasses from her left hand. On the opposite side of the room is a young queen in a blonde wig, a white blouse and a black pencil skirt, also barefoot. The queen holds up swatches of green against the bare stone walls.

Ginny puts her finger up as I walk in. "Get the purples, darling. I'm thinking less like a plum and more like a bruise. Take your time though. Momma has a meeting."

The ingénue disappears and Ginny turns to me. She shakes her head at me like I'm a child who wet the bed. I take the hat off and hang it from a nail sticking out of the brick, and smooth out the indentation it left in my hair. It's warm, so I take off my jacket too, hang it up next to the hat. Ginny points at the bandage on my arm. "I see you've been busy."

"I made a new friend. But I think I'll wait three days to call. I don't want to seem too eager."

"You're punchy today."

"Sleep deprivation and blood loss."

Ginny pulls two folding chairs out of the corner and hands me one. We sit in the circle of light cast by the bulb hanging from the ceiling on a frayed wire.

She leans forward, interested. I don't know if she knows why I'm here. She likes to play head games, fine. I'll wait and let her start the conversation. Let her be uncomfortable.

Except she doesn't take the bait.

After she realizes what I'm doing, she sits back and smokes on her cigarette, occasionally bringing a curled hand up to her face to check her nails.

I give up, ask, "Ginny?"

"Yes, darling."

"Why did you lie to me when I was here?"

Her eyes go wide and she presses her spread fingers to her chest. "What reason would I have to lie to you?"

"Maybe a good one. But when I asked if you had seen Chell around, you neglected to mention you had brunch with her the day she died."

For the first time since I have known Ginny Tonic, there is a split-second, a tiny fraction of an instant, that she doesn't have a comeback. This is what it's like to watch someone drown.

"Well," she says, drawing out the word. "It didn't seem relevant."

"I think it's pretty damn relevant that she was spying on the hipster community in Brooklyn."

She narrows her eyes and breathes out slowly through her nose. "How did you know that?"

"There's a reason you keep me around. Things like this."

Ginny sighs. "I'm impressed."

"I'm not, because I thought better of you."

We sit there in silence. Me staring at Ginny. Ginny staring

off at the wall. Neither of us speaks because neither of us wants to.

Finally, in a quiet voice, Ginny says, "There's a war coming."

"Don't be so fucking dramatic."

She swings her head around, then gets up and paces the room as she lights a cigarette. "You know how the districts work, right? And the power structure?"

"I know enough."

"Good." Ginny says, the words spilling out. "So the most powerful districts had always been in Manhattan, and the outer boroughs barely even registered, but all of a sudden Brooklyn is on the map. Like it actually matters or something. The districts out there are amassing power. We believe they're going to push their way into Manhattan."

"Like a turf war?"

She sits down in the chair and slows herself. "They have numbers. The Manhattan districts are fractured. So now I'm trying to build coalitions." She pauses. "And meanwhile I had Chell working her way into the inner circle of the guy who runs Bushwick and Williamsburg."

"What's his name?"

"People call him The Hipster King."

"Fucking wow. And what did you have Chell doing?"

"She was hanging around, listening, letting me know what she heard."

"So you just sent her out like that, unprotected?"

"They're a bunch of hipster brats. The most dangerous thing they could do was criticize her taste in music."

I slide my chair toward Ginny. "Then why are you afraid of them?"

Her eyes frost over. "Numbers count. And they have more."

She gets up and paces again but doesn't say anything. I ask, "Any idea where The Hipster King hangs out?"

"There's a bar in Bushwick. It's called Slaughterhouse Six."

Convenient. "So the king is tied into this game she was working for?"

Ginny pauses and smiles. Impressed, and not entirely thrilled to be showing it. "Very good. Very, very good. You're right. This is exactly why I keep you around."

My cell phone buzzes. I can't believe I'm getting a signal down here. Text from a blocked number: *It didn't work.*

"Time to go," I tell Ginny.

She says, "Ash, like I said, down-low."

"I practically invented the term."

Ginny doesn't laugh.

EIGHT

SNOW WHITE HANDS me a crumpled twenty. "Partial refund. Didn't you know this lady was black?"

I never met Miss Hudson. When I got into the apartment there was some barren, dusty furniture. No photos.

Seems I'm not as clever as I like to think.

And thus ends my reign on Tenth and First. Aziz's parting message to Snow White was that he would have an ad for the apartment posted within ten minutes. The place would probably be gone ten minutes after that.

There's a very good chance I could get home and my things could be at the curb. I can't find any words and Snow White has something caught in her throat, so we shuffle our feet, looking at everything else but each other, like a solution is going to magically drop from the sky.

Shaking her head, she says, "I hope this doesn't mean I'm

losing my best customer."

"C'mon. I never bought volume."

"You're the only person who ever asks about my grandkids."

For a very brief moment, I see her for who she is: An old lady no one would care about if she wasn't running the drug game on this block. I imagine her apartment is filled with afghans and cats, an image that stands in stark contrast to the time she had a rival dealer tuned up for slinging across the street.

Her eyes are wracked with what appears to be genuine sadness. I don't know how to feel about that, with it coming from my dealer.

But that's the way this place works. We are constantly losing the things that we know in favor of whatever can afford to take our place.

I kiss Snow White on her cheek and leave her on the stoop.

I STAND OUTSIDE MY apartment for a long time with a fresh pack of smokes, inhaling them one after another, staring up at my building.

The bricks are beaten and faded. Windows in steel black frames. Most of them are covered with dingy curtains. It looks like a million other buildings. I wonder if anyone who lives in the building will notice I'm gone.

Probably not.

I trudge up the stairs to my apartment, dreading what I'm going to find. The door is propped part of the way open, which is about what I expected. Inside the apartment is the sound of rustling and crashing.

Aziz must be trying to clear me out already. He's got to give me a week, a few days at least. If I'm going to stay with Bombay or Lunette, I really should ask before I just show up on their doorstep with a duffel bag.

I push open the door of my apartment and yell, "Dude, c'mon."

The person who looks up at me is not Aziz.

It's a small guy, his slim frame and face obscured by a baggy gray hoodie. He doesn't wait for me to register what's going on, just puts his shoulder down and finds an opening, slams me up against the wall of the hallway, and he's gone.

It takes me a second, but then I'm right after him.

He's heading for the roof. Probably how he got into the building, considering I've been standing on the front steps and being glum for the past twenty minutes. He's small and fast and has a lead, but I work to close it, throwing myself up the stairs. As I'm on the last landing, I hear him burst through the metal door to the roof, and find it swinging when I get there.

The air is cold and the sun is brighter than the dark hallway. It takes my eyes a second to adjust. He's running across the rooftops toward Second Avenue.

Each roof is flush to the next one. There are no pits or drops or patio equipment to trip him up, and I think I know where he's headed: The fire escape at the end of the block.

He's two floors down by the time I get there, and we fling ourselves down the stairs, trying to maintain speed on the narrow metal steps without tripping. The clanging of our feet draws people to their windows and some of them yell things I can't make out.

When he hits the street, he takes off toward First, back toward the front of my building. I hit the ground and follow.

There's a group of tourists careening down the street and he can't get around them so he hops onto a cab parked at the curb, and proceeds to run across the tops of the cars parked down the stretch of the street.

As I hop onto the cab behind him, he changes course, leaping across the hood of an idling car in the middle of the street. The driver leans on the horn and gives me the finger when I land on the hood a few seconds after him.

This guy is built for endurance, and I'm not. Already my lungs are crumbling like newsprint in a tight fist. Not enough oxygen getting to my brain. The ankle I twisted in the drop outside Chell's apartment is protesting hard.

He turns down First. The streets are crowded with people stopping to take pictures in the middle of the sidewalk, like there aren't people trying to chase each other across it.

I'm not going to catch him in a fair race, but then I get an idea. He's glancing behind me to keep track, so I go out wide, to the far edge of the sidewalk. He sees this and takes it as an opportunity to duck down the next side street, to put some more distance between us.

He must think he's pretty smart. Except I know in about a block, he's going to run into the street fair I passed earlier. When he hits that, I'll catch up.

Then I'm going to break his fucking legs.

But when I turn the corner after him, he's gone.

I put my hands on my head, give my lungs room to expand, take in huge gasps of air. Down the block is the fair, one of those generic gatherings that mysteriously pops up to sell socks and belts and arepas. He couldn't have made it all the way down and disappeared into the crowd. I was right behind him.

There's a homeless kid sitting up against the scaffolding set against the building next to me. He's crusty and grimy with a sign in front of him that says: TRYING TO GET HOME. PLEASE HELP. I recognize him. He's been trying to get home for two years now.

He doesn't say anything to me, just points up. I look at the scaffold and even though it hurts I hold my breath and I hear scraping and pounding above me.

There's no way I'm going to get him now. He'll bust into a window, climb through an apartment, and he has an entire block worth of exit points.

I drop a few singles into the cup in front of the homeless kid. Then I go home, the whole way walking slow and breathing deep, trying to ease the knot out of my side.

H E WASN'T HERE to rob me. Most robbers tend to take valuables. So the fact that my iPod is sitting on the counter sort of discounts that.

I check my pockets for my phone so I can see what time it is but instead I turn up the thumb drive. The mysterious self-destructing thumb drive I found at Chell's. If the guy was looking for something it was probably this. Because now apparently Chell is a spy or something?

I don't have a computer, or else I could keep plugging away at the password, for however many tries I have before this thing is useless.

Why did Chell have a military-grade self-destructing thumb drive in her goddamn possession? Why are there so many people breaking into my apartment? Why am I suddenly in the middle of a turf war that sounds like it came out of a movie from the eighties that only plays in the middle of the night?

My thoughts are scattered. I can't concentrate. I can't be inside right now. There's not enough space to think. I should go to Brooklyn. In Brooklyn there'll be something I can hit.

I GET OFF THE L train at Bedford and Grand and there's a store on the corner renting VHS tapes. This trip is going to be a big test of my patience.

I'm feeling a little faint and across the street is a boutique coffee joint. Standing behind the counter is a girl with a nose ring and wild purple hair crammed under a knit cap. She's cute, but she looks too innocent for this place. Her eyes are too bright, too clean. Like freshly fallen snow waiting to be trampled.

When I tell her I want a large black coffee she asks me which region I'd like the beans from. She waits like I'm supposed to know how to answer that. I tell her to surprise me.

On the bench outside the door is a copy of the *Post*. I forgot to check today's edition. There's another picture of Chell on the cover. It was taken outside, at night. She's wearing a white top, a black bowler hat, and her eye is caked with heavy dark makeup. Halloween last year, when she went as a droog.

The story doesn't say much, but there's a part near the middle that catches me.

A law enforcement official told the Post that the killer did leave behind traces of DNA, which are currently being tested. Given the heinous nature of the murder, they believe this is the work of a serial rapist, and hope to make a connection that will bring the killer to justice.

Police sources also said they've questioned the victim's boyfriend, but no arrests have been made at this time.

Meanwhile, bar owners in the East Village are feeling the effects of the crime, saying that the number of nightly visitors has plummeted in the wake of the death of the Greenpoint Goth.

DNA is good and bad. Good, because it could point to the guy who did this. Bad, because it could point to him before I find him. If the cops find him first, I have to get arrested so that I can go to prison and murder him there. That's Plan B, of which I am not a great fan.

What bothers me is who the *Post* and the police considered to be Chell's boyfriend. Me or Quinn. I know they questioned me. I don't know if they questioned him.

The story leaves a bad taste in my mouth. I wash it down with a gulp of the coffee, which incidentally tastes very good.

Time to find the bar. I'm not familiar with the area, so I pick the direction I think is correct. I pass a pickup truck with a young couple dressed like circus performers, selling vintage clothing from the back. On the corner is a furniture store, fronted by a jumble of wooden chairs that don't look sturdy, but carry price tags in the triple digits. There's a taco truck manned by white kids and so many places to get coffee this block must be keeping Latin America afloat.

A real estate office on the corner has fliers plastered on the inside of the window, advertising lofts with reclaimed wood and stainless steel kitchens and price tags I can barely fathom.

It's hard to peg why I dislike hipster culture so much, but walking around here, I think it's that they're selling Bohemian culture at a premium. The vinyl stores and organic markets and restaurants with three items on the menu and bars built from driftwood, it's all artifice. Nostalgic propaganda. This neighborhood is just like Times Square, inauthentically authentic, just on a different end of the spectrum. The thing no one seems to get is that just because you love something doesn't mean you can have it back after it's gone.

I'm in a mood. I swallow the last of my coffee and end up with a mouthful of grounds.

THAT THEY CALLED it Slaughterhouse Six should impress me because I'm a Vonnegut guy. It doesn't.

Looking through the big window in the front, if I didn't know this was a bar, I would assume it was a garage full of trash. It's barely lit, and when I step through the door, I can't see anything around twisting columns of furniture. Chairs with tables stacked on them, less for sitting and more for presentation. A few people dot the couches and small tables that sit close to the ground. They twist around to see who walked in, and when they don't recognize me, they go back to reading books, or poking at laptops, or staring off into space.

There's music playing through a hodge-podge of speakers, balanced on piles of books and empty crates. The walls are cluttered with signs and Christmas lights and pages ripped from magazines and abstract art printed on computer paper.

At a very brief glance it might look like Apocalypse, but at least we have a theme.

The bartender looks at me with a mixture of smugness and disdain from behind a repurposed jewelry display case. He's wearing a white t-shirt, a vest, and four scarves. I tell him I'm looking for The Hipster King. I cringe as I say it.

The guy shrugs. "Never heard of him."

I lean across the bar and put my hand on his shoulder. He tries to pull away so I dig my fingers in. "Tell me where he is."

His eyes dart to the back, toward what looks like a doorway, then to me. "I don't know what you're talking about."

"Thanks," I tell him.

The guy protests, but I don't listen. I climb through a narrow hallway with an uneven floor and come out into a space that looks like a junkyard, fenced in with corrugated aluminum sheeting and piled with scrap wood. There are four guys standing around a fifth, and it's pretty obvious who's king.

He's seated on an easy chair propped up by cement blocks. Big handlebar mustache, waxy and curled. A pair of shiny faux-gold aviators is folded into a dirty yellow t-shirt, its red wording cracked and faded. Draped over his shoulders is a tweed jacket. His jet-black jeans are so tight I can see that he's not Jewish.

Perched on top of his head, kicked to a slight angle, is a cardboard Burger King crown. I can hardly believe he's a real person.

He nods at me with his chin, a sneer stretched across his face like a gash. He barely moves from where he's slumped into his throne. He asks, "What's up?"

"You know, I'm usually pretty good at this, but I am just speechless right now," I tell him.

"What do you mean?"

"I don't know if I can handle this."

"Handle what?"

"You. This whole thing you've got going. You are the most

ridiculous thing I've ever seen in my life. And I live in the East Village."

The guys flanking him are standing at attention now. Two of them break off and move around me so that I'm surrounded, which would normally make me nervous, but they all look malnourished. Though that could be hubris. I brush my hand against my umbrella to make sure it's there.

The king brings his hand up to his mustache and twirls it. It's a tic, he's not doing it on purpose, but still it feels like he's challenging me to keep a straight face. He doesn't betray any emotion, just surveys me as if I were a jester. After a few moments he asks, "Who are you?"

"My name is Ash."

"Ash?"

"Short for Ashley."

A few chuckles. The king says, "That's a girl's name."

"I didn't realize that, ever. What about you? The Hipster King? I thought hipsters didn't self-identify."

He rolls his eyes. "It's ironic."

There's nothing polite for me to say, so I pull out the picture of Chell from the *Post*. It's worn and beaten from being in my back pocket. I unfold it carefully so I don't rip it, then hold it up. "Do you know this girl?"

He stares at it and exhales so deeply he sinks a few inches down in the seat.

I tell him, "I guess you do. Why don't you tell me everything you know about her."

"I know she's dead."

"Good place to start."

"What do you want me to say?"

"I'm trying to find the guy who killed her so that I can

kill him. Anything you can tell me would be appreciated." The killer could also be someone here, and we'll see how that plays out.

The king purses his lips. "I don't know anything about that."

"You know what? I have another question. What qualifications does it take to get named king of the hipsters? Biggest trust fund?"

"Actually, yes."

"I was kidding."

"I own this bar. I own several buildings on this block."

"Good for you. How about Joel Cairo. Is he around?"

On the edge of my vision there's movement. Someone ducking out of the backyard. I turn and there are three people blocking my path.

Someone today outran me. Not happening again. I put both my hands on the chest of the guy in front of me, pivot my hips and put all my weight into pushing him as far as he'll go. He crashes into a pile of tires.

Then the rest of them jump on me.

It happens quick. Two guys are holding my arms behind me. They're strong and my leverage is off, and I can't get to the umbrella. I lunge forward and try to loosen their grips so I can twist out, but it doesn't work.

The king stands in front of me. He's more solid than I would have guessed. Taller too. He looks like he could hand out some damage. He says, "I had this theory that she was working for someone in Manhattan. I guess that's bearing out. Now, tell me where the drive is."

"Get fucked."

He punches me in the stomach and my lungs compress. The king waves his hand in the air like he hurt it, smiling like a kid who just discovered jerking off. He gears up to hit me again, like he wants to make it count.

The guys on either side of me are holding me too tight. Can't break free. One is wearing steel-toe construction boots and the other is wearing beaten Converse sneakers. I pick the kid with the Converse and slam my foot down on top of his.

He yelps and his grip gives. My right arm comes free. I turn and push my weight into the guy holding onto my left arm, slamming him up against the metal fence. I level my elbow and jam it into the eye socket of the guy coming up from behind me. I catch it right on the funny bone. My arm jolts with electricity.

I turn to the king, but there's another guy standing between us to protect him. I put my boot into his stomach and he goes to the ground.

The ones who aren't convulsing on the floor have fled. Then it's me and the man in charge. And he looks pretty scared without anyone to back him. I wrap my hands around his throat and pull him so close I can taste the Thai he had for lunch. I tell him, "Now you and me have some things to discuss. First up, tell me why you want that fucking drive so bad."

Before the king answers, someone inside the bar yells, followed by the whine of a police siren. Rushed footsteps, crashing around the debris inside the bar.

I tell the king, "You are a dick." Then I hit him in the face as hard as I can. He collapses in a heap on the floor and I hop the fence, only a little sorry for hitting him but mostly pissed because this is way more physical effort than I was prepared for today.

NINE

I FLICK MY CIGARETTE into the corner where it burns a mark onto the polished hardwood floor.

I can't blackmail Aziz into letting me stay. If he has skeletons, I'm not privy to them. I could find a lawyer, but I don't have any legal standing. Not that I could afford an attorney. Nor can I afford to pay Aziz what he's going to end up charging for this place.

This day was inevitable. Shame on me for not having a backup plan.

I wander through the apartment, which doesn't take long. Head back the other way. There's not much to bring with me. The furniture was either here when I showed up or scavenged. All of it can be replaced.

On the kitchen counter, I make a pile of things I want to keep. It's not a big pile. Mostly clothes. A few books. Thumbtacked to the wall is a photo of me and my dad standing outside Yankee Stadium. It's not a great picture. The frame is pulled back too wide, so it's just two little dark figures you can barely make out against the stadium wall. I take that and put it with the pile. Grab the little things lying around the apartment—cards, scraps of paper with important notes, my phone charger.

Margo's bag is gone. She must have picked it up. I hope things with Lunette are going well because she's going to need a place to stay.

The scanner is buzzing on its little table. A veil of static pierced by an occasional voice. "10-28, Astor Place." Smoke condition in the subway.

I yank the plug out of the wall and the buzzing stops. The apartment is draped in silence. I take a shirt from my duffel bag and wrap it around the scanner, nest the bundle in the middle of my clothing.

And that's it. I've reduced the entirety of my life into a green duffel bag.

YOU LOVED MY apartment. The brick walls held the heat like an oven. We spent some good winter nights in here, lounging around, soaked in sweat, ripping lines and smoking cigarettes and drinking whiskey and listening to David Bowie.

Those nights, the whole world fell away and it was just us.

One night we were sitting by the window, blowing smoke through the screen, watching snow accumulate on the street below. The forecast called for more than two feet. The following school day had already been cancelled. The block was quiet, the snow white and soft.

You said, *We should go down and play before the snow gets New Yorked.*

What?

It gets all dirty and slushy.

I've never heard that term before.

There's always a first time.

We got dressed and went outside and avoided the avenues and cut down the side streets. The streetlamps made the snow sparkle like the sky was filled with stars whipping in lazy circles over our heads.

We hit each other with powdery snowballs and stopped for shots in the bars brave enough to stay open and tried, unsuccessfully, to build a snowman in Tompkins Square Park. We sat in the middle of Fourth Street, facing the direction of traffic, wondering when a car would turn the corner, savoring the look of the unblemished snow.

Finally, when the cold got to be too much, we retreated to my apartment where it was so hot we dropped our clothes by the door. You slept on the couch, and the next morning, the snow was filthy and gray.

TEXT BOMBAY: *EVICTED. Crash with you?*

He writes back: *WTF?*

Long story.

Okay. Girls are here.

One last look. There's nothing else to take. Nothing else to do.

At the murder chart on the wall I use the crappy camera in my phone to snap a photo. Next to it I write a note to Aziz:

You're a greedy fuck. I'll call you if I need a reference.

I don't close the door behind me when I leave.

Part of me stays in the apartment.

BOMBAY AND LUNETTE and Margo are drinking beer and watching a black-and-white B movie. Desert mountains and giant lobsters on the horizon. Bombay pauses the movie and they all turn to look at me as I find a spot to drop my bag.

Lunette says, "Not really your week, is it?"

"It is not," I say. "How come you're all in? Figured you would all be out tonight."

Bombay says, "No one's out."

"What do you mean no one's out?"

"We popped into a few bars. Didn't see anyone."

"Really?"

Lunette says, "Rage, rage against the dying of our social life."

I drop my bag and put my umbrella on top and sit on the floor, the bag between me and Margo. She looks over and pokes at the umbrella, then picks it up. She curls it like a dumbbell.

"This thing is really heavy," she says.

I shrug. "Those bodega umbrellas aren't very sturdy. They snap in a strong wind."

Bombay scoffs. "Sturdy. Right. That's why you have it."

To me, Margo says, "What happened to your apartment? It looked like a bomb hit."

"Some friends stopped by," I tell her. "It got out of hand."

Lunette says, "Will you two shut up? We're watching a very important work of cinema." She takes the remote from

Bombay and turns the movie back on.

I look at Margo. "Want to go upstairs?"

"This movie sucks anyway," she says.

Lunette says, "You suck."

"Now we have to rewind it," Bombay says.

I bring Margo to the roof. It's cold, but I'm too tired to go back downstairs for my jacket. I find a spot and fall onto my back, let the sky swallow my vision. Margo sits next to me, her knees pulled up to her chest, and says, "I'm sorry about your apartment."

"Just a matter of time. And don't apologize to me. You came here to visit, and now I'm homeless. I'm the one who should be sorry."

"It's fine," Margo says. "I got my stuff and Lunette said I can stay with her." She pauses, afraid to say the next thing. "How are you?"

"I've been a bad host. Tell me what you've been up to."

She pauses. "Spending a lot of time with Lunette. Walking around the city, going to thrift stores, stuff like that. A lot of coffee. Coffee here is good." She laughs. "It's funny. It's not what I thought it would be like."

"What did you think it would be like?"

"If I tell you, you'll laugh at me."

"Why would you say that?"

"Lunette did."

"She's Russian. She doesn't have a normal sense of humor."

"It's just that, the only things I really know about New York is what I saw on *Sex and the City*," she says, like she's admitting to an embarrassing kink.

"Ah."

"What?"

"I've seen a few episodes. Nothing about it looks familiar except the sidewalks. It's all gallery openings and fancy fucking bars." I pull my jacket a little tighter around me. "So any second thoughts yet? Still want to move here?"

"I think so."

"What's so bad about Pennsylvania?"

She laughs. "Let me tell you about a typical Saturday night. Me and my friends get dressed up like we're going out for a night on the town, and we go to the pool hall or the bowling alley. They're full of the kids we went to high school with. We all want to drink, but we have to fight over who's going to be designated driver because we can't walk home and there's no public transportation. These places close around midnight, so we end up going to someone's house and sitting in the basement. And all anyone ever talks about is stuff that happened in high school. Why would I want to live there anymore?"

"The quiet must be nice though. The space. You don't get that here."

"I'll get used to the noise."

We smoke some cigarettes in silence. I feel like she wants to ask me a question, but she's afraid. And if she's afraid, I don't want her to ask it. I consider moving us inside, back where it's warm and I can find a snack, but then she says, "Lunette told me about Chell. You know, a little. She said you two didn't exactly have a... healthy relationship."

"We all express ourselves in different ways."

"Why do you feel you need to do this?"

"Someone needs to."

"What if you get hurt?"

I want to tell her I don't care about that, but she'll take it the wrong way. Maybe she'll take it the right way. Either way, it's going to produce a lot of drama so I tell her, "I can take care of myself."

"Lunette thinks this is about your dad."

"What about him?"

"That the people who killed him are dead and you're looking for someone to lash out at."

"That's an interesting theory."

"My mom still talks to your mom a lot, you know. She said you were planning on taking the test to be a firefighter. Like your dad. How did that go?"

"Everything went fine until I got to the drug test."

She doesn't say anything to that. I don't expect her to. I don't even know how to feel about it anymore. The memory has spent so much time kicking me in the ribs that now I'm numb to it.

She slides her hands into her sweater and pulls the arms around her, says, "Cold."

"Head back in. I need a few minutes."

She nods and leaves. I stare at the city for a long time, at the tops of the buildings jutting into the dark sky. From here I can only see the apartments stretching from here to the West Side Highway. I've got this feeling inside me like I want to cry, but I can't remember how. I try to focus on the things I need to focus on and my mind wanders down dark paths.

I keep coming back to the same thing.

You promised.

Who promised?

This isn't the first time I've blacked out from drinking. This is the first time that a blackout has scratched at the back of me, daring me to figure out what happened during the course of it.

The question I haven't been asking because I don't want to

know the answer is, did I see Chell the night she died?

And I can't answer it.

My phone buzzes. Text: *Can you help me move out tomorrow?*

Good Kelly. I respond: *Sure.*

Great!! Tomorrow afternoon?

Sure.

At least I have a few hours to grab some sleep.

Then I notice I've got another text that I missed. This one says: *Dymphnas.*

Let's see who sent it.

ST. DYMPHNA WAS the patron saint of the mentally ill. St. Dymphna's is our backup bar, a small British-style pub with an older clientele and a chill atmosphere. There's also a back patio that's covered and heated, so it's perfect for those especially cold winter nights.

At the front door, there's a guy checking IDs. They've never checked IDs. When I get inside I see why. The place is overflowing. Tommy is drowning, trying to fill orders for Jaeger bombs and Amstel Lights for overeager college students. He sees me come in and screams through the crowd, "You drinking yet?"

"You'll be the first to know." I push up against the bar, shoving some kid wearing a trucker hat aside. "What's with the crowd?"

"Who knows," Tommy says, blowing off a group of sorority girls who want lemon drops. "This stuff is cyclical. One person finds out about a bar that's not too crowded, suddenly it gets slammed."

"Good for business at least?"

"I prefer the regulars. These kids are assholes, and they don't tip."

The guy next to me says something to win Tommy's kinship. Tommy ignores him. I head to the back.

Bad Kelly is sitting at a table in the corner by herself. The patio is just as crowded as the front and there aren't any free seats. On my way to the rear, some kid gets up to go inside so I take his seat and drag it over to Kelly. Someone yells about it being saved, and I hold up my middle finger over my shoulder.

She looks up at me like she's looking down at a roach. I sit and light a cigarette and wait for her to say something.

I ask, "What?"

"You're lucky I like you."

"If it was such a big deal why did you do it?"

"Chell was my friend. I did it for her."

"What did you find out?"

Bad Kelly takes a sip from her glass of white wine, then places it down and holds it to the table by the stem. "There were two sets of DNA."

"Two different guys?"

"One male, one female. They can't identify either. The guy, the cop. A friend of his is working the case. So he's hearing it right from the source."

I lean back and wish I had a drink. That's weird. Even weirder is, I know there's a girl who was gunning for Chell. Fanny Fatale. It helps and it doesn't, because I don't know anyone in the burlesque world aside from Cinnamon West, and she's not going to help me.

Bad Kelly waves at me. "It would be nice if you at least said 'thank you.'"

"Thanks. I owe you one. Two actually."

"Yes you do."

I figure that's all there is so I get up to leave when the girl working the tables stops at ours and drops a folded-up piece of paper in front of me. I open it. Rushed scribble, on a blank bar receipt. Tommy's handwriting. *Hipster assholes asking about you.*

Inside the bar there are two guys, both in tight jeans and tweed jackets with massive plaid scarves looped for miles around their necks. One is heavy and has a thick, sloppy beard. The other is scrawny, wearing an old pair of Ray-Bans converted to real glasses.

The thin one's hand is in a cast.

My friends from the other night.

I reach down to my belt and it's empty. My umbrella is sitting on top of my duffel bag at Bombay's apartment. I consider picking up a chair to use as a weapon, but after last night, they might be carrying something heavier than a pocketknife.

Better to duck out. I kiss Bad Kelly on top of her head. "I need one more favor. You didn't see me here."

"If only."

I vault myself onto a spent keg and over the wooden fence at the back of the yard. No one seems to notice, and I try to land on my good ankle, but I screw that up too and take the full force of the fall on the bad one.

The adjacent yard is an empty box of concrete dotted with piles of scrap wood behind an apartment building. No one is looking down from the windows, and I'm covered by just enough shadow that this spot should be safe for a little while.

I crouch down and listen. Bad Kelly is sitting right on the

other side of the fence and maybe they'll ask her something. But I can't hear anything, not over the din of people talking and laughing and yelling.

After fifteen minutes of having my ear pressed to the fence, I give up and climb back over and Bad Kelly is gone.

A S I'M SMOKING a cigarette outside Bombay's apartment, trying to decide if I should go inside or check on the groper situation, a massive pair of arms wraps around me and picks me up off my feet. I'm shoved into what I'm pretty sure is the trunk of a car, because my head bounces off something rubber and slams into something metal and then it's dark.

A car engine roars on and that confirms it.

Most people would panic in this situation, but it's par for the course for how much fun the last couple of days have been, so I roll with it. No sense in getting worked up until the trunk opens. I stretch out as much as I can in the slight space. The car isn't moving fast, and I start to doze. I can't tell if it's because I'm tired or carbon monoxide, but either way, at least it means I can get some rest.

It's not long before the trunk swings open, and I can't make out who's standing over me. I reach for where I think there's a throat but a large hand grabs mine, crushing it.

A massive figure hauls me out without much effort, and once my eyes have adjusted I can see it's my best buddy in the whole wide world.

"Hey Samson," I tell him.

He throws me against the car and pats me down. I consider wising off to him, but his hand is way too close for my junk for that to be a good idea. When he's done, he turns around and walks away. In his language, it's an order to follow.

I don't know where we are, but it feels like the West Side somewhere. Some anonymous street full of big blank industrial buildings. I can't see the Empire State Building or the Woolworth or the Chrysler, or any other tall building I can use to orient myself.

Samson leads me down a narrow alley between two buildings and I run through the events of the last few days in my head, wondering whether Samson or Ginny might have any reason to kill me. But I'm pretty sure I haven't screwed up that bad. I know I said I wouldn't hit anyone, and I kinda fucked that up, but I've also done worse.

We walk through a metal door and into a room so dark I can't see in front of my face. There's a sound of shuffling and then Ginny says, "Thank you, Samson. Please wait outside."

Something drops to the floor, feet shuffle into the distance. Complete blackness. I hold my breath, still myself. Can't hear anything.

A light clicks on.

It's a small lamp. Antique, skinny, and a little bit shorter than me. It has a beautiful pink shade with beaded tassels, and it throws off just enough light to show that it's flanked by two red leather wingback chairs, a small coffee table in the middle of them. Underneath it all is a blue shag carpet. It's a living room set floating in a vast, empty concrete warehouse.

But that's not the thing that throws me.

Ginny stands before me in a tight gray t-shirt, threadbare and ripped at the seam on the left shoulder. Ratty black jeans torn at the knees. Her head is shaved, but growing in just enough that it's clearly thinning around the temples. The only give-back to her true identity, the one I know now, is a carefully applied layer of pink on her thin, skeleton lips.

Even seeing her like this, I still refer to her as 'she.' I know a lot of people get hung up on the pronoun, even when she's still in her armor. Thing is, I can't picture her as anyone but Ginny anymore.

"I look dreadful," she says, smiling like she's carrying a planet on her back.

She gestures to the chairs. We sit and she lights her cigarette, her body weak and loose at the joints. Even her poise has evaporated. She takes a drag, rests her head on the back of the chair, her legs splayed open, and asks, "How was the ride over?"

"Great." I light my own cigarette. "Samson has the nicest trunk I've ever been in."

"He made you ride in the trunk?"

"Didn't give me much choice."

"I'm sorry for that. I told him you were irrational and that you might not come easily. I guess he decided to take some liberties with my instructions."

"That he did." I lean forward to knock a pile of ash off the end of my cigarette and adjust the fedora. "So, why no hissy fit over my hat this time?"

"Because I'm exhausted. I didn't even want to get dressed for this meeting. Luckily, you knew me before Ginny was born. So you can see me like this." She raises one hand, the hand that doesn't have a cigarette, and waves it in front of her face. "No one sees me like this anymore."

"Should I be honored?"

"Don't be cute." She pulls a bottle of wine and two glasses from the floor next to her seat and pours one, then looks up at me. "Still not drinking?"

"Not yet."

She nods, doesn't fill the second glass. Leans back, resting the base on her knee. "You have pissed off some people."

"Well, hey, everyone's got a talent. This is mine. What's the use in hiding from it?"

"I need you to focus." Ginny exhales. "I got a phone call. It seems as though your visit to Brooklyn didn't go over too well with the king. There's a bounty on your head."

"All I did was hit some people in the face."

"At a time of great unrest. This isn't a joke. You don't understand the full scale of what's happening right now, and what you just did puts months of planning and work at risk. Because I'm not ready for what's about to happen."

"What is about to happen?"

Ginny pauses, but not for effect. "I'm about to lose a great deal of money, power, and influence."

"I need to understand this, because I don't. There's a turf war. That I get. A bunch of goofy fucking hipsters are trying to, what, depose you?"

"Yes."

"Why? I understand there's money to be had. But honestly, a lot of this sounds made-up and ridiculous."

Ginny looks past me, like she's searching the room for something. "New York is not a city. It is an idea. And one of the most prevalent ideas is the romanticism of Old New York. These... children believe that New York has lost its authenticity. They have fantasies about how they think things should be, versus how they really are."

"So I was wrong when I called it a turf war. It's ideological."

Ginny laughs. "All wars are about ideology. Ideology and

money. They want my neighborhood for two reasons: One is because they'll get keyed into all my business. But they also want the bragging rights. They want to be in control so they can say they're in control of the most prime real estate in Manhattan."

"I know this city has a problem with gentrification, but this sounds a little extreme."

"Then let's call it that, darling, for the sake of simplicity. Extreme gentrification."

"But you've got soldiers lined up from here to Battery Park, right?"

"I don't have as many people in my corner as you think I do. That's why I'm trying to broker deals with the other Manhattan leaders. But everyone wants something. There are less and less people on our side because the city is emptying out. The natives are leaving. And meanwhile, the gents get stronger every day."

"So," I ask. "What does this mean?"

"It means that the hipsters have been waiting for me to escalate. Biding their time and building their power base. And today, they believe that I escalated."

Damn. "So whatever happens now is on me. Ginny..."

Ginny waves her hand. "It was going to happen soon. I would have preferred more time, but no one ever gets what they want. The point is, it's happening. I'm going to leave here, get dressed, and go see the leader for Harlem. I think he's interested in working together."

"Think you'll get him on board?"

"I hope so. The truth is, I have more to gain from an alliance with him. There are a lot of goofy white kids moving into Harlem for the cheap rent, so his territory is already in danger, but where do you think they all want to come? The

East Village. The Lower East Side. These are the historic neighborhoods for New York City's youth. This is what they really want. My district."

I ease back into the chair, stretch out my legs. This is just ridiculous enough that I can't question it. "What do you want from me then?"

"To be ready. You already told me that you owed me one, for the information on Chell. Now I'm telling you that I'm going to cash in on it pretty soon."

"What do you need me to do?"

"I'll tell you when you need to know."

We sit there in silence for a little while. It's nice to sit across from Ginny like that. Like we're not in a stage play.

Finally she says, "I'll do my best to protect you."

"Why?"

"Because you're my friend."

"Friend is a strong word, isn't it?"

She looks hurt. "To me it is."

I get up. I'll take her call when I get it. Right now I need to be doing other things. Which means anything other than this.

"Before you go, there's something you should know," she says. "I poked around a little bit at the police department. Some people I know. Your name keeps coming up in the investigation into Chell's death."

"Well. How about that?"

"They don't have much to go on, and they're looking into your past. Obviously there are politics involved."

"Politics?"

"With your dad. Given his hero status, they don't want to move on you unless it's a sure thing. Don't you have an alibi? Something? Just get this out of the way?"

I look at my palm.

You promised.

Who promised?

"I'll figure it out," I tell her. "Go to work. Call me when you need me."

Ginny stands too. She smiles, the one she wears under her wigs, and the lilt returns to her voice. "Yes, darling. Off to defend this city from the conquering hordes."

THE GIRLS ARE gone and Bombay is in bed. I go to my duffel bag and dig out the scanner, plug it in next to the couch and turn the volume down until I can just hear it.

"10-35 code 2, Greene and West Fourth." Unnecessary alarm caused by construction activities.

I sit in the dark for a little while until I realize that I am desperately in need of a shower.

The bathroom is next to Bombay's bedroom so I put the water on low and I hope it doesn't wake him. The bandage on my arm sticks a little so I yank hard. It hurts like hell, but it comes off without ripping the wound open.

I climb under the hot water and stand there, let it flush the grime off me. I check the cut on my arm and poke it around the edges. Doesn't look or feel infected.

My ankle is feeling pretty rough. Landing on it twice has left it swollen. I can put my weight on it but it feels like a wooden joint. There's a bruise on my stomach from where the king hit me, and a lump on my head from where Samson tossed me into the car.

Delightful. I turn the water as hot as it'll go and lean my

head against the porcelain tiles, think through what Bad Kelly told me.

Two sets of DNA. Maybe the killer raped someone else? Maybe he had a female accomplice, which is a little heavy, but not impossible.

I know someone had been giving Chell trouble, and I know she had at least two people angry at her: Fanny Fatale and The Hipster King. Either one of them could have been working with a partner. Maybe they were working together.

The hot water turns lukewarm. I turn off the shower and towel dry, redo the bandage on my arm. I find a sports bandage in the medicine cabinet for my ankle.

The shower felt good and it woke me up. I nestle into the couch and reach for a laptop, scroll through apartment listings on Craigslist. After reading a few dozen ads, I make the following conclusions:

An apartment of comparable size to the one I lived in will be at least three thousand a month.

A studio apartment will be at least two thousand a month.

There are plenty of people looking for roommates, which would knock the rent down. Most of them are looking for people to split one bedrooms or studios. Some are even offering closets.

As I move uptown, the apartments get more expensive. As I move south, they get a little less pricey. The cheapest apartments I find are in Chinatown, but I'm vaguely familiar with those neighborhoods, and those buildings are nightmares. I'd be splitting my room with roaches and rats. And they still rent for around fifteen hundred a month.

Things get a little cheaper as I head out to the boroughs. Williamsburg is off the charts. Lofts going for four thousand a month. But there are apartments in Bushwick and Bed Stuy going for eight hundred, nine hundred. What's funny is that the listings say the apartments are in Park Slope or Williamsburg.

I think of Good Kelly and click over to Texas, scroll through the options in Austin. Right off the bat I find a one-story house with a back yard and two bedrooms. The kitchen is big enough to prepare meals more complicated than toast and there's even a driveway. It's eight hundred a month.

If I lived in Texas, I would get a dog. I've always wanted a dog, even got tempted a few times, but people who get dogs and force them to live in small apartments are assholes. Dogs need room to run around. Dogs need yards.

A yard would be nice. Sit outside at night, stare up at the sky, not feel like there's a bunch of people crowded on top of you. I wonder if you can see the stars in Austin?

The real question is what I would do in all that quiet.

The thing about living in New York City is that it's never really quiet. It's like when there's a television on in the next room and you know it's on, because you can feel the electric hum of it. To live in a place like this is to live in the middle of an electric hum that never stops.

So what do you learn about yourself when the world goes quiet and the humming stops and you can't hear anything but what's inside?

I concede defeat and dig the jump drive out of my pocket. Plug it in and the password prompt appears on the screen. I try Kent, the town in Ohio where Chell was born. Doesn't work.

What would matter to her? Enough that she would use it as a lock?

She had an imaginary friend when she was a child. She told me about it once. He was a clown in a yellow and red outfit.

Giggles. I try that and it doesn't work either.

Has to be something important. Something really important. Something meaningful.

Before I can even formulate a coherent thought, I type in 'Ashley' and hover over the return key.

It wouldn't be the first time she used me to protect her.

Was I important enough for this?

I yank the drive out and toss it onto the coffee table, close the laptop, and push myself further into the plush cushions.

The radio crackles next to me. "10-32, caller states male robbing woman. Southeast corner of Tompkins Square Park. Send a bus to assist?" That's right on the corner. I'm in my pants and out the door before I hear the response.

B Y THE TIME I get there, the cops are already talking to a shaken girl wearing a beige coat and hugging herself. Against the chill or the fear, I don't know. She doesn't have a purse with her, so I imagine it did get stolen. I light a cigarette and look at my phone and act like I'm waiting for someone, get close enough to hear the description: Two guys in ski masks, both of them wearing glasses through the masks.

One guy with his hand in a cast.

I'm caught in a loop and I can't see the boundaries of it.

The cops lead the girl into the squad car to bring her to the station for paperwork. They close the door and one looks at the other and says, "Second one tonight. Fourth this week. Un-fucking-believable."

An old guy walking a French bulldog stops and asks me what happened. I tell him it was a mugging. He asks for a cigarette and I know from his accent he was born here so I give it to him.

He talks at me like a person who's very lonely, says, "This city is too goddamn safe, if you ask me. If you wanted to live here, you used to have to earn it. Now you come here and you get shit handed to you. Shame about the girl, though."

"It's still pretty safe."

He shakes his head. "I miss the old days." He doesn't wait for me to say anything, just tugs the leash and leads the dog down the block.

CAN'T SLEEP, EVEN though I'm desperate for it. Too wired. I don't like that I missed the mugging. I check into Apocalypse and Dave tells me there's a patrol out, even though it's a little early. I walk over to Tompkins Square Park and find Katrina in pumps and a skirt, walking around the park and talking on her cell phone. Her bodyguard is Todd, a nice guy with a mean right hook who bartends in the West Village. I catch a glimpse of him, moving through the trees like a wraith. They don't see me.

The sidewalks are crowded and I drift south, my shoulders tight, my jaw clenched so hard my teeth creak. I feel like a screwdriver in a house made of nails. Who the fuck are these assholes terrorizing the people who live in my neighborhood?

My feet carry me independently of where I think I want to go, or should be going. I just walk, further south, down past Houston, to Delancey. I cut across to the Williamsburg Bridge, to those dark streets underneath that are veiled in shadows. I can't do drugs, and I can't drink. All I can do is walk.

I think about the man who wants to go back to the bad old days. Back to an authenticity that came in hand with a constant threat of violence. I don't know that those days are even gone. The bad guys didn't go away, they just got smarter. They wait and they think. They're a dangerous breed, able to operate in a city that renders them invisible, as long as they don't draw too much attention.

Doesn't matter that the city is safe. People still get hurt.

TEN

THE RAIN MAKES the street smell like urine. The first ten minutes of rain always does that, bringing the stench up from the sidewalk.

As I pass Curry Row on First Avenue I get an idea and duck into the spice shop underneath Milon. I ask the disinterested clerk for anything that smells like lavender. He points me toward the back and I find an ornate wooden display of scented oils.

I take one, crack the top open, and pull it in. The smell of it floods me, makes it feel like Chell is standing next to me. I like it.

At a bodega, I snag a copy of the *Post*. On the front page there's some jingoistic crap about a war somewhere. The saga of the Greenpoint Goth is relegated to a small banner at the bottom of cover, and then the fourth page on the inside. Not much new to report. People must be losing interest.

What troubles me is the opinion piece running next to it.

After some nonsense about the heinous nature of Chell's death, the columnist hits a point that makes me ball up the page in my hands.

What continues to haunt me about this attack, more than the brutality, is the photos of a once-beautiful young woman, her body scarred with ink like it's a canvas meant to be on display. The question I have to ask, and the question all of us should be asking is: How does this help?

We have photos of her in a stiff bra and low-cut shirt that displayed her cleavage, leather pants that were so tight the killer had to cut her out of them, and heels worthy of the stage at The Hustler Club.

The "feminists" are going to crow about this and call it victim-blaming, but I prefer to think of it as preemptive-shaming.

How are our daughters supposed to respect themselves if they think this is appropriate? They're the ones doing the real damage—by telling their daughters it's okay to dress like this.

I pitch the paper over my shoulder. I want to punch the brick wall next to me. I take back everything I said. Fuck the *Post*.

Another few blocks and I find a rental truck sitting outside Good Kelly's apartment. Tibo is sitting in the back, smoking a cigarette. He's also wearing a pirate hat and an eye patch.

I pull myself on the truck bed alongside him and ask, "Why are you a pirate today?"

"Because I haven't found the silver yet."

"That's... not the answer I was expecting. Though I guess I

don't know what I was expecting."

Tibo takes the hat off and runs his hands through his dreads, trying to flatten them to his head. "I'm going to tell you a secret, Ash. You can't tell anyone." He pulls a map out of his pocket and smoothes it on his lap. I recognize the shorelines of Staten Island and Brooklyn, with the Verrazano Bridge connecting the two. It looks like the map he was studying in Apocalypse a few nights ago.

Tibo says, "In 1903 a barge capsized. It was carrying seven thousand silver bars. They only recovered about six thousand. There's a bunch still left down there, and by today's standards, they're worth more than twenty-five million."

"That's not nothing."

"The Army Corps of Engineers has had to dredge and detonate parts of the canal to make it deep enough for cargo ships." He pulls out a smaller map. "These flow charts? There are some strong currents that lead in this direction." He pulls out the first map and points to a spot a quarter of a mile to the east of where the barge sank. "There's a little trench here, and I think this is where the bars ended up."

Tibo believes the world is going to end in five years. Every two months he comes up with a new scheme designed to help him fund a sustainable commune, so he and a select group of people can ride out the end times. Get enough booze in me and his logic doesn't sound too crazy. I tell him, "Best of luck then."

"I need a boat."

"I can't help you with that." I take out a cigarette and stop halfway to lighting it. "Actually I can. Talk to Kuffner. His dad has a boat."

"Didn't know that."

"Well, there you go then. Happy to help. Cut me in when you find the silver."

"Deal." He shakes my hand and folds up the maps.

I ask, "Where's Kelly?"

"Errand. She told me to stay here and watch the truck. Dave and Todd are upstairs getting shit together right now."

"Good then. I'll help you watch the truck."

The rain picks up. We pull our legs inside. Tibo asks, "How are you holding up?"

"Could be better."

"It's a hard thing to parse out, you know."

"How someone could hurt someone like that..."

Tibo pauses, confused. "Oh, you're talking about Chell. I thought we were talking about Kelly. But yes, the Chell thing sucks, too. How's the hunt?"

"Coming up empty."

"Can I be nosy?"

"Sure."

He arches an eyebrow at me. The eyebrow that isn't covered by an eye patch. "Are you prepared to deal with the consequences?"

I pitch my spent cigarette into the street and place a fresh one between my lips, but I don't light it. "I'm only doing what my dad taught me. He raised me to believe that you don't hit women and you stick up for people."

Tibo nods. "Maybe this guy just didn't have that positive influence in his life."

"Is that supposed to be an excuse? Bad is bad. Wrong is wrong. There's no fucking gray area here."

Tibo looks around and takes out a small psychedelic stained-glass pipe with a nugget of weed packed into the bowl.

He holds it in my direction, and I shake my head. My body doesn't handle pot well. Last time I got high, I threw a chair at someone, which I'm to understand is the opposite of the intended effect.

He takes a long hit and holds it in his lungs, taps his knee four times, lets the smoke explode from his mouth. In a gravelly voice he says, "We were animals before we developed social contracts. We're still animals, just smarter now. Evolution can only do so much. The animal part of us never leaves." Cough, cough.

"How high are you, exactly?"

"Look, I'm not saying you're a bad person. A thought is a seed of something that doesn't have to take root if you don't let it. The point is, we have these base instincts and urges inside us, and this is where nurture comes in. That's what we need to learn, to suppress our urges. But more than that, to be better than them. What sets us apart from animals? We can dream of a better world."

"I guess the answer is 'very high.' You are very high."

"Don't blow me off. I'm not trying to drop some deep fucking sage wisdom on you. I'm just saying you're going to kill yourself before you get the answers you're looking for. Some people just can't get past those animal urges."

"So you're saying this guy didn't have a choice? He just wanted to get laid and couldn't control himself?"

"You're oversimplifying it," he says. "First, rape is not about sex. It's about power and anger. It's about rage. And I said nothing about choice. Choice is a whole other conversation."

"So if it weren't for my dad teaching me to do the right thing, I'd be the same as him?"

Tibo shakes his head. "Oversimplification. Don't look for

openings to argue. Not the point. Just think." He reaches his hand up to my head and taps it with his finger. "Think. You're like a wrecking ball. Smashing into shit, not thinking."

He picks up his pipe and takes another hit. We sit and watch the rain, at the rivers pushing trash into the gutter, scrubbing the grime from the streets and leaving them fresh and clean. I reach my hand out and the drops fall between my fingers.

Good Kelly shows up and we work for a few hours, hauling boxes down four flights of stairs. Me and Todd do the heavy lifting while Dave helps Tibo maneuver items into place on the truck. It's slow work and by the fourth time I'm climbing the stairs to Kelly's apartment, my chest constricted and my lungs filled with cotton, I question why I smoke as much as I do.

When the truck is ready to roll out Kelly asks if anyone wants to grab a pizza. One last pie before she leaves. No one can stay so I raise my hand. She disappears, and I climb onto the small space in the back of the truck that's empty. She reappears ten minutes later with a full pie.

"Are we going to kill this whole thing?" I ask.

"Yup. It'll be a while before I have this again."

We dig in. It's a plain pie from one of those anonymous corner joints you don't even know the name of. Halfway through my second slice I look up at Kelly and ask, "So, Texas? I mean, c'mon."

"Don't knock Austin until you've been there. You would not even believe it's Texas."

"When's last call?"

"I think one-thirty in the morning."

"Madness."

Kelly picks up her third slice. "Being able to drink until four in the morning isn't a good reason to stay here. This place is too expensive and too loud and it's turning into a playground for yuppie rich kids. Eleven bucks for a pack of smokes. I paid twelve bucks for a Jack on the rocks last week. Someday there's going to be a fun tax, and if you're out having a good time some guy in a uniform is going to run up to you and demand five dollars. And then we may as well live in Iran."

"It's not that bad."

"It will be."

"How are you going to adapt?"

"Just fine. The cost of living is lower. I can pay a rent that makes sense. And I love the idea of living in a town where the natural thing to do on a lazy afternoon is get margaritas."

"We can get margaritas here. You can get pizza and bagels here. What are you going to do the first time you want pizza or a good bagel?"

"I'll have something to look forward to when I come home." She picks up her fourth slice. "This city isn't going anywhere."

"Not until someone tries to blow it up again."

"More reason to go."

"You're sure about this?"

"You make it sound like I'm moving to Siberia. I'm going down to try something different. If I don't like it, I'll be back."

"Then I wish you luck."

"Will you come visit me?"

"Will you pay for me?"

She pauses. "Do you need money?"

"I'm kidding. I'll come visit. I've never been against country music."

Kelly offers me the last slice, but I let her have it because where she's going, pizza as we know it does not exist. When she's finished, I help her make sure the back door is down and locked and then I hug her goodbye. She climbs in the cab of the truck, starts it, and pulls away from the curb. I watch as the truck turns at the end of the street and disappears out of sight.

BEFORE I HEAD back to Bombay's I take a walk by Washington Square Park and find Craig sitting by himself at a chess table. We play two games and he butchers me on both but I'm not paying attention. When I knock over my king for the second time I ask, "Anything?"

He doesn't look up at me, just goes back to resetting the pieces on the board. "Still looking."

I slide a twenty across the table and pat him on the shoulder, walk cross-town to Alphabet City, to follow up at the bar across the street from where Chell was snatched. It's closed so I knock on the door to see if maybe someone is setting up, but no one answers.

Then to Apocalypse. Nothing on the groper. There are a few familiar faces floating around so I collect some phone numbers to fill out my contacts.

I should be looking for Fanny Fatale but Cinnamon West isn't going to back my play. I could pop into the bars where the burlesque performers hang out and ask around, but that raises issues of the creeper variety.

Outside KGB I look up and turn in a circle. Directionless.

I get hungry again and I need more cigarettes so I head to the ATM. This time I check my balance. I stare at the number for a little while and hope I'm not reading it right. But no, in yellow numbers on a blue screen it says $60.24. I take out forty and resolve to look for some work to fill things out a little.

BOMBAY IS PLAYING video games when I get back to his place. I sit on the couch next to him and watch as he stalks a pixilated battlefield and slaughters aliens that look like a cross between lizards and gorillas. He sticks a grenade to the chest of one of them and I tell him, "I guess I'm not the only one who gravitates toward violence."

He doesn't take his eyes from the screen, just switches to a rocket launcher and blows up a platoon advancing on his flank. "False equivalence. I'm not hurting anything."

"Nothing except your sex life."

"You are not as funny as you think you are."

"Sure I am."

Bombay's space marine is suddenly smashed to the ground by an enormous beam of green light. He turns and finds an alien encased in tank-like armor. The fight doesn't last long. He puts the controller in his lap and wipes his eyes. "I have something for you. And you're not going to like it."

"Par for the course."

"I found the guy. Cairo. His real name is Rick Paulsen."

"What is there to not like about that?"

"The fact that I also found out he got accused of sexual assault two years ago in Boston."

The room freezes. Pieces snap in place.

Rick Paulsen runs Noir York, which has some sort of tenuous connection to The Hipster King and the crew at Slaughterhouse Six. Chell was working in the game and that's how she was spying on them. Maybe they found out and killed her to cover what was going on with the coup.

Maybe that's why the thumb drive is such a hot item. It could belong to Paulsen, or to the king. And those hipster assholes tracking me want it back.

Though it raises the question of how they know I have it.

But maybe Paulsen was sweet on Chell and that's who was harassing her. He made himself scarce when I asked about him at the bar in Brooklyn. Sexual assault isn't a momentary slip in judgment. That kind of thing is a black mark on your soul that doesn't wash off, no matter the penance.

I ask Bombay, "No other details on the assault rap?"

"Charges weren't formally filed. Could be nothing."

"Could be something."

"Look." Bombay says. "I almost didn't want to tell you. I don't want you to go off and just kill this guy over something that could be a coincidence."

"I wouldn't kill him without asking first."

Bombay slams the controller down on the table. "Will you stop being so flip about this? What do I need to say to get it through your thick fucking head, man?"

"Chell was your friend, too. Are you saying you're okay with all this?"

"Yes, she was my friend. And now she's dead and gone. And then you're going to be gone, because you're going to be dead or in jail."

"When did you become such a fucking pacifist?"

"When have you ever known me to approve of violence? When have you ever known me to support this kind of thing? I spent my whole fucking life getting shit on because I was raised Muslim. I can't walk outside without some fucking asshole looking at me like I'm a terrorist. Life is fucking hard. I get over it."

I walk across the room, completely spent. I don't want to have this conversation. Bombay follows and pushes me against the wall, holding me in place. We're both so shocked by the physicality of it that for a moment neither of us say anything.

Finally he says, "You are not going to find peace from this."

"Don't tell me what I will or won't find. You don't know that."

"What would your father want?"

I pull out of Bombay's grip. "I don't know. Let me ask him. Oh wait, he's fucking dead now, because he put his life on the line to do the right thing and protect people."

"What he did and what you're doing are two very different things."

"I know that." I reach down and pick up my umbrella, tie it into my belt. "Thank you for your input, but I'm going for a walk."

Bombay says, "Ash." But he doesn't say anything after that, just stands at the center of the room, his shoulder slumped. I turn to the door and he whispers something. Over my shoulder I ask, "What?"

He doesn't answer so I head to the roof.

THE RAIN HAS stopped and the clouds have parted. The city and it's broken skyline sparkle on the horizon. I take out my phone and call my mother.

She answers the phone with a tone like she's expecting bad news. "Ashley?"

"Hey Ma."

"Honey? I've been trying to call you."

"I know. I'm sorry. Been busy."

"I spoke to Margo. She said you looked tired."

"Is that all she said?"

"Is there more?"

"I don't think so. I haven't been sleeping well."

A few seconds of silence. Then she says, "You're thinking about him right now, aren't you?"

"I'm not."

"What do I tell you about sitting around and crying about him?"

"You don't cry anymore?"

She pauses. "I didn't say that." Clears her throat. "How's Margo adjusting?"

"Fine. She seems to be having a great time."

"Good. Your Aunt Ruth was in hysterics, after that girl was in the news. You know, the girl who got killed."

My turn to pause. "Margo has nothing to worry about."

"Honey, what's wrong?"

"Nothing. Tired. I'm sorry. And I'm sorry I didn't call you back. I'm a bad son."

"You're not a bad son."

"I wish I was a better son."

"Stop it. Come over for dinner. Bring Margo so I can see her. And bring Bombay. You can bring any of your friends. It's so quiet here. It would be nice to have people over."

"Sure Ma."

"Do you promise?"

"I promise."

"And Ashley? Please answer your damn phone when I call."

"Love you too, Ma."

The line goes quiet. I close the phone and hold it in my hand.

PART OF LOVING my dad, my mom would tell her friends, was learning to love the scanner. It lived on the nightstand next to their bed, and he never turned it off.

Behind the nightstand was a hundred feet of orange extension cord, wrapped up in a neat coil. Sometimes I would find him sitting in the kitchen, the lights off, the cord stretched through the house, the scanner in front of him. His ear cocked to the speaker, his brain translating the numbers and codes.

I would wake up for a glass of water and he'd smile and say, "Can't sleep. Neither can you, I guess."

Even if it was a school night, he would let me sit there with him and he would explain what the codes meant. If a call came in that was close by, he would leave to see if he could help.

He listened to that scanner all day. Sometimes it was like he was afraid of quiet.

That's not why he listened though.

A lot of firefighters in this city have scanners, in bedrooms and kitchens and basements. They all listen, waiting for one single moment. The kind of moment you don't even know you're waiting for until it happens.

Half an hour after Tower 2 was hit, the FDNY issued a total recall. Every firefighter in New York City, no matter where they were, no matter what they were doing, had to drop everything and report for duty.

A total recall only happened once before, the day after Christmas in 1947, for a blizzard.

This wasn't a blizzard.

It didn't matter that the call went out. Most of them were on their way in as soon as the first plane hit. They didn't need some guy in a white hat and gloves to tell them it was time to go to work.

I was asleep when it happened. Home sick from school. I don't know if my dad came into my room before he left. He probably figured I needed my rest. And he had no idea where he was headed. I never asked my mom about what happened when he left that morning, but I've pieced some of it together.

She was making coffee. I know she was making coffee because after she shook me awake, dragged me to the television as the first tower collapsed, I remember dry grounds spread across the counter and floor, the coffee maker half full of water, the acrid smell of burnt bread that had been left too long in the toaster.

On the kitchen table was a copy of that day's *Post*. It was opened to the sports section.

My dad's last words to my mom were: "You are beautiful in the morning. I'll see you for dinner." I know this because sometimes my mother would whisper it to herself, standing at the kitchen counter in the dark, her voice shaking like glass about to shatter.

I know that twenty minutes later he was on a truck riding heavy with two shifts, aimed at downtown Manhattan.

They never found his body. His lieutenant said that means he probably fought his way to the upper floors to evacuate the people who were trapped there.

That was my father.

This is how I honor his memory.

THE BUSINESS CARD for Noir York is still in my pocket. So is the scrap of paper with the number Bombay found on the website. I wipe the tears from my eyes and click it into my phone.

A woman answers. "Is this line secure?"

I tell her, "Whatever."

"How many in your party?"

"One."

"Name?"

The hipsters probably know my name so I pull one out of the air, hope she's not a fan of The Smiths. "Johnny. Johnny Marr."

"Address?"

I begin to give her my old apartment but then think better and give her Bombay's. On the other end of the phone is the sound of a pen scratching on paper.

The woman says, "Five hundred dollars, cash. You'll receive your instructions shortly."

"That's not specific."

Click.

This is it. I know this is it.

Joel Cairo or Rick Paulsen or whatever his name is. I'll find him at the end of Noir York. The bogeyman who's been looming over this neighborhood, over my life. He's the guy. He has to be. It just makes sense.

I'm going to stop him. No umbrella. I'll do it with my hands.

I just need to find five hundred bucks.

If I'm going to do this, I need to adopt a new investigative style. The worst thing I could do here is charge in and spook the guy at the end. He could ghost and I'm left with nothing. I'll play the game. Maybe I can get through this without losing any more blood.

My phone buzzes.

Time to cash in on that favor. Come to the club.

ELEVEN

'THE CLUB' IS not Chanticleer. I wish I were meeting Ginny at Chanticleer. The club is a black door on a street next to a bar. It's the plainest door in the city, and if you don't know what happens behind that door you'd never even notice it was there.

It's not like I have a problem with what people are doing in the club. It's just that if you're not into leather daddies, it's hard to feel comfortable when they're practicing their art.

I knock twice. The door swings open a crack so I can slip through, and leads into a small partition created by black curtains.

Seated in the center is an old man wearing an accountant's visor, drenched in red light. He's at a card table, a lockbox in front of his folded hands. I fish out ten bucks and hand it to him. He nods, puts the cash in the box, hands me a casino chip, a condom, a handy-wipe, and a mini packet of lube. Which I don't want to take, but I also don't want to be rude, so I shove them into my pockets. He doesn't look up from the table at any point during the transaction.

Past the black curtain there are glass bowls filled with more condoms and more lube, and curtained booths, and a lot of red lighting. The people I can see are mostly talking and lounging. Mostly. A few heads turn toward me as I enter. They see I'm not there for fun and go back to what they're doing.

Perched on a stool in the middle of the room is a young guy, pretty enough to be a model and dressed only in a bathrobe. He's not watching anything too intently so I figure him for an employee and not a voyeur. I slide up next to him and say, "I'm looking for Ginny."

His eyes dart to a door in the back, partly hidden by a red curtain. He says, "Never heard of her."

"I bet you haven't."

I don't bother to knock. Maybe I should have.

Ginny is in the middle of a room with a concrete floor, stone walls, and candle holders bolted into the walls. It looks like a dungeon. She's wearing a leather dress that covers her entire top and her arms, cut off right above her knees. Long leather boots and a big black Elvira wig.

When I close the door she looks over her shoulder and leans forward, fumbling with something at her crotch. Stretched out on a plastic tarp is a handsome man in a gray suit. The front of the suit looks like someone just spilled a bottle of water on him, but the smell tells a different story.

Ginny says, "Christ, Ash."

The guy on the floor picks his head up and says, "Actually, I'm good with this."

I ask Ginny, "Do you want me to leave?"

"We're all grownups here. But next time, knock."

Ginny turns, her situation rectified, and smiles. "So you got my text? Oh, and..." She points at my head. "Off please."

I take off the hat and hold it in my hands. The man lying on the floor hasn't moved and it's making me uncomfortable. Ginny notices this because she waves at him and he climbs to his feet. "Ash, this is my lawyer."

The man gets up and brushes at his drenched suit. He looks vaguely familiar. He smiles and extends his hand toward me and I look at it. It's wet. I tell him, "No."

He nods, first like he's hurt, then with the realization of what's on his hands. He stares at the floor like a dog waiting for a command.

"So," I say. "This is the most awkward I have ever felt in my entire life. And I went to a Catholic grammar school. How about we get down to it?"

Ginny snaps her fingers. The lawyer goes to the corner to pick up a briefcase propped up against the wall. Before he can grab it I tell him, "Just leave it."

The lawyer returns to Ginny's side. She pats him on the shoulder and says, "Please wait outside."

He nods and leaves through another door in the back. When the door closes behind him I say, "Ginny. Seriously. What the fuck?"

She shrugs. "Darling, I'm sorry. If I knew you'd be so quick, I would have waited. And if you would have knocked, we could have relocated our meeting to another room. He's one of the best lawyers in the city and we have an... arrangement."

"Getting peed on."

"The technical term is urophilia."

"Why did you call me?"

She nods over to the briefcase. "You know that favor you owe me? Deliver that."

"That's it?"

"That's it, darling. There's a card on the top with the address it needs to go to. Drop it off with a man named Rex. Keep it quick and quiet. I want you seen and not heard. No names."

"Seems like a simple task."

"Nothing is ever simple. Especially when it comes to the Latinos. They're excitable."

"That's a little racist, isn't it?"

Ginny exhales. "I have spent my entire life being stepped on because of who I am. Even in the liberal bastion of New York City, I often find myself judged and ridiculed. I have a lot of pent up anger to express." She pauses, smiles, and adds, "You know a little something about how that feels, don't you?"

"Whatever." I cross the room and pick up the briefcase. "Listen, I know I'm paying off a debt on this, but any chance you could kick me five hundred bucks? I need it for something. I'll get it back to you as soon as I have it."

"I don't have any cash on me. Come back when you're done."

I check the address, which is in Hell's Kitchen. Or Clinton, as the yuppie gents have taken to calling it. I ask Ginny, "Why me? Anyone else could do this for you."

"Because Ash, Samson is otherwise occupied, and you are the only person I know who doesn't care enough to open the case. I should add, please don't open the case." She pauses. "And one other thing."

"What's that?"

"I hear it's supposed to rain tonight. It's good that you have your umbrella."

"The skies have cleared up, Gin."

"Oh, I know. But better to have it and not need it."

THERE'S A FOLDING table set up at the entrance of the subway station where a gaggle of cops stop me. A young officer, tall and ginger and gangly, asks, "Sir, could you please open your briefcase?"

"How's your wife doing?"

He stands at attention. "What?"

"I'm sorry, I thought we were playing that game where we violate each other's personal boundaries."

"Sir, the case."

"Forget it."

He crosses his arms and his cop friends stand behind him, like they're intimidating someone in a schoolyard. "Then you can't ride the subway."

"Fine. Fuck you. There are plenty of other ways to get around Nazi Germany."

I leave before the cops get the bright idea to search me.

That's new. Never been stopped before. I guess the cops need to pull a white kid out every now and again so they can argue against racial profiling.

I remember when Snow White had to tack a surcharge onto her product because the runners couldn't take the subway anymore. The times, they are changing.

THE CAB GETS stuck in traffic at 43nd and Sixth. Should have cut crosstown further south, when we still had a chance. I can't afford to sit with a running meter so I tell the guy to let me out and hand him the last of my spending money. I am now broke. I hope Ginny is good on the loan.

I hit the sidewalk, head west, and as I get closer to Times Square I can feel the neon buzzing on my skin like a swarm of insects.

When I step onto Seventh Avenue, the street is bright enough that when I look at the ground I could swear it was daytime. The glare of mammoth LCD billboards and the building-sized advertisements suck the color from the sky and turn it into a vacuum devoid of color.

Crossing the street is a simple task because traffic is stopped, but the further I get to the center the thicker it gets, until the air is like water. The crowd swallows me. There's a fog of people wearing fanny packs and speaking different languages. They move without reason or thought, bouncing in different directions. Every step I take is impeded. I duck and weave through the crowd, a frenetic ballet of stupidity. People cross my path in my blind spot and nearly end up on the floor and I don't feel bad for them. I nearly trip over a man who has stopped in the middle of the sidewalk to tie his shoe.

Those people in movies who are overtaken and devoured by crowds of zombies? This is what they see before they die.

It's loud. So loud. The blaring horns and the screaming people and the chain restaurants pumping Top 40 hits. The cacophony of this place makes my vision blur. I take a knee next to a large potted plant on the median, jam my earbuds in, and crank The Dictators, just so I can block some of it out.

Back in the day this was a great place for crack or a handjob.

It's still dealing in opiates and sex, except now it's aimed at the pleasure points of middle-America.

Traffic is moving a little better on the western spur of Seventh but I don't want to wait at the corner, so I push through the crowd and dodge taxis and buses until I'm on the other side. I push through the crowd on the sidewalk to the less-traversed side streets. When I break through, I suck in a big gulp of the cool night air.

Outside Times Square, 43rd is a bit more quiet. I wander past young kids from the suburbs breaking their city cherry, past scared tourists lined up outside the theaters, peeking over their shoulder and holding their kids tight. Past scalpers offering me jacked-up tickets to Disney movies that have been turned into Broadway shows.

Occasionally I pass another native, lost and terrified. We share nods of recognition.

The building I'm supposed to go to is near the water. The contrast between Hell's Kitchen and the square is staggering. It's so quiet I can hear a television blaring from a third floor apartment across the street.

I find the building easy enough, a drab little brick number that would disappear into the scenery if I weren't looking for it. There are a couple of unmarked buttons on a buzzer by the gunmetal door, but no clear sense on what I'm supposed to do next, until I notice the security camera bolted into the corner of the doorway. I hold the bag up and say, "Delivery."

The door buzzes. Inside the hallway it smells like bleach and some other chemical I can't place. An overweight Latino guy pops out of the doorway. He's wearing designer jeans, sneakers, and a long white t-shirt. So long it looks comical, but nothing about his face says this is funny. I brush the umbrella hanging from my belt. He waves at me to follow.

Maybe I read too much into what Ginny said. Maybe the forecast is for rain. I should have checked. But the security cameras inside the hallway are pushing my heart down my chest. By the time we get to the second floor it's sitting in my lower intestine.

He leads me through another door and into a hallway, throws me against the wall, and pats me down. His hands check my pockets and reach around toward my junk. No way is the umbrella going to pass the test. Once he feels the weight it's going to be a problem. I play the only card I can think to pull out.

"Buddy, buy me a dinner first, and I'll let you do a full cavity search," I tell him.

"Faggot," he says.

"That's sweet. Do I see Rex now?"

"T-Rex."

"What?"

"As in, Tyrannosaurs. As in, my man will swallow you, bitch."

"How is it I'm the gay in this scenario?"

He opens the door to an apartment, the look of disgust on his face so strong I want to make another pass at him, just to fuck with him. I don't, in spite of my ability to make terrible decisions all the time.

The next room is small. There's a mahogany desk surrounded by blank walls. There's another door in the back.

And there's no camera in this room.

Behind the desk is a sharp-looking guy in a suit. The kind of guy who spends a lot of time worrying about his eyebrows. There are three teardrops tattooed below his left eye, which means he's killed three people, or he wants me to believe he has.

"What have you got for me," he says, not asking, looking at the bag and not at me. His voice is condescending even though I don't think he means it to be.

People like this scare the shit out of me: The ones who think Scarface's death was about honor and not atonement.

The fat homophobe stayed in the room. He's behind me. Standing between me and the desk are two more guys, both of them in matching blue denim outfits, flanking me like decorative suits of armor. Neither of them appear to be breathing.

My new friend takes the briefcase from my hand and brings it to the boss. I throw my hands up and say, "Guys, thanks for having me, but I have to run. No, I wouldn't like anything to drink. See you later. Tell everyone I said hey."

T-Rex says, "We count first."

This doesn't feel right. I never stay long enough at these things to see the package get opened.

As T-Rex lifts the top of the case the two guys in the denim tense up, like they're getting ready for something. I play the angles in my head, because if this goes south, I have to be quick. The homophobe didn't look like he was carrying a weapon, but the two guys in the Canadian tuxes could be strapped. They would have to go first.

The problem is if T-Rex is packing too. I may not have enough time to get to him.

Then again, I could be overreacting. Ginny is a lot of things, but she's still a friend. She wouldn't put me four heartbeats from a coffin.

"What the fuck is this, *mama huevo*?"

Maybe not.

T-Rex turns the briefcase upside down over the table. Piles of multi-colored Monopoly money fall out, bundled with rubber bands.

Before the play money hits the top of the desk the umbrella is out. I swing it toward the guy closest to me and it extends with just enough time to crush his jaw. I let the momentum carry my elbow into the second guy's throat. Before the two of them hit the ground the homophobe is on me. My stomach drops as he lifts me into the air and slams me into the wall. It's cheap sheetrock and my body leaves the imprint of a snow angel flecked with blood. I land hard on my shoulder.

The umbrella slides across the floor. By the time I get to my feet the homophobe has got it in his hand and he's figured out why I carry it. T-Rex is sitting at the table, his arms folded behind his head, watching the fight.

The homophobe swings it like a baseball bat. I jump back but the umbrella clips me on the arm. Not hard enough to break it, just enough I won't be able to lift it over my head tomorrow.

He's strong and quicker than he looks, but he's sloppy. As he finishes the swing he leaves himself wide open so I slam my fist into his kidney. He arches his back and opens his chest up to me. I fold my hands together, reach high overhead, and slam them down on his breastplate. He hits the floor and doesn't move.

T-Rex is up from his seat and I'm on him before he has the chance to pull the gun. It's a little six-shooter, strong enough to do damage in a tight space. I swing the umbrella and smack him on the side of the head. His body folds and he fires off a shot that takes a chunk out of my thigh.

Adrenaline is gunning through my veins, hard enough the

bullet wound doesn't hurt, it just feels hot and tight, like a hand gripping my leg. The gun skids across the floor, and I use my good arm to punch T-Rex, and the lights behind his eyes go out.

My blood is buzzing. My leg is bleeding. On the desk is a piece of paper. In thick, curled calligraphy, it says: *Courtesy of The Hipster King.*

T-Rex groans at my feet. I kick him in the ribs a couple of times, less for trying to kill me and more for his stupid fucking name. I check his pockets and come up with his wallet. There's a thick wad of high-denomination bills inside. I stick the wallet in my jacket, grab my umbrella, and tear out the door.

I CAN'T TELL HOW badly I'm bleeding because my jeans are black. The skin surrounding the gunshot wound is hot and swollen. Every time I put pressure on my left leg something explodes in my thigh. I search the street for a cab, but I'm too far on the outskirts of Times Square to find one.

I pass a street vendor selling plastic replicas of the Statue of Liberty and I Heart NY t-shirts and piles of multicolored scarves. I grab a black one, hand him a bill from the wad I took off T-Rex, not even looking at it, and limp to a dark doorway. I wrap it around my leg and tie it tight and oh, fuck man, there's the pain.

That much solved, I limp east, not wanting to look over my shoulder, listening for the patter of footsteps or the hard click of metal. Anything to indicate I'm about to take another bullet, this one placed with a little more care.

As I get closer to the beating neon heart of the city, the

midnight sky is washed out by white haze that amplifies the darkness behind me.

Head toward the light. Ha-fucking-ha.

An open yellow cab turns the corner and coasts toward me. I flag it down and jerk the handle of the back door, but it's locked. The driver lowers his window to ask where I want to go, so he can blow me off if it's not where he wants to go.

I lean down to the window and put on my 'not-to-be-fucked-with' face. He recognizes it and hits the button to unlock the door. I climb in, spread myself onto the leather bench seat, careful to keep my leg from touching anything. Not because of the pain, but because I don't know what's been on these seats tonight.

The cabbie doesn't ask me where I want to go, just stares at me in the rearview mirror while cars line up behind him, drivers smashing their horns. His eyes hover in the reflection, sepia and bloodshot.

I can't go home. I don't have one anymore. Bombay won't take me like this. Not without some big fucking lecture and a fight. Ginny could funnel me to an off-the-books doctor, but she also might have sent me into that room to get killed. There's only one place I can think to go.

"Brooklyn," I tell the cabbie. "Greenpoint. Get to Driggs and I'll know where."

He drives. I can't see his face but there's not a smile on it. This late, he won't get a return fare into Manhattan. A lot of driving for a little money. I want to tell him I'm bleeding and maybe he should cut me some slack, but then he'll kick me out. No one wins.

The interior of the cab smells like an air freshener with a scent that doesn't exist in nature, like 'cool breeze' or 'mountain fresh.' The floor looks recently vacuumed, and the tears in the leather seat are patched with electrical tape. Spanish music whispers from the radio up front. Best case scenario, as far as cabs go.

The video screen on the partition lights up. Overlay of the weather—intermittent rain for the next three days—and a pretty brunette sitting at a desk, talking about how the city has experienced massive drops in every major crime category. Her voice is calm and reassuring.

The screen swipes to a segment about a television show that's filming on the Upper West Side, full of preppy kids who look like they were designed by a focus group. I stab at the touchscreen until the video stops. The screensaver illuminates the red swirls of my bloody fingerprint. I wipe it off with the sleeve of my jacket.

I take out my cell and click through until I find Ginny's number, send her a text: *Still alive, asshole.*

The driver stops at a light. I close my phone and hold it against my chest. Think about sunshine and cupcakes. Not about the chunk of my leg that's missing or the white ball of pain that replaced it. I take out T-Rex's wallet, count off the money. Close to three grand. At least something's looking up.

As the cab turns a corner I hear a sharp tap against the window. I look up and there's a fat drop of water smacked against the glass, trailing down and leaving a path in the dirt.

Then another, and another one after that, until it's raining so hard everything outside the window blurs. The driver slows to a stop. Car horns ring out around us. My phone buzzes. I flip it open and find Ginny's response: *I told you to bring your umbrella.*

TWELVE

THERE'S NOBODY SITTING outside Chell's apartment this time. Just a quiet Brooklyn street. The only sound is the wind rustling leaves on the trees lining the block.

The key is still there, dug into the soil of the basil plant. The plant is wilted and browned despite the rain. I hold onto one of the leaves and it crumbles in my hand.

Something goes my way: The key works. My leg is blazing now, the full brunt of the pain having made itself at home. I push into the apartment and shut the door, quick but without a sound, then lean on the door and listen. Still quiet.

The curtains aren't all the way drawn. The apartment is empty, save some cardboard boxes stacked in the corner. Chell's stuff ready to be sent out? Who knows where. Probably to the trash. I doubt her family would care enough to come and get any of it.

In the kitchen I spread out the results of my stop at the bodega and the liquor store.

Antiseptic. Bandages and surgical tape. Bleach. A sewing kit, just in case.

And a bottle of Jay.

The water in the shower turns hot right away. I strip off my clothes and climb underneath and watch as the water runs down my body, coming off pink at my feet, circling the drain.

The gash is on the outside of my thigh, halfway between the knee and my hip bone. I've lost a chunk of skin, but it's not a huge chunk. I don't even know that it's worth sewing. It's more like a deep scratch. Lucky. I pour on antiseptic and the burn snaps every muscle in my body to attention.

Something I didn't anticipate: The apartment has been cleared out, and I don't have a towel. There's a roll of paper towels under the sink so I use it to dry off, then work on bandaging my leg. I twist the gauze loose around my leg until I get to the end, and fashion a knot. I hold my breath, pull it tight. It feels like getting body-checked by a truck. I scream loud enough I actively hope no one calls the police.

After that I redo the bandage on my arm, unscrew the Jay and smell it, feel the woody sting in my sinuses. I stare at the bottle for a long time without any real internal conflict because I'm resigned to this, and take a very long chug.

The booze kicks a path straight to my brain and it is so, so good.

I take another for good measure, because my first time being shot deserves some sort of commemoration. Shot for a shot.

After getting dressed, I retreat to the corner and crumple into a ball on the floor, my hands on my knees, the bottle cradled between my feet. I switch between the bottle and a cigarette. The alchemy of whiskey and tobacco tastes like the best parts of the last four years of my life. I hold onto that feeling until I'm afraid it's going to snap.

The apartment is empty. I try to remember where everything was. The carpet at the center of the living room. It was a rectangle, light beige bordered by dark brown. Heavy. It didn't move when you walked on it.

The floor was always covered with throw pillows. Chell liked sitting on the floor but I never did, even though I tried to like the things she liked.

None of the pillows matched. One was polka dot and one was plaid. Another was a paisley print and one was just a regular pillow, like the kind you'd sleep on. All on that beige carpet. I'm a guy and even I knew Chell's color coordination was shoddy.

This was where she lived. This apartment was her. Hidden away like it was a secret. Small and sort of perfect.

And now she's gone. The city took her away. This goddamn city. It does not discriminate. It takes and gives nothing back.

Before I realize I'm drunk, the bottle is half-gone. The booze is hitting me fast but that's my own fault for being out of practice. For pretending I was something I'm not.

There's a scraping sound at the front of the apartment. A key in the lock. I watch the knob as it jiggles back and forth. I know it can't be true, but the dazed and drunk part of my brain expects Chell to come through the door. For her to stand in front of me and shake her head, but then kneel down next to me and cradle me in her arms and tell me that I am not my mistakes.

The door opens and a young couple enters. The guy is

wearing a plaid lumberjack shirt and has a thick, elaborate beard. The girl is wearing a skirt over her jeans and a purple leather jacket. They're happy and laughing and they see me in the corner and stop. We stare at each other.

The guy asks, "Why are you in our apartment?"

"Your apartment," I tell them, climbing to my feet. "Your apartment. Chell's body is still fucking warm."

The guy reaches out and grabs my arm, says, "Hey man, did you take anything?"

I put my hand on his forehead and shove him to the floor. The girl backs up against the wall and pulls out her cell phone. I make myself scarce before the cops show up.

YOU NEVER REALLY judged me, Chell, but you never really approved of the way I am, either.

One night Apocalypse was hosting a dramatic reenactment of that episode from *Saved by the Bell* where Jessie Spano takes too many caffeine pills. It was a bunch of kids dressed like characters from the show, acting it out like it was Shakespeare.

The show had ended and we were sitting around drinking with the cast. This was during one of our cold periods. I had been sort of seeing this girl, and you were sort of seeing this guy, and who knows where Quinn was, and we were sort of avoiding each other. But it was difficult to not cross paths.

I didn't like the guy you were seeing. He would talk forever about how he really understood filmmaking and books, and if anyone would dare to disagree, they would disappear from his field of vision, as though having a differing opinion rendered them inert. He was just some guy from someplace else who was so full of himself he oozed onto the floor. You didn't even bother to introduce him to me.

So this night, you were wearing a black dress and yellow heels, your hair pushed back on your head, like you had just come from someplace fancy. I was doing my best to ignore you but failing miserably, and just when I had settled into a nice drunken groove I saw a flash in the corner of my eye.

He had slapped you across the face.

You took it like a pro, didn't budge, didn't say anything, just stared daggers at him so hard he actually took a step back.

He stepped right into me. I grabbed him by his hair and dragged him outside the bar and threw him to the ground and told him to get up. That if he wanted to fight someone he should fight someone his own size. His eyes were so wide with fear they nearly fell out of his face.

I was going to let him take the first shot, knowing I'd put him in the hospital no matter what, but he lingered too long, so I lunged. You got in between us. You didn't say anything, just stared at me almost as hard as you did him. I tried to get around you and you wrapped your arms around me and I melted because I didn't want to risk hurting you. The guy got up and ran away.

You asked, *What the hell was that about?*

He hit you.

Yes. Me. I'm a big girl, Ashley. I don't need you fighting my battles.

Doesn't matter. Guys don't hit girls. It's a rule.

Whose rule?

Doesn't matter. It's a rule, and I'm not going to watch some guy take a swing at you and walk away like nothing happened.

So you're judge and jury now?

That's not the point, Chell.

Is this a morality play? Or are you just looking for someone to beat up?

You want to date guys who slap you around, that's your prerogative.

Sometimes I think you'd like that, because all you ever do it act like I'm some soft little thing that can't survive without your protection. It's how you treat everyone.

I want to say something back but you didn't give me the chance. You spun on your heels and stalked off down the street. I watched you turn the corner and then I felt the eyes of the crowd on me. I left, like I was following you, but instead of walking west, which is where you were going, I went north, toward home.

We didn't talk for a little while after that.

IT'S NOT UNTIL I'm on the subway, fighting to stay awake so I don't miss my stop and end up in some far away land, that I really have to ask: Is Ginny deliberately trying to kill me?

She knew there'd be trouble, which is why she told me to bring the umbrella, happy coincidence aside with the rain. Ginny knows me. She knows under duress, I'll punch my way out. And maybe that's why she sent me, because it was her way of sending a message to T-Rex, whose name I can't even think about with shuddering. Where do these people get their names?

She clearly wanted to make him think The Hipster King pulled the trigger on that, but why not loop me in?

Unless she actually was sending me there as a sacrifice.

Knowing I'd get killed, but take a chunk out of them along the way, so she could protect her more valuable players. If she lost Samson, she would lose a one-man army. I'm just occasionally useful. The cost-benefit analysis is pretty clear.

I can't think about this anymore. My head hurts. I lean forward and rest my head against my palm, eyes closed. Then I look up at my hand. The words are washed away but I can still read them.

You promised.

Who promised?

Chell's face twists in pain.

A voice across from me says, "Hey."

I look up at a homeless man with hair that was once white, is now some shade between gray and brown. His skin is wrinkled and dirty like he's rubbed mud into it. It's only now that I'm looking at him that I realize what that smell was, the smell of hot garbage that's sent everyone to sit on the other side of the subway car.

"Hey," the guy says. "Can I get a sip of that?" He's pointing at the bottle of Jay still in my hand.

I probably shouldn't have the bottle out in the open like this, and I'm lucky a transit cop hasn't bagged me for it. There's only a sip left, so I down it and toss the empty bottle toward the end of the car, where it shatters. The people on the other side of the car jump.

"No," I tell him.

He mutters under his breath. "Motherfucker."

"I'm sorry. Want to repeat that?"

An octave louder, he says, "Motherfucker."

"Say that one more time, I'm going to come over there and break your fucking jaw."

On the other side of the car there's a stage whisper. "Should we pull the emergency brake?"

I close my eyes. "Don't pull the fucking emergency brake, because then the car will be stalled between stations and you'll be trapped with us. Seriously, what the fuck is wrong with everyone in this fucking city?"

The people on the train look away from me and lucky for them, or maybe just lucky for me, the next stop is mine.

SO I'M DRINKING again. Time to celebrate. I hope that, as a bonus, I'll run into one of the several people trying to kill me, and we can see how things shake out.

I stop into Apocalypse and it's jammed. More than for Chell's memorial service, more than I've ever seen. I fight through waves of college kids just to make it the bar. First Dymphna's and now this.

Dave looks up with a lost expression on his face. He shrugs and gestures toward the crowd. "Dude, I have no fucking idea."

"Whatever. I don't give a shit. I need a whiskey."

"Glad to see you back among the sensible." He pours me a stiff glass then gets a good look at my face. "Ash, what the fuck?"

There was a mirror in Chell's bathroom. I purposely didn't look at it. "You should see the other four guys. They'll be waking up in ICU any time now."

Dave shakes his head. "Your cousin is here. People are hanging out downstairs."

"Thanks." I take a pile of bills out my pocket. Drinks courtesy of T-Rex. "Keep me in Jay until this is gone."

Dave hands me the bottle.

"Slainte, then," I tell him. I take a swig and head downstairs, where I find Margo standing in a corner with a bunch of kids I don't know. Everyone is drinking PBR. When she sees me through the crowd, she waves me over. She grabs my hands and yells, "Guys, this is my cousin Ash." With a healthy dose of pride she adds: "He lives around the corner." It's nice of her to tell that lie.

She points to each person in turn and says their name. I don't bother to remember them. They regard me like cats looking at a wall.

Margo turns away from the group. "Are you okay? You look a little rough."

"Long story. Who are all these people?"

"They're in the program I want to be in at NYU. They were looking for a new place to hang out so I suggested this place. I guess word is getting around."

"You're lucky you're blood."

"What?"

"Nothing."

People are crowded from wall to wall. I don't like it. I take a pull from my bottle and listen to her friends. One guy, wearing skinny jeans and a black button-down shirt and an actual real-life mullet, is holding court. I don't know where the conversation started, but I don't like where it's headed.

The guy says, "You know, a lot of people thought 9/11 would have been a transformative moment for this city, but instead it acted as a catalyst for an economic earthquake that's really wreaked havoc on the poverty line. It's been moved so many times, we don't even know what class we are anymore. I mean, do any of you even know?"

At that everyone turns, rapt. Like he's dispensing some kind of wisdom, like that's even possible in a fucking bar.

First sign someone isn't really from New York: Their excitement at discussing 9/11.

I move forward a little into the circle and ask, "What's your name?"

"It's spelled like Ian, but it's pronounced Eye-Anne."

"Where are you from?"

"Michigan."

"And when did you move here?"

"About a year ago."

"Maybe it's best if you didn't pretend like you knew what you were talking about."

"What's your problem?"

"You."

I take another sip from the bottle without taking my eyes off him, Margo puts her hand on my shoulder. I yank it away from her. The asshole asks, "And where are you from?"

"Here."

"So you were born in Manhattan?"

"Staten Island."

"Well, that doesn't count."

I stand closer to him. He recoils.

"At least my birth certificate says New York City on it. Assholes like you, they should stop at the fucking door and turn back. Fucking children, ruining everything for the rest of us." I look at Margo. "I'm leaving. Your new friends are fuckheads."

Margo chases after me and stops me as I reach the stairs. "What was that?"

"Nothing."

"Ash. Look, whatever. I was going to ask, can I stay with you and Bombay tonight? I just got a text from Lunette. She said she has a friend in town and she's going to be busy."

"Who's the friend?"

"Jacqui. Which, whatever." She waves her hand and looks away. "I can take the floor at Bombay's if you want."

"I'm staying with someone else tonight. You take Bombay's couch. It's fine."

She nods, looks at me worried. "I want to ask you if you're okay but you're going to lie to me. You don't look okay. You don't sound okay. What the fuck is going on?"

"I'll be fine." I take out some of the money I lifted off T-Rex and hand it to her. "If it's late, take a cab to Bombay's. The door to the building doesn't lock. And pay attention when you're going in, to make sure no one's coming in after you."

She pushes my hand away. "I don't need the money. And I'll be fine Ash, really. This place you're going right now, will it involve sleeping?"

"Hopefully."

"Then please go do it. You look like you need it."

I kiss Margo on the forehead and head back inside to drop off the half-empty bottle. When I place it on the bar Dave waves me over. I lean close so I can hear him.

"Listen," he says. "I've told a couple of people but I want you to hear it from me. We're closing in a week."

I smash my fist against the bar and the Plexiglas surface cracks. Dave jumps back. I ask, "Why the fuck would you do that?"

He puts his hands up, like he's worried I'll take a dive at him. "Not my call. The people who live upstairs, they complain they can't open their windows because of the smoke and the noise. They filed complaints, it turned into a thing."

"They live above a fucking bar. Why are they complaining? They can go live somewhere else."

"Look, is what it is. The owner of this place has been considering an offer. It's a lot of money. And he wants to be done with this bullshit."

"Who made the offer?"

"Starbucks."

"Fuck!" I take the bottle of Jay and wing it against the wall. It shatters, and so does a mirror behind the bar. Dave ducks away from the flying glass, his hands over his eyes. Everyone in the bar stops and looks in our direction. The place falls silent, so we can only hear a mellow song from The Notwist pumping over the speakers.

Dave looks up at me, his eyes wide. "Dude..."

I take a couple of big bills out of T-Rex's stash, throw them on the bar, say, "There. Fix it."

Outside I light a smoke. Watch the kids going in and out like it's a fucking playground, and not the only place left in this city that I feel like I can call home. Something else that's being taken away. The thought of it not being here opens a jagged hole inside me.

My head fills with fantasies of benefit concerts and fundraising drives, to get the money to buy the place. Then we'll tell the people who live upstairs to fuck off and they should move to Nebraska if they want it to be quiet, and we'll keep running the place, keep things the way they are, won't change a damn thing. And we won't let people in unless they can prove they're native-born.

I put it out of my head. Right now I should go see Lunette, because what Margo doesn't know is that Jacqui isn't a person.

AFTER RINGING LUNETTE'S buzzer three times I assume she's passed out. I'm not looking forward to climbing up the fire escape. My leg feels like someone is hitting it with a hammer. Then the intercom crackles and Lunette says, "Yeah." Her voice sounds further away than three floors up.

"It's Ash."

The door buzzes. I climb up to her floor, leaning heavy on the railing, and the door to the apartment is ajar.

The air is stale, like she hasn't left in days. It's been less than twenty-four hours since I saw her, but Lunette is good at letting her life crumble at lightning speed.

I find her on the couch, wrapped in a blanket despite the fact that it's already pretty warm in here. The coffee table in front of her is a mess of discarded bottles of orange juice and empty bowls crusted over with the remnants of things I hope were food.

There's a dead needle, a spoon, and a pile of cotton swabs lying on the table, next to an empty balloon that previously held heroin. Code name: Jacqui.

I pick up the works, put them in a plastic shopping bag, and leave it in the kitchen. She doesn't try to stop me. I don't even know how she got up off the couch to buzz me in.

I drag a chair next to the couch and sit by her side. I figure she's asleep but then she says, "I'm sick." She talks in a sing-song voice, drifting between this world and another. She stares at the ceiling, her eyes opening and closing.

"You're not sick." I go back to the kitchen and get two glasses of water, place them on the coffee table between us. I down half mine, she doesn't touch hers. "So, what happened?"

"Me and Margo. I don't know. We got in an argument about something."

"And this was how you handle it?"

Her face turns down and tears form at the corner of her eyes.

I ask, "Do you remember what it was about?"

"No."

"Then why are you so upset?"

"I can't control myself."

There are a lot of things I could say at this moment, about self-control, or about how when something bad happens your first response shouldn't lean toward self-destruction. I can't say that with a straight face. So I slide my hand under the blanket, find hers, and hold it tight.

"You know I love you," I say.

"I know. I love you, too."

"You know it hurts all of us to see you like this?"

"I'm sorry."

"Don't apologize to me. I don't deserve it."

I take out a cigarette and get it lit, take a deep drag, and hold it up to Lunette's lips. She takes a half-hearted pull, then chokes when it gets caught in her throat. She says, "Thank you."

Lunette drifts off and I think she's fallen asleep, so I go to the closet and find some blankets and pillows and pile them up on the floor next to the couch. I strip off my shirt, my shoes and socks, and click off the lamp. The apartment plunges into darkness, save the narrow beams of light slowly tracking across the ceiling from the headlights of cars passing down the street.

As I'm getting comfortable Lunette says, "I lied to you, Ash."

"What did you lie to me about?"

"I saw Chell the night she died. And I saw you."

I prop myself up, lean a little too hard on my leg, and bite my lip to keep from yelping. Deep breath. "What did you see?"

"Chell was walking out of the subway. She looked upset about something. And I saw you stumbling down the street. You were so drunk you could barely stand up. You bumped into someone and then started screaming at them."

"Why didn't you tell me?"

"Because you didn't kill Chell. I know you didn't. But I was afraid."

"Afraid of what?"

She doesn't say anything, and I think she's fallen asleep again. I think about it for a little while, consider quizzing her on exactly where I was, and exactly where Chell was, but she's so far gone, I doubt I'd get a straight answer.

Think back to that night, try to shake my memories loose. But the only thing I can see is Chell's face twisted in pain.

No. It's the heroin talking. That's all. She didn't see me.

Just as I'm drifting off Lunette says, "Can we go to a museum?"

"Why?"

"Because all we ever do is sit in bars. There's so much more we could be doing. There's so much culture. I want to do things that are different. Different things."

"We'll do that."

"Ash?"

"Yes?"

"I miss Chell. I don't want to miss you, too."

Then she's snoring and I can go to sleep. And as I'm drifting, the same thought plays in my head on repeat: What if I just left?

I could get up and leave and be done with all of this. Margo and Bombay and Lunette don't need me. My mom doesn't need me. No one needs me but me. I could go live in a cabin in the woods. Chop down trees and look at the stars and sleep in the quiet. No one would try to kill me in the woods. I'd only have to worry about bears. I can handle bears.

The problem is this place is all I've ever known. I haven't traveled. I haven't wanted to. I've always loved New York for the diversity, because the entire world crosses right at this intersection. Anything you could ever need is right here, always available.

But at what point is that not enough for a person?

Because otherwise, seriously, fuck this place.

Does that make me selfish?

My phone buzzes. Bombay.

Envelope under the door. Says meet at Blue Moon Diner. 9 a.m.

Thirteen

THE THREAT OF morning hangs over my head until I give up on sleep and climb into the shower. I try to wash away the exhaustion and the shame but it coats my skin like oil.

After I get dressed and change my bandages, I check my phone. It makes me angry. Fifteen minutes to get to Blue Moon. Lunette hasn't moved but she's still breathing so I figure she'll be fine.

The walk down the stairs is the worst. Every time I take a step down and put pressure on my foot I feel a little pop in my leg. But once I'm outside and stretch a little, it evens out. The pain fades to a small electrical current. Bearable if I don't think about it.

Chell isn't even on the front page on the *Post* today. The article inside the paper doesn't say much, other than the cops being unable to find the killer, but that they're following some promising leads, which probably means they have nothing.

BLUE MOON IS crowded and there's one girl sitting alone. She looks like she showed up for a fancy party fifty years late, with her cream-colored gloves and bobbed, shoulder-length hair. Her outfit is monochromatic. She's nursing a mug, scanning the room for the person she wouldn't know if she saw.

I slide into the booth across from her and wave over the waitress. Retro-girl snaps out of her daydream and says, "Can I help you?"

"You tell me. My name is Johnny. I'm meeting someone here."

She goes to say something about my face, then stops. "So you're the private detective I heard about?"

So it's like that.

"Yes I am," I tell her, and take the envelope with the money out of my pocket, slide it across the table. The waitress shuffles over and I order a coffee, black.

The girl takes the envelope and puts it in her purse, reaches a gloved hand across the table to shake mine. "I'm sorry, I should have introduced myself. My name is Iva. Iva Archer."

"Johnny Marr."

She looks at the thick bandage wrapped around my arm and asks, "Are you okay?"

"Fell down some stairs."

"Well." She doesn't believe me, and I'm fine with that. She continues, "Mister Marr, the reason I called you is because my sister has gone missing. Two years ago our father took ill and we moved out to Chicago to be with him. She fell in with a rough crowd and flew back out here about a month ago with her good-for-nothing new husband. They were supposed to be staying in the Hotel Chelsea, but when I went there today, they didn't even have a record of them checking in."

She speaks with a very practiced poise. And she's good, too. I can barely tell she's reciting a script from memory. And this feels comfortably familiar. It's what I do professionally. Sort of. I treat it like I would anyone asking me to help them find someone. I rip off a piece of the placemat, dig in my pockets for a pen, and ask, "What's the girl's name?"

She pauses, a little surprised. "Lindsay. She's using her husband's last name now. His name is Terry Lennox."

"Do you have a picture?"

She hands me a black-and-white photo. Not Chell. It's a pretty blonde with bedroom eyes and full cheeks. They look enough alike they could be real-life sisters.

"Mister Marr, I heard you were the best private detective in the city, that if anyone can find my sister, no matter where she is, it'll be you." She places a gloved hand over mine and even though I know it's an act, my heart races a little.

"First of all, call me Johnny," I tell her. "Second, if someone doesn't want to be found, this city is the place to do it. That's even if she's still here. But we'll operate on the idea that she's with Lennox. What can you tell me about her habits? Places she goes, routines?"

Iva looks very pleased at all of this. "I know where you can start. There's a bar on Staten Island, right on the other side of the ferry. I don't remember the name of the place, she goes there Sunday nights to play pub trivia. Someone there might know something."

The waitress puts down my coffee and a glass of ice water. I toss a couple of cubes into the mug to cool it. Iva smiles, says, "I just gave up coffee." Her voice drops and octave. She's off-script.

"Why would you do a silly thing like that?" I ask.

"I'm trying to be healthier."

"I know that feeling. I'm trying to get off a couple of bad habits. But coffee will always be there. No matter what happens, I think it'll always be my last vice."

"How many vices did you have?"

"Pretty much all of them."

She nods, says, "Johnny? Terry Lennox is a very dangerous man."

"So am I."

"I'm not kidding. He worked in Chicago's financial district. That's where Lindsay met him. I was never able to figure out what he did, but I'm pretty confident it wasn't legal. He comes and goes at all hours and disappears for days at a time. One time he came home with the most terrible black eye, and he said he got it in a bar fight but I knew he was lying. I don't know why they even came back here to the city, but I know he's up to no good." Iva drops her eyes and frowns. "I'm afraid."

This time I put my hand on hers, caught up a little in the story. I can feel the warmth of her skin through her glove. "I'll find your sister. Now, when should I head out to this bar?"

"As soon as possible, if you can. Oh Johnny, please be careful."

I sip my coffee and put my elbows on the table, lean forward, resting my chin on my folded hands. As I move, the sleeves of my shirt slide up. Her eyes dart down to the blob of black ink poking from the corner. She slides her hand across the table, but she stops her delicate fingers a hair-length from my skin.

Her eyes meet mine and she asks, "May I?"

I nod and she reveals the tattoo I got when I was nineteen and way cooler: A skull and crossbones with the words "trust me" underneath.

She giggles and asks, "So, can I?"

"Can you what?"

"Trust you?"

"You shouldn't believe everything you read."

I want to ask her about Chell. I've been itching to drop her name since I sat down. But I'm invested in this lighter-touch approach. I can't scare off Paulsen. Not when I'm this close.

We finish up and she pays the bill. As we step outside the diner she says, "I'll handle your expenses, of course." She hands me an envelope packed with Monopoly money, says, "That ought to cover it. Call me if you need anything, and I'll speak to you soon."

She turns to leave but then looks over her shoulder at me. "By the way, nice hat. Very appropriate."

I tip it in her direction. "Glad someone likes it."

And with that, she turns, her hips swaying to the tune of a song I wish I knew.

IT'S JUST AFTER the morning rush and the Staten Island Ferry terminal is packed with tourists, crowded around guides holding up red umbrellas and plastic light sabers so no one gets lost in the throng. As the doors slide open and let us on, I try to remember the last time I rode one of these orange and blue boats.

Inside the gate, a Coast Guard officer clutches an automatic weapon to his chest and scans the crowd. On the butt of the gun is a little white sticker with what I imagine is his last name. Something long and probably Polish, in desperate need of vowels. I want to ask him if he expects to lose the gun, but people with firearms usually don't have a sense of humor.

No one goes down to the lower level because you can't see the skyline from there. That's where I ride, out of the way of the tourists clicking cameras and chasing screaming kids. The horn blares and the boat slides out of the slip into the harbor. The engine is loud enough that it drowns out the scattered conversations around me. I pull my legs up onto the yellow bucket seat and tip my fedora down over my eyes so I can take a nap.

THE FIRST TIME I rode the ferry was with my dad. My earliest memory of him. We were going to my first Yankee game. I don't remember who played or if the Yankees won. I remember being outside on the front deck of the boat, and the wind, and the spray of the water, and my dad picked me up and sat me on the wooden railing. He dug his fingers into my waist so I wouldn't fall.

It was sunny and the city sparkled across the water. Like it had a light source underneath it that shone even in the day. I had just seen *The Wizard of Oz* and I was convinced we were going to the Emerald City. That's the way it looked. I told him that and he laughed.

I remember a lot about the way my dad looked. Stubble,

dark hair with peeks of gray. Broad shoulders. The thing I remember most is that he was tall. He always seemed to be the tallest person in every room.

After the towers, after I was old enough to want to go into the city for things, I wouldn't take the boat. I didn't want to walk across that deck again, or spend the ride staring at the fractured skyline. So I would take the bus over the Verrazano Bridge into Brooklyn, and then take the R train. It took nearly two hours.

I didn't take the boat again until I took it with you, Chell. Do you remember that?

One weekend the R train wasn't running and my mom needed me home because the basement flooded. I didn't have the time or the money to come up with a good alternative. A cab would cost four days-worth of food.

You were laying on my couch. I was standing in front of the door with my hand on the knob but I didn't want to open it. I don't know how long I had been standing there when you asked, *Where are you going?*

Gotta go see my Ma.

The odyssey begins.

Nope. Taking the boat.

You're taking the ferry?

No choice.

You didn't say anything. Just put on your boots, took my hand, and led me out the door. The whole train ride to Whitehall you held my hand tight. When the terminal doors opened so we could load, of course it was the same boat I rode with my dad: The John F. Kennedy. Still in rotation all those years later. I froze and you wrapped your long thin fingers in mine and pulled me forward, past that same railing he sat me on, led me to the bottom of the boat, even though I knew you would have wanted to sit outside.

We hid in the shadows of the bottom deck. You bought us tallboy beers from the snack bar and you pointed to things outside the window and asked me what they were. You asked me about the apartments I lived in before the one I had. You did everything you could to keep my mind off the trip.

When we got to St. George you didn't want to come meet my mom because you had a thing about parents, but you offered to wait for me until it was time to go home. I told you it wasn't necessary. As you were going to get back on the boat I stuttered and looked away from you, trying to say what I wanted to say and drowning in that feeling.

I'm glad I met you too, Ashley, you said.

You didn't need to do this.

I don't need to do anything.

And you stretched up to kiss me on the cheek.

I never told you this, but I borrowed some money from my mom and took a cab home that day. One trip was enough at that point. But after that, I was able to get used to the ride again. Which was nice. The boat only takes twenty-five minutes.

I'M SKIRTING THE edge of sleep when the loudspeaker blares with the voice of a deckhand telling people that to ride back to Manhattan, they have to get off the boat and go back through the terminal.

The ferry pulls into the slip lined with wooden poles and scrapes against them with the sound of fingernails on chalkboard amplified by concert-grade speakers. As it strikes the wall of the dock the few tourists that ambled down here lose their footing and nearly fall.

I knew a girl whose dad piloted a ferry. They hit the sides of the docks on purpose. It's a fun little game for the deckhands: The tourists stumble and the local don't. I don't know if that's a true story, but I like to think it is.

The bar Iva was talking about is Cargo, because unless there's been some drastic change, it's the only bar in this neighborhood that does pub trivia.

My last apartment on Staten Island, before I scored my digs in the East Village, is right up the block, so I used to drink at Cargo on the regular. It's a squat building across the street from a crack motel. The outside is painted with a mural that changes every six months or so. Last time it was giant parrots, one of which was devouring a person. Now it's a giant, rustling American flag.

Inside there's nobody I recognize, just a few people saddled up to the bar, drowning themselves in amber liquid. I pull the photo of Iva out of my pocket, go up to the closest drunk and put it on the bar in front of him. "Know this girl?"

He stares at the photo and slurs his words when he says, "Wish I did. She's a pretty one. You got any more photos?"

"Keep it clean. Ever see her around here?"

He holds up the photo, shakes his head, motions for the bartender. The drunk says, "Clyde, do I know this girl?"

The bartender tosses a towel over the shoulder of his brand-new vintage-style t-shirt and adjusts his glasses. He shakes his head, "No Ronnie, you don't." Then he looks at me. "But I do."

"Well then. You and I need to talk."

He looks me up and down and asks, "What do you want?"

It's not even noon. All the more reason to drink. "A glass of

Jay and some answers."

"Jay?"

"Jameson." Idiot.

He pours me a finger without ice and I toss a few bucks worth of fake money onto the bar. He rolls his eyes and stuffs it into his back pocket, says, "It's customary to tip."

"I tip for good service. Tell me about Lindsay Lennox."

"Tell you what about her?"

"Tell me about the last time you saw her. Was she here Sunday night?"

"She hasn't been here in a while. Who are you, anyway?"

"Her sister is looking for her. She tapped me to find her. You keep up with the attitude you're not getting that tip."

"Nothing in life is free, pal."

I down the drink and toss a handful of the play money onto the bar. He shakes his head and takes it. An old man at the end of the bar pulls himself out of his beer long enough to watch the exchange with a look of shocked disbelief.

Clyde says, "She was in here two weeks ago. She was looking for a contact."

"What kind of contact?"

"She was in trouble. Some kind of trouble with her boyfriend or husband or whatever. She was looking for someone to talk to him."

"Talk to him how?"

"I think it was the kind of conversation she wanted to end in a hospital bed."

"And why did she come to you?"

"Because I know a guy."

"Tell me about this guy."

"Right."

He goes back to wiping down the bar. I am done playing. I get off the stool and reach over, wrap my hand around the back of his neck, pull his close face to mine. His eyes go wide. I tell him, "I'm just looking for the girl. My understanding is that her husband is bad news so you're really not doing her any favors by playing hardball."

He yanks himself away from me, eyes spiraling around the room, trying to decide if he should ask for help or just do whatever he can to get me out of there. He settles on the latter. "The Communist."

"What?"

"The Communist. Russian dude, hangs out in Coney Island. If you go there now, you'll probably find him on the boardwalk. Don't tell him that I told you about any of this." He slides a menu to me. Through gritted teeth, clearly not wanting to, but out of some sense of obligation, he says, "Before you go, you should have brunch. Our specialty is a full English breakfast."

"Thanks, but no." I slide the menu back at him.

BAY STREET IS heavy with cars and buses. Bringing people to the ferry terminal. Bringing people away from it.

I spend a long time standing on the corner, thinking about hopping on the S48, taking the ten-minute ride to my mom's house. She would be pissed if she found out I was on the island and didn't come visit. Probably already someone has driven past, recognized me, and called her to tell her how much I've grown. Staten Island is like that. The small town America of New York City.

I could do that. There's even a bus down the block headed my way. But when I turn and look in the general direction of her house, I feel something pulling me back.

The bus coasts by. I can't let her see me like this. Booze on my breath before I've had breakfast and beaten like old meat. Her heart's been broken enough already.

TIME IS SUPPOSED to heal all wounds. Which is a thing people say when they've never been cut to the bone. The big wounds, even when they do heal, they don't heal right. Every time you move you feel the tug of the scar tissue.

I think about the feeling that gripped me as I was falling asleep at Lunette's. That feeling of being done with this place. Part of it was the exhaustion, and I'm feeling a little kinder now that I'm on my feet and have some booze in my system. But not much.

Growing up on Staten Island, it's like being behind the velvet rope of the best party in the world. Welcome to stop by every so often, but ultimately relegated to the outside. Standing at the crest of Victory Boulevard, just north of Forest Avenue, and watching the skyscrapers poke above the tree line. People live their whole lives and die on Staten Island and are perfectly contented by that. I never wanted to be one of them.

All I ever wanted was to live in Manhattan, for a million reasons, ten million. But right now, I can't think of any of those reasons. Now the skyline looms like a threat. Like I've seen it too many times and I've learned things about it I don't like.

I consider going inside the boat, but the cold air is keeping me sharp. The beer I bought at the snack bar upstairs tastes like stale bread but I drink it anyway.

An older couple next to me mutters to each other in French. They stare at me and whisper like I'm dangerous. The man approaches me, one hand on his expensive camera, and in halting English says, "Sir, can you tell me where the trade centers was?"

I know the spot exactly but tell him, "Doesn't matter."

The man nods even though he doesn't understand what I mean. He goes back to his wife and they point and take pictures. First at the city, and then at the U.S. Coast Guard boat with the massive machine gun attached to the front, escorting the ferry back to Manhattan.

The wind is kicking hard enough to make my eyes water. I put my hand on the railing of the Kennedy. On the spot that I think may be where my father held me.

I TAKE THE R into Brooklyn, then at Atlantic-Pacific switch over to the N train. As the door closes a man stands up at the end of the car and insists that he's not on drugs, he's looking for a job, but things are tough, he just needs a little help to get by, but if anyone has any food to spare he would happily take that, too. The sincerity is so practiced it actually sounds legit. The torn clothing and worn knit cap lend him an air of credibility.

He walks down the car and shakes an empty coffee can and people either dig through their pockets for change, or pretend to be asleep. I think I recognize him, as in he's done this before, but when he gets to me I pull out a twenty and shove it in the can. He extends his closed fist and invites me to bump it. I do, but I don't feel I deserve the camaraderie. It's not really charity if it's not your money.

He ducks off at the next stop and gets on the adjacent car, ready to start the spiel again.

After so many stops I lose count, the subway comes barreling out onto the above-ground tracks of South Brooklyn and the sun screams into the car, turning every aluminum surface into a blinding source of light. It doesn't feel right to ride a subway in the sun. The grime doesn't look romantic. It just looks like grime.

The train barrels toward Coney Island, looking out into the yards of trim two-family homes. At the last stop, as soon as the doors open at Stillwell, I can smell the salt air. The summer season has been over for a while now and the neighborhood looks like it's been wiped out by a plague. Graffiti mars the walls and trash clogs the gutters. Storefronts turn over so fast the awnings and signs are tacked up three or four deep. Stray newspaper pages drift across the wide expanse of Surf Avenue. The only real activity in the area is the jumble of customers in Nathan's.

Coney always makes me nostalgic. Not just because it's where I first met Chell. The neighborhood is dingy and glitzy in equal measure. The chain restaurants and million dollar condos haven't reached this far yet. It's the last true refuge for the city's freaks, of the people who remember what it means to say you grew up here.

I actually wouldn't mind looking for a new place down here. The minority population is high enough to scare the white folk away, which means the rent is cheap, and maybe it'd be nice to live by the sea.

Not that it'll last. Before long, they'll tear down the Cyclone to put up an organic coffee shop and a parking lot for strollers and call it Park Slope South. Funny thing is, no matter how hard people try to redefine this city, it's the real estate agents who have the most success.

THE BOARDWALK IS dormant. There are some joggers and dog-walkers and sightseers. I'm wondering how I'm going to find the Communist, and then I see him. Tall and bald, wearing a black bubble jacket with a red t-shirt underneath. On the t-shirt is a graphic of a yellow hammer and sickle.

Just when I was giving this game a little credit.

He's spread out on a park bench, dark sunglasses slapped over his face, staring off into the distance. He's got his head cocked to the side, and when I get close, I can see the Bluetooth headset in his ear. He's having a loud conversation in Russian, looking up and down the boardwalk, and then his eyes settle on me, like he thinks I might be the guy he's waiting for.

"*Zdravstvuite*," I tell him.

He pulls the Bluetooth out of his ear and sets off on a long string of harsh syllables.

I put up my hands. "That and *na zdorovie* are the extent of my Russian. I have no idea what you just said."

"Who are you?" His accent is thick enough to serve on a plate.

"Guy named Clyde sent me, although he told me not to tell you that. I'm looking for a girl." I reach into my back pocket and find the folded-up photo of Chell from the *Post*. I'm about to show it to him when I realize what I'm doing, so I pull the picture of Lindsay out of my other back pocket. "Seen her?"

Without a blink he takes off running toward the Parachute Jump.

I don't hesitate, head right after him, immediately regret it when the first explosion goes off in my leg. I throw myself forward, try to be faster than the pain.

The boardwalk is treacherous, hammered together by weathered planks of graying wood that curl up and threaten to trip me. We're both slowed down by the poor condition of it and the occasional person who gets in the way.

We cover a few hundred yards when the Communist veers off toward the sand, glancing over his shoulder, staying far enough ahead of me to make it feel like a real chase. I doubt he'll really try to get away from me, but I'm annoyed so I step up my pace, and before he has another chance to look around again, I throw myself into his legs and we tumble into the sand.

My lungs are over-smoked. Like trying to breathe through a wet sock. I hold him down and will the pain in my leg to fade. He's sprawled on the sand looking up at the sky.

I ask him, "Why did you run?"

"Are you cop?"

"No, I am not cop. Why did you run?"

"I thought you might be cop."

"You could have asked."

He sits up and I show him the picture again. "The girl?"

He nods, still breathing heavy. "She see me last week. Say boyfriend needs to be taught lesson."

"I assume she didn't mean English lit."

"What?"

"Never mind. What kind of lesson?"

"What do you want know?"

"Everything."

He nods. "She want him dead. She pay me to do it, but then she call me and say not to kill him. I keep money she paid up front."

"Can you tell me how to find her?"

"I have phone number."

"You seem pretty helpful all of a sudden."

"You hit like truck."

"Well, whatever." I get to my feet and yank him up.

He pulls out his cell and reads the number off to me. I put it in my phone.

He's about to leave but he stops. "You look hungry. You go to Nathan's. Get hot dog. They have frog legs too, if you want try. Not bad."

"Why does everyone think I'm hungry? I'm not hungry."

This game is silly. I consider stalking the guy, throwing him under the boardwalk, and pounding on him until he explains how this whole thing works. But the wind ruffles my hair and I realize my hat is gone. I wander up and down the sand for a little while until I find it kicking around in the breeze, right on the edge of the surf.

When I'm back on the boardwalk I call the number the Communist gave me and it goes straight to voicemail.

"Hi, this is Lindsay. Leave me a message."

Chell.

It's Chell's voice.

I'd know that voice upside down and underwater.

This is the role Chell played. She was the girl. The missing girl. The one I need to find to find out who killed her. Whether that's poetic or ironic, I can't really tell for sure, so I settle on calling it batshit.

I call the number twice more just to hear it. To hear her say a combination of words I've never heard so that it can be new. Chell has only been dead a few days. They must have forgotten to change this.

So, there's that. I have a phone number that when I call it, no one's going to answer. But it's enough. It's concrete, something I can point to. It doesn't prove anything, it doesn't help anything, but it's her voice. Exhaustion rolls off my back.

My specialty lately is hitting things, which isn't helping. So I think about what Bombay would do, which is reach for a computer. There's a library up on Neptune Avenue. It's open and not crowded. I sign up and find an open terminal, plug the phone number into Google, and an address in Chinatown pops up.

Bombay would be proud.

THE BUILDING IS on a stretch of Mott Street where you can buy live frogs from garbage pails alongside fruit that could double as a medieval torture device. The place is a four-story walkup that looks like it's been forgotten by time. The front door isn't locked, not on the building, not on the apartment.

It's just as sparse as Chell's. I have to remind myself it's a prop, that she didn't live here. It's a studio, with a bathroom made for a midget and a hobby-kit stove crammed into one corner. The bed is neatly made and I run my hand over it, but the sheets are cold. Inhale, but it doesn't smell like her.

I turn the place upside down because I can't think of anything else to do. The only thing that seems out of place is a crumbled napkin in the waste basket. Written on it is *BB-M*. I pull out a chair, put my feet up onto the kitchen table and stare at the wall with my hands behind my head.

This is what it must feel like to run into a wall at full speed. I run combinations of words through my head, try to come up with something for *BB-M*. Can't even come close to it. There must be something else I need to do and I'm just not noticing it.

The phone rings and I nearly tumble onto the floor.

I pick up the plastic handset and press it to my ear. On the other end of the line a man says, "Go to the R station at Canal Street. On the Brooklyn-bound side there's a pay phone at the end of the platform. Ten minutes."

Click.

I GET DOWN INTO the subway and run into a gaggle of tourists. They're crowded in front of the turnstiles, wearing foam State of Liberty headpieces, carrying street maps and I Love New York bags, bleating like geese.

Ten deep at each turnstile, and none of them can figure out how to swipe their MetroCards through the machines. Either too slow or two fast or not all the way, so that the fare doesn't register. The phone should be ringing any minute.

The trains around Canal Street are connected by a labyrinth of tunnels. If I ran back to the street and found another entrance, I wouldn't even know how to get around. I wait, and they just laugh and point, and they swipe their cards like it's a game that's fun to lose.

My blood hits a simmer. I'm not the only one waiting for this mess to resolve itself. There's a puff of air from a train pulling into the station, then the high-pitched whine as it pulls out. I shove my way through the crowd, not worried about who gets pushed to the side.

An older guy with a baseball cap and a fanny pack, trying desperately to exude the authority of a chaperone, says, "You can't cut the line like that."

"Fuck off." When I say this some of the kids look at me with expressions that land somewhere between disappointed and afraid.

As I shove more people out of my way the guy says, "I can't believe this."

"Welcome to New York. It's just like you heard."

By the time I make it to the phone, it's already ringing. A curious skateboarder is making his way toward it so I duck around him and grab it off the receiver. I can't believe there are still working pay phones in this city.

The voice on the other end is the same guy who called the apartment. He says, "Meet at the usual place. No funny business. Come alone. And leave soon. It'll be crowded." Click.

The usual place. I don't know the usual place.

I slam the phone against the receiver until the plastic earpiece cracks off and clatters to the subway tracks. My body is shaking so hard I have to grip the steel support pillar and hold my breath and slow myself down. Just slow down. This is hard, but they wouldn't make this impossible, or else no one would ever solve it.

There's got to be something here, something in the vicinity. Some kind of tip.

On the phone is a sticker with a picture of the Brooklyn Bridge on it. The rest of the phone looks like it's been dragged through a field of rocks but the sticker is bright and clean. I run my finger over it. Not even scratched.

The napkin from the apartment. *BB-M.* Could mean Brooklyn Bridge, Manhattan side. It makes sense as a meeting place. Plenty of public transportation nearby. And it's crowded. Way too many people to pull a stunt.

That could work.

THE PEDESTRIAN WALKWAY is packed with joggers and walkers and bikers. It's sunny and it's not too cold and it's difficult to find a clear footpath. I look for open spots, dive through them, push forward, but spend most of my time stopping and stalling. I fumble through my pockets for a smoke but can't get it lit because the wind is too strong.

At least it's pretty up here, the city stretched out in the sun, clear and crisp in the afternoon air, windows catching the sun. I rarely see it when it's not shrouded in darkness. I walk past the bench where me and Chell sat, where I made the biggest mistake of our relationship. Four children eat sandwiches being passed around by a frazzled mom. They're sitting there like it's just a bench.

At the foot of the first tower is a guy in a trench coat holding a briefcase in one hand, a big soft pretzel in the other. He looks the most out of place among the gawkers so I figure he's my guy. As I approach, he backs up a little, and through a mouthful of pretzel asks, "Who are you?"

"Terry Lennox sent me."

"Do you think I'm retarded?"

"That's offensive. But it would also make my life a whole lot easier if you were."

He takes a step away from me, placing a hand over the

briefcase. Which means, clearly, I need the briefcase.

"What'll it cost?" I ask.

"What do you mean?"

"The transaction fee. Like an ATM. To let me take the case. How much?"

He thinks about it. "Two hundred."

Fancy that, I've still got a few hundred in play money stuffed in the envelope. I guess they made this one easy, considering the last step was a bit of a brain bender. I count off the money and hand it over to the guy.

"Not a word to Frankie," he says. "This was supposed to go to Terry."

"I don't even know Frankie."

"When you're done, you should check out the pretzel cart at the foot of the bridge."

"Are you fucking kidding me?"

He tilts his head and bites off another chunk of his pretzel.

I take a knee and flip the case open. It's holding two phone books, probably there to give it enough heft so that whoever picked it up would have thought it was full of something else. Nestled between them is a note.

Dear Frankie,
Consider us even.
Owen Taylor

Makes me think of the package I brought to T-Rex's. My life is stupid lately. When I look up the guy in the trench coat is gone.

I toss the briefcase onto the ground and lean onto the railing. This time I get a cigarette lit. I look north, up the

Hudson River. This is exhausting. I wish I could skip to the end. But feeling sorry for myself isn't going to figure this out.

Next step, next step, next step...

The way you find something you've lost is to retrace your steps. It's the only thing that makes sense.

I turn and smack right into two bearded hipsters assholes. I think maybe they're just in my way so I try to walk around them but they box me into the corner against the railing. It takes a moment before I recognize them from Dymphna's.

The big one is a redhead, with a beard showing blonde and white in spots. He smiles. "Hey Ashley." He leans on it heavy, like he doesn't want me to forget I have a girl's name.

The thin one, his blond, salon-quality hair floating in the wind, says, "Our friend is looking for you."

I ask, "So, you're the guys who tried to stab me."

The blond strokes the cast that extends from his fingertips, down to the middle of his forearm. "Thanks for this, by the way."

"You pulled a fucking knife on me. What did you think was going to happen?"

"Most people cool it when they see a knife."

"I'm sorry to disappoint. But I'm not sorry for breaking your hand. You deserved it." I lean against the railing, contemplate my cigarette. They're standing in my personal space and I don't like it. "So your friend wants to see me? The king? You can go back and tell him I'm busy. I don't have time for his bullshit."

"You don't understand." The redhead pats the waist of his jeans. There's a bulge, and it's not a penis. "You're coming with us."

Another one of my rash decisions comes around to bite me in the ass. The problem I'm having is this: If they saw me talking to the other guy, then the game is blown and Cairo or Paulsen or whatever the fuck his name is, he's going to get wise to what I'm doing.

But maybe they were just following me, and they don't know about the game. That's within the realm of possibility, I think. I don't want to ask and tip them off. So I settle on another question. "What's on that drive that you want it so bad?"

The redhead shakes his head. "Don't know. Don't care."

"Fine. I don't have it on me anyway. How'd you guys find me?"

The blond says, "We have people everywhere."

"So if I come with you guys, what happens?"

"The king has some questions for you."

"Well, you're not going to shoot me in the middle of the bridge. That gives me a pretty distinct advantage."

The redhead says, "It doesn't matter how fast you run, you have to slow down eventually."

I smile. "Point taken."

We're on a public landmark with a lot of foot-traffic, which means there's got to be some sort of anti-terrorism SWAT team hidden around here somewhere. At the top of my lungs I scream, "These two guys have a bomb and they're trying to blow up the bridge!"

Fear takes hold like an electrical storm.

People run and scream, but they don't know what direction to go so they swarm us. The redhead can't pull his weapon. Within moments there's a cop working his way toward us but he's moving slow, pushed back by a tide of terrified tourists.

The two hipsters are looking at me with wide eyes.

"See ya, assholes," I tell them.

And I jump over the railing.

FOURTEEN

WHEN I WAS lost in thought, staring over the railing and feeling sorry for myself, I noticed traffic was moving pretty slow. About a hundred feet from where I was standing it opened up like a floodgate after passing a construction crew.

So I do the absolute dumbest thing I've ever done in my entire life, which is saying something.

First I feel air, and then the sharp crack of roadway as I tuck my legs underneath me and try to keep my head from rolling under the tire of a moving car. I land on my right leg and pain hits me like a tidal wave. My hat falls off and rolls in front of a truck. I grab it just before it's crushed.

Cars slow down to avoid hitting me, drivers slamming on their horns. There's a cab to my left so I open the door and crawl inside. The driver yells at me in a language I don't know.

I tell him, "My car broke down. I'll pay you whatever you

217

want, just take me to the bottom of the bridge. Get me down to Chambers."

He argues with me while keeping with the flow of traffic. "Sir, I cannot pick up a fare on the bridge. Please get out of my cab."

"I bet it's against the rules to discharge a fare on the bridge, so it's sort of a catch-twenty-two then. Help me out, my car broke down and some guy bumped his car into me and knocked me down."

"Where's your car, sir?"

"It's back there, it doesn't matter, just keep up with the traffic and let's get out of here."

"Twenty dollars to Chambers."

Actual cost on the meter, probably three bucks. I don't say anything because twenty is much less than I planned on giving him.

When we get down to street level I hand him a hundred dollar bill. He looks at it and back at me. I tell him, "Forget what I look like."

"Sir."

"Forget me."

And with that, I limp my way into the crowd to find another cab. I take it north, change cabs at Union Square. The third one I get into is the one that takes me back to the apartment in Chinatown.

M Y PHONE BUZZES as I climb the stairs of the apartment building. The number is blocked.

A voice on the other end asks, "Johnny?"

I get confused for a second, forget that's my assumed name, but then recognize that it's Iva and she's talking to me. I tell her, "Yes."

"Just wanted to see how things were going. If everything was okay?" Her voice is confused, expectant. Like she wants to be able to see me right now. I wonder if she's setting me up, trying to figure out where I am so the hipster thugs can come back after me. Or maybe I'm being paranoid.

I tell her, "Just got a little tied up taking care of something."

"How's the search?"

"Good. Going good."

"Okay. I mean. Just wanted to let you know. Sometimes the easiest way to find someone is to retrace your steps."

"I'll take that under advisement." And I hang up the phone.

I must be running behind, which means I need to move faster. The lines here are crossing way too close.

The apartment is exactly how I left it. Doesn't even look like there's been anyone in here since me. I flop onto the bed and the cheap springs squeak underneath me. I lay there, just to catch my breath, until I realize the light on the answering machine is flashing. I press the 'play' button.

"Terry, you moron, it's Frankie. Get up to the courts at Astoria Park."

Click.

Queens. Goddamn Queens.

For the first time in a long time, I'll have to consult a subway map.

I FLASH LINDSAY'S PICTURE to a dozen people around the Astoria Park basketball courts and they all look at me sideways. Just a bunch of young kids playing around, none of them looking like they're expecting a mysterious stranger.

So I get a cup of coffee and a pack of smokes from the corner bodega and sit on a bench and use the two to keep me awake. I can't remember the last time I was in Queens that I wasn't trying to get somewhere else.

I keep waiting for something to happen and nothing does. Iva called when I was running late and now I'm sitting here and no hints, no nothing. Granted, I played express train roulette, hoping between the subways that skipped stations, and probably shaved a good twenty minutes off the trip. But still. Nothing.

Unless I'm wrong.

The guy on the message said to meet him at the courts. He didn't specify which courts, he just said courts. And he sounded like a *Goodfellas* reject.

I'm an idiot. An old Italian guy isn't going to be playing basketball.

It doesn't take long to find the bocce courts, and a couple of goombas in polo shirts and slacks. One of the guys, with slicked-back hair and a heavy gold chain around his neck, looks up at me and stares. He looks away, hoists a lime-green ball, and tosses it at a bunch of yellow balls, scoring a couple of points. At least I think he does, because the guys on the opposing side don't look happy.

I call out to him. "Frankie."

He waves to his friends and walks over to me. Stares at me like he's trying to exert his dominance, says, "I do not know you." He talks like he's bored with me. "What's your name?"

"Johnny."

He swings his arms so wide he nearly hits my face, as he talks to everyone in the world except me. "Nice hat. Did it come with a free bowl of soup?"

"I saw *Caddyshack* too. Let's get serious for a moment. I'm here about your business with Terry Lennox."

He snaps his fingers. Two burly guys, both in velour track suits, materialize at my side. Frankie steps forward and asks, "Where is Terry?"

I take a shot in the dark. "I have no idea. But I do know where your case is."

He pauses. His eyes narrow. "Do you have it?"

"I do. Not here."

"Bring it to me."

"Not for free. But I'll trade it."

"What do you want?"

"Information."

He crosses his arms. "What do you want to know?"

"I need to find Terry."

"That's too bad. Because I need to find him first."

"Well, really, I just need to find the girl he's with. So I'll make you a deal. I won't touch Terry. I won't even tell him you're coming. But I need to know how to track him down."

Frankie looks at his men, then at me. He waves them off. They walk away but they keep staring at me like they want to murder me. Frankie says, "I don't know where Terry is. But I know where you can find his girl. Little bar down in Tribeca called The Patriot. She's a bartender."

"Back to fucking Manhattan then."

I turn to leave and Frankie calls out after me. "What about the case?"

"It won't be of much use to you."

"Why not?"

"It was full of phone books and a note from some guy named Owen Taylor. I could go get you the case but all you'll have is a briefcase. It's not even that nice."

"Owen." Frankie shakes his head. "Damn it. Damn Owen, damn Terry." He takes out his cell phone. Without looking at me he says, "You can go now. But you should stop up the block at Ray's." He kisses the tips of his fingers and fans them out. "They make a beautiful slice of pizza."

I FIGURED IT OUT. Or I figured *something* out, which is better than all the nothing I've been figuring out.

This is a game for tourists. It's an interactive walking tour. That's why everyone is pushing food on me. The restaurants and bar are probably helping sponsor the thing, for the increased foot traffic. Between not stopping to eat, and knowing how to get around quick, I've been able to keep pace.

This is the perfect sort of thing for a tourist with a little adventure in his heart, some time to kill, and a desire to see the far-flung neighborhoods that don't make it into the movies.

I must be getting toward the end. The sun is starting its downward arc and I'm being sent back into the heart of the city.

A black gypsy cab is sitting at the curb, the driver leaning against it, eating a sandwich wrapped in white butcher paper. Gypsy cabs aren't supposed to pick people up on the street, but when he sees the wad of cash he doesn't ask questions, just points toward the back as he crams the rest of the sandwich into his mouth.

When he asks me where to go I tell him Tribeca and we pull into traffic. But then I figure, I'm in Queens, in a car, and I may have some time to spare. So I tell him to take me down Merrick Boulevard first.

YELLOW PLANKS WITH sloppy red lettering, just like I saw in the aerial shot on the television the morning Chell died. I tell the driver to stop and wait.

I wander into the lot, where there's some ripped-up police tape caught on a pile of broken wooden planks, flapping in the wind. Other than that, no evidence of what happened here. The cops must have picked this place clean.

I walk around the property, a small patch of dirt covered with broken glass and old tires and scraps of metal, blocked from the street and the surrounding sidewalks. A little alcove the people who live around here probably don't even know exists. I could scream my head off and the nearest apartment building is so far back no one would hear me.

I take a knee, run my fingers over the ground. It's cold and unforgiving and doesn't smell anything like lavender.

Is this where he did it? Or did he do it in his van?

Did he strip her naked before he did it, or after? Was she drugged, or fully aware of his body crushing her?

Why am I asking these questions?

I close my eyes and I see Chell's face, contorted in pain. So clear, like she's right in front of me.

You promised.

Who promised?

Behind me there's a crunch and I hear, "Mister McKenna."

Detective Medina walks toward me a smile so wide it looks painful. "You know, we've had a guy sitting outside here for the past few days. Some crazy idea about maybe the killer returning to the scene of the crime." He points over his shoulder at Grabowski lurking by the car like a mountain in the mist. "As luck would have it, me and my partner here decided to do some thinking, talk the case over, and we figured maybe we should do it here. He was just saying, and I mean *just saying*, how it was a waste of time. That no one would be stupid enough to come back to the scene of a body drop. So, Mister McKenna, do you want to tell me exactly what the hell you're doing here?"

I shake my head at him. "I'm sorry, are you still talking?"

He pulls a pair of handcuffs from his belt and lets them dangle in his hand.

"Mister McKenna, we'd like to ask you a couple of questions down at the station. Would you like to take a ride with us?"

"Not really, no."

"It's not a request."

"Well, you fucking framed it like a question, asshole."

Medina sticks his finger in the air and twirls it around. I turn and as he slaps the cuffs on me, the cab driver shrugs his shoulders, salutes me, and drives off.

SMALL WONDERS. INSTEAD of some station in Queens they bring me back to the 9th Precinct, a few blocks from Bombay's. At least I got a free ride back into the borough, even though it was an awkward trip. No one said a thing the entire way. Grabowski shot Medina a couple of long, judgmental looks from the passenger seat.

The interrogation room walls are mental-institution green, polka-dotted with hard water stains. There's a big, scratched window that I think I can see flashes of movement behind. Other than that there's a scratched metal table and scratched metal chair across from me. Everything is scratched. It smells like mildew and sweat.

It also looks so much like the set of *Law & Order: SVU* that this feels like someone is playing a joke. I expect Benson and Stabler to come in to question me.

The cuffs are digging into my skin and I've been sitting here for fifteen minutes already. This doesn't bode well. I need to be at The Patriot. I need to be out of here now. I need for rational things to happen. I've stopped holding my breath.

The door slams open and Medina marches in, dragging a chair across the floor. The harsh squeal echoes in the small room. He undoes the cuffs and I stretch my arms, get the blood flowing into my hands.

He places a tan folder on the table in front of me. Next to that he puts down my umbrella, then pokes it with his finger. "That's an interesting thing to carry around."

"Those five dollar bodega umbrellas can't stand up to a gust of wind. I wanted something a little more sturdy."

"This is a weapon. I can throw you in a cell just for this."

Fine. If this is the way it's going to be, then I'm going to play to my strengths by making it worse. I tell him, "Guns are for pussies. What model firearm do you carry?"

"Funny. We'll see how long you're laughing."

"Look, I don't know what kind of power trip you're on today, Detective Keystone, but I'm exhausted and my tolerance meter is completely run out. Am I under arrest?"

"Being a wise guy isn't helping your case."

"Now I'm on trial? What's your name again?"

"Medina."

"Great, thanks. You're so insignificant to me I forgot. What were you saying about being a wise guy?"

He nods and smiles, lifts up the folder and lets it drop open in front of me. It's an old file, the pages inside yellowed with age. I don't even need to read it to know what it's about. I nod toward it. "Funny that you have files. There were never any formal charges filed."

"Well, the police department likes to keep files on individuals such as yourself."

"Such as myself."

I knew this would never be behind me. It's the reason I don't like cops. Very long story told short: Back in high school I knew this girl, and she got raped at a party, and I found the kid who did it. The way I hear it, he still walks with a cane.

It was the first time I felt skin split under my fists.

Problem was, the kid's dad was a cop.

The memory of what came after stings. The cops harassing me on my way to school, confiscating my books as evidence in some crime they could never describe. The nighttime phone calls to my mom telling her I was dead. The broken window on her car. My dad was gone at this point, but my mom got in touch with his friends in the fire union. They got things settled.

It goes away and you think it's gone, but it's not.

Medina says, "You beat up a cop's kid. Hurt him real bad. Violent individuals, such as yourself, tend to get an early start on that kind of thing. And you got started all the way back in high school. I guess this is a long time coming."

"And I guess that paperwork doesn't say that cop's kid was a rapist. Look him up now. He's doing a stretch his daddy couldn't get him out of."

"I don't see that report here. In fact, there's no indication of any kind of rape claim from when you were in school with him. So you know what I think?"

"That you're ignoring the rape that put him in jail so you can fuck me? This is a stats thing, isn't it? It's easier to arrest me so at the end of the month the brass doesn't wonder why stuff's not getting done. This is why no one trusts cops. Even the ones who claim to be good will protect the bad ones without question."

He smiles, not listening. Hungry. "I see a history of violent behavior. I see someone who doesn't have a good alibi. I think you see what I see."

"I see a detective who needs to close a case and is willing to smack it on an innocent person to keep his numbers up. That's what I see."

He closes the file, asks, "Want to tell my why you were in her apartment after she died?"

Dammit. The couple who found me after I cleaned up the gunshot wound. They must have called it in, Medina matched the description. I take it back. He's a passable cop. I tell him, "She borrowed my blender. I loved that blender."

"Let me tell you what I think. You were looking for something."

"Wow. You'll make captain in no time."

He's getting angry but he doesn't want to show it. Not sure if that plays in my favor or against. He asks, "You left quite a mess back there. Why don't you tell me the truth, huh, about why you went back?"

"Why don't you believe me about the blender?"

He puts aside the report and folds his hands in front of him on the table, asks, "Did you kill her?"

"You know what? I don't even think I'm under arrest. I think you're just an asshole. I want a lawyer."

"I know who you are. I know who your father was. Don't think that gives you any kind of special treatment in here. In fact, I thought I would get a little professional courtesy."

This suddenly stops being funny.

I tell him, "In one day my father made this world a better place and then he died for it. You're a bully with a badge. And you will never, ever deserve to be spoken of in the same tone as him. He was a hero. You're a joke."

I'm spitting by the time I finish the sentence, choking on my words. Medina pauses, wide-eyed. Then he shakes it off, pushes out from the table and comes to my side, looms over me. "I like you for this. Which is why we're going to swab you for DNA, match you to this murder, and put your ass in jail."

I laugh at him. "You want my DNA? Here."

And I spit on the table.

He nods his head, puts his hand on the back of my neck, and slams my forehead into the wet spot. Pain ricochets through my skull like a rubber ball. Over the course of my life I've taken many blows to the head, and this is the first time I've ever seen stars. I didn't even know that was possible.

When my vision swims back into focus there's a splotch of blood on the table where my forehead connected with it.

Medina says, "Are you all right? You seem to have slipped there."

I get up and take a step, fall to the floor. He puts his hands under my arms and pulls me to my feet, or tries to because

I don't want to cooperate, when another cop comes into the room. The new guy looks very angry. "Detective. Outside. Now."

Medina lets me fall to the floor and leaves the room. I stumble around like I'm dizzy. I figure if I pretend to have a concussion they'll feel obligated to take me to the hospital instead of putting me in holding.

Also, I might have a concussion.

Another officer comes in, this guy clearly a desk cop, because he's too heavy to be expected to chase people down a street. He's also way too earnest. He asks, "Are you okay?"

I steady myself on the chair and stare off into space, shake my head like he asked me a question about nuclear physics. He takes my arm and leads me through the station and I see Medina through the glass window of an office where he's getting screamed at by a guy in a fancy uniform. Grabowski is standing there too, off to the side, arms crossed. Good. I flip Medina off but he doesn't see it.

We get outside and the cop brings me to a squad car. "Look, this is a tough case, kid. Everyone's under a lot of pressure. Medina can be a little gung-ho… he's just trying to do the right thing. Maybe we can just call this no harm, no foul?"

"You're kidding, right? This asshole brought me in and tried to split my skull open and you want me to forget it? Like it was a happy accident?"

The cop shrugs. Smiles. He's genial. Probably used to doing this. "We're going to get you to a hospital. Get this taken care of. We'll make it right. No need to turn it into a thing, you know what I mean?"

"I don't need a hospital. I need to go."

"Regulation. Sorry kid."

There's no one else around and he's not spry enough to chase me so I fall to a knee and tell him, "I need orange juice."

"What?"

"I'm diabetic. I need orange juice or a candy bar or something."

"We're getting you to a hospital right now."

"No, orange juice first. If you don't get me some sugar I'm going to have a seizure and I could crack my head open on the pavement." I look up at him. "Please. I'll wait right here."

The cop pats me on the shoulder and nods. He looks genuinely concerned. Which makes me feel bad for the fact that by the time he comes back out, I'm gone.

Me disappearing isn't going to look good, but now the pressure to get this thing solved is weighing on me a little heavier. If only because Medina clearly has some kind of misappropriated hard-on for me.

As I duck around the corner the world spins on an invisible axis. I grab the side of the building to steady myself. I probably should go to a hospital, but I'm passed the point of patience.

I just need something to set me straight first.

SNOW WHITE IS sitting outside, just like she always is when I need her. I sit on the step of her building and tell her, "Sixty."

"No small talk, huh?" She reaches into the coin pocket of my jeans for the money. Then she gets a good look at the welt on my forehead. "Babe, you're bleeding."

"I'm sure it'll be fine."

She shakes her head. "Your call."

When she pulls her hand away the vial of coke has replaced the money. I duck into the bathroom of the bar next door.

The first rip wakes me up.

The second brings the world into focus.

I'll save the rest for later. The mirror shows me things I don't want to see so I try not to look, just get myself straightened out, wipe down my face with a wet paper towel. It comes back pink with blood.

At the bar I order three shots of whiskey. The bartender looks around to see who else I'm with as he pours them. I throw them back one after another. Outside I light a cigarette, let the tastes mingle at the back of my throat.

Fuck moderation.

My umbrella is back at the precinct. It would probably be bad form to go and ask for it back. Doesn't matter. I don't need it anymore.

FiFTeeN

AS SOON AS I walk into The Patriot, I fall in love with the place. The wood is stained and rotting, the floor sags, the stools don't look safe, and the paint on the walls is peeling. Cheap drink prices are scrawled on blackboards in multi-colored chalk, and country music is blasting from the juke box. The entire place reeks with the sweet bread smell of dried beer. It's a real dive, not dive-chic.

First thought: I can't believe I've never been here before.

Second: I wonder if the bars in Austin are like this.

Third: I need more coke.

After topping off in the bathroom, I climb the uneven stairs to the second floor. There's a lot to take in but only one thing I notice. Up on the bar is a girl in jeans and nothing else, swinging her hips in time with Willie Nelson's voice. Her body is so perfect she looks like a mirage. There's a crowd of guys belly-up to the bronze, drool pouring in rivers down their faces.

I slide up to the bar and she shimmies over, leans down and ruins the mystique when she opens her mouth. She has a harsh Jersey accent, the kind that sounds like she's kicking her vowels in the ribs. She asks, "What can I get you, honey?"

Her fantastic breasts are literally hanging in my face. The lengths I go to.

"Three shots of Jay," I tell her.

She jumps down and pulls on a gray t-shirt. Every other guy in the bar looks at me like they want to shank me.

The girl puts down the shot glasses and pours the bottle of Jameson across them, and she even manages to keep from spilling too much on the bar. She asks, "Who else is drinking?"

I respond by downing all three of them. Then I put the photo of Lindsay on the bar, ask, "Where is she?"

"Lola?"

"Lindsay."

"She called herself Lola. It helps when the regulars don't know your real name."

"Fair enough. Seen her lately?"

"Maybe."

"When?"

She hesitates, looks around.

I ask, "Is she here now?"

"She just left. Half hour ago."

"Do you know where she was going?"

"She came to get her pay but we didn't have her envelope, so I..."

"You what?"

"Look, I'm sorry, I probably told you too much already. I

shouldn't be saying so much about Lola. Who are you anyway?"

The whole paying-for-information thing is getting old, and I'm pretty sure I lost the play-money at this point, so I lean over the bar and drop my voice. "I'm tired of this fucking game. It's been a long night."

"I don't..."

"Just give me the address."

The floor creaks behind me. A voice says, "Is this guy giving you trouble?"

The guy is in his mid-thirties, gelled hair, Ed Hardy t-shirt, but also dress slacks and wingtips, so he must have been wearing it under his suit in anticipation of going out. Wedding ring. Probably told his wife he was working late and he's in love with the bartender and he wants to be her hero so she'll blow him in the back.

I ask, "Do you work here?"

"No."

"Are you a cop?"

"No."

"Good." I grab his shirt and twist it up in my hands, pull him close and whisper into his ear. "Then mind your fucking business."

I push him into a stool and he crashes onto the floor. Everyone watches but no one goes to help him up. The bartender is standing with her back against the bottles that line the wall.

"Give me the address and I'll leave," I tell her.

She reaches in her pocket and pulls out a scrap of paper, tosses it across the bar at me. It's an address in Alphabet City. I nod, stick in my pocket, and leave. No one tries to stop me. The guy hasn't even gotten off the floor.

That wasn't graceful. And she's probably calling Paulsen to tell him I'm coming.

Which is fine. I think he knew that anyway.

CRAIG IS SITTING at the top of the subway steps with an empty paper coffee cup and a cardboard sign at his feet that says he served in the Vietnam War and could you please spare some change. When he sees me climbing toward him he waves at me but I keep going. "Not now."

He says, "I have something."

The two of us walk out of the way of the crowds filing up and down the stairs. He shakes the cup a little. I pull out three twenties and cram them into the cup.

"Found someone who saw the girl," he says.

"Where?"

"Astor Place train station."

"What was she doing?"

"Ran onto the train, like she was trying to get away from someone."

"Did your guy see who she was running from?"

Craig nods, slowly. "You."

A hand grips my heart, squeezes.

He holds out the cup again, like I'm going to give him some more money. I knock it out of his hand. Changes scatters across the sidewalk. "Fuck you, and fuck your friend. He's wrong."

Craig stoops down to pick up his money and says, "Nice knowing you." When he's done he gets up and walks away like I'm not standing there.

It's not true. I know it's not true. So someone saw me

stumbling around and they saw her running to catch a train. It's a small fucking city. I didn't hurt Chell. I see her face when I close my eyes. Twisted in pain. It's a reminder. That's all it is. All it has to be.

Paulsen did it. He's the one I'm after.

THE CITY IS in twilight, and I am more awake and more alive than I've ever felt, because in front of me is a building, and inside that building is Rick Paulsen. And he is the person who killed Chell.

I know it.

I'm going to kill him. I know that, too. I don't know how. With my hands, I think. I want to feel the life leave him. He has to die. You can't do something like that and come back.

The front door is locked. I ring some bells, figuring someone will buzz me in, but the intercom doesn't light up so I go to the building next door and use the roof to cross over.

The door leading inside has a heavy padlock on it. I find a cinder block, come back, and smash it off. This clearly isn't the way I'm supposed to be going in, but at this point, I don't fucking care.

The apartment is on the third floor, one of three doors on the landing. I press my ear to the door, slow my breathing, try to hear what's going on, can only hear blood gushing through my body like a river.

I try and formulate a plan, but I'm still not even sure what I'm going to do when I find out who's inside.

Completely bereft of ideas, I knock, and when the door opens, for a second I think I'm going to see Chell, and that this has all been a terrible, mean-spirited joke.

Instead there's a gun in my face.

The gun is connected to the arm of an older guy with salt-and-pepper hair and a nice enough demeanor, despite the firearm.

He says, "Ashley McKenna."

"That's me."

"I've been waiting."

"So I guess I shouldn't even bother pretending my name is Johnny?"

The more my eyes adjust, the more I can see of the guy. Nice face, like an aging movie star. Gray at the temples. He's lean but not stronger or faster than me. I would kill him in a fair fight.

He says, "We made you right at the start."

If I try and take the gun from him, I could get myself killed. No matter how bad I want to jam it down his throat, now is not the right time. I ask, "Are you going to shoot me in the face? Because at this point, you may as well warn me. I think I deserve the chance to turn the tables."

He regards the gun, all without pulling his eye off the sight that's aimed squarely at my nose. "No, I'm not going to shoot you. Not here. You know, it's funny. I use this gun in the game, in Noir York. It usually has blanks in it. Do you know how hard it is to get real bullets in this city?"

"Well, I'm glad we're both winning at today."

With his free hand he tosses a black cloth at my chest. "Put this on. Play any games, I will shoot you in the back."

"Firing a gun isn't as easy as it looks. If I break off on a run, are you good enough to hit me?"

He smiles. The worst kind of smile you can see on someone's

face when they're holding a gun. "I'm not worried."

I pull the hood over my head. He leads me down the steps, letting me swing my foot out to find each individual stair so that I get to the bottom safely.

The two of us head outside and walk down the street, him leading me, and I have to wonder if there are people walking by, and if they see a hooded man being led down the streets of Alphabet City, and whether that gives them pause.

I feel like the gun should give me pause. I've seen guns, tucked into waistbands, sitting on tables. Never had one with the business end pointed into my direction. T-Rex aside.

If Rick wanted me dead, he would have done it in the building. That's what I keep telling myself.

At least that's one mystery solved. The man in the hood. Which gets me thinking. I still haven't given much thought to the actual parameters of this game. Like, the whodunit. Not that it really matters, but with not much else to do right now, I'm curious.

Lindsay is a ghost. Everywhere I go, people know her but no one really seems to know her. Terry, on the other hand, is clearly a bad guy. He has money issues. So how does Lindsay play into it?

Maybe the family has money and he's working on getting some of it. That makes the most sense. Maybe he's killed her, but that seems a little too fatalistic. Even in New York, people want happy endings.

Then there's the question of Chell. I'm operating on the assumption that the girl who Chell played was Lindsay, only because there's no other clear option. The only thing throwing me is one detail: Lindsay's photo. The resemblance between Iva and Lindsay is uncanny. Iva and Chell don't share the same facial features. Chell's face is sharper, her eyes bigger. She's couldn't pass for Iva's sister, not the way Lindsay does.

My sinus cavity feels empty. I need another line. My breath is making the hood damp and I don't like the feel of it against my face. I hope they wash it between uses.

Coming down the block is the click of high heels, and a woman exhales. There's the sound of two people kissing quickly on the lips, and the guy grabs my shoulder.

"I still have the gun," he says. "Don't try anything stupid. I will kill you."

There's a groan of old metal, and he leads me down a stone staircase, guiding my head for what's probably a low clearance. Then we're in a hallway. My shoulders brush up against the walls as I sway back and forth. He's behind me. When we've walked about a hundred feet he stops me and fiddles with a lock. It smells like cigarette smoke and mold and hard water.

We get through a doorway and he sets me down on a chair and ties my hands behind my back. I keep them at an odd angle so that maybe I'll be able to wriggle out of them. After a few moments Terry pulls the hood away from my head.

We're in a basement room, probably below a bar, not entirely dissimilar from the one below Apocalypse. A concrete box with exposed brick walls and a scuffed floor.

The room is empty save the chair I'm tied to and another chair to my left, a coil of rope sitting on the seat. There's a small table by the door with a beer bottle on it. No label. Paulsen is standing directly opposite me on the other side of the room, the gun dangling against his leg.

He's flanked by Iva Archer. She's smiling. This morning it was warm and vulnerable. Now her lips are set like blades.

"So," I ask the man with the gun. "What should I call you?

Terry? Joel? How about Rick?"

He tenses, tilts his head. "How did you find out my real name?"

"It may come as a surprise, but I'm actually pretty clever."

Iva laughs. "Clever enough to get tied to a chair with a gun pointed at you."

"Yes, please note the sarcasm," I tell her.

"Rick," says the man with the gun. "You can call me Rick."

To Iva I say, "And your name?"

"You can use my professional name. Fanny Fatale."

"Well then. I've been looking for you, too."

If it was Rick's DNA on Chell, then she must have been the female set. Fanny must have wanted the part Chell had, but Chell didn't want to give it up. They decided to kill her. Maybe they did it together, maybe he did it after they fucked and that's why there were two sets of DNA. Regardless. Doesn't matter. I'm here now, and this bullshit ends.

Fanny leans down into my face. Her breath smells like chocolate. I want to smash all the bones in it. She asks, "Do you know why you're here?"

I ask, "The game or the real reason?"

"You figured out the game?"

"I did."

Rick shakes his head. "No you didn't."

"You were looking for a patsy. Iva or Lindsay or whatever her name is, she posed as her own sister and sent me all over town. Anyone looking for her would find people who remember me, so I'd come back as a suspect. But you were going to double-cross her. You would pull the bag off my head, she'd be tied up too. Once we were down here you'd leave us alone, I'd get out of the chair and use that stage-prop beer bottle to get the gun away from you when you come back into the room."

Rick smiles. "How'd you figure it out?"

"I told you, I'm clever. Current circumstances aside."

"If it makes you feel better, I'm impressed. No one's ever figured it out that quick. Now, tell me where the drive is."

"Not on me."

"So it's at the apartment."

"I was evicted."

Rick takes out his phone and taps at the keyboard. "I know. You're staying at your friend's place. The Indian kid."

"The drive isn't there."

"You're lying."

"If you send someone there and he gets hurt, I will murder you much harder than I had planned."

"I'm not terribly worried about that." Rick finishes what he's typing, puts the phone into his back pocket. "So, there's not much left to say here."

"Tell me why you did it, first. At least give me that."

"Did what?"

"Killed Chell. Why did you do it?"

Fanny and Rick look at each other like they've walked into a conversation halfway through. Rick says, "We didn't kill Chell. We didn't even find out she was playing us until after she died."

"You're lying. You found out about the drive or you found out about Ginny or something, and you snatched her and you killed her to cover up, I don't know, this dumb fucking turf war you're having. Which, you better believe that if you hurt me, Ginny is going to cut through you like a fucking howitzer."

Rick laughs. It's a high, unsettling laugh that makes me think he knows something I don't. He reaches the gun up to his head and uses the barrel to scratch his scalp, then drops it back to his side. "Ginny signed off on you. I can do whatever I want."

"What does that mean?"

"You seem to have a passing familiarity with what's going on, so I guess you'll understand me when I say we've negotiated a cease-fire. We're going to back off on the robberies and assaults, and we're stalling the direct attacks on Ginny's turf while we sort some things out."

"What robberies and assaults?"

Fanny shakes her head. "He doesn't know as much as he thinks he does."

Rick leans down in front of me, and speaks like he's lecturing a child. "The robberies and assaults The Hipster King has been overseeing. On one hand, it messed with Ginny's relationship with the local cops. Made it look like she couldn't handle her neighborhood. And on the other, we wanted to bring a little danger back to this neighborhood. This place has gotten soft. We're bringing the authenticity back to New York City."

"Are you kidding? That was you? Are you guys behind the groper around Tompkins Square Park, too?"

"Make an omelet, break some eggs, all that jazz."

The gears in my brain grind and nearly snap. "You killed Chell to make some ideological fucking omelet?"

"I told you we didn't kill Chell."

"And I think you're a fucking liar."

Rick smashes the gun across my face so hard I almost fall to the side. I run my tongue across my teeth and find one is loose. I know it should hurt, but I'm over the threshold. My body can't process any more pain.

Rage bubbles in my stomach, forces its way up my esophagus. I put my feet flat on the floor, roll my weight onto my toes. Rick doesn't notice. I try to get him to lean forward to me, just a little. I tell him, "You got bagged for a sexual assault up in Boston. Once a degenerate, always a degenerate. I know Fanny wanted a part in the game and Chell got it. You two killed her together, didn't you?"

Rick shakes his head. "This is getting tiresome." He moves forward to bring the gun up, which gives me just enough room to reach him. I lean forward onto my feet and launch myself into his stomach. We crash against the wall and the gun goes off next to my head. My hearing cuts out and I see the gun leave his hand, but I don't hear it clatter against the floor.

Rick is doubled-over in pain so I take a look over my shoulder. Fanny is picking the gun up. I kick it out of her hand and turn to the wall. I'm stooped over, bent at the knees, still tied to the chair, so I give it a crack against the wall and it shatters.

Fanny scrambles for the gun again. She grabs it, but doesn't have a good grip. I take it out of her hands, go over to Rick, who's just gained his composure, and bash it across his face.

WHEN RICK COMES to, he's sitting on the floor, his arms tied around the water pipe in the corner of the room. While he was dazed, I was a gentleman and offered Fanny the only unbroken chair in the room. Then I tied her to it.

A couple more lines of coke and I'm just about right. My ears are still ringing from the blast of the gun but I can hear a little better now.

It's my first time holding a gun. You'd think that wouldn't be true, given my line of work, but it is. I don't like guns. They're a coward's weapon. Still, I know the basics. Check the clip. I know that in order for it to fire the safety has to be off, which it is. And I know which end is the dangerous one. It's heavier than I thought it would be. Cold, too. I hold it down at my side.

"Why the game. This whole ridiculous thing?" I ask Rick.

"Access to people and information. Money." He shrugs. "And it's fun."

"And Chell was a threat to all that."

I train the gun on him. Rick looks up at me with pleading eyes. He says, "We didn't kill Chell."

"Bullshit. It fits. She was a spy in your organization."

"We didn't..." He trails off, still woozy from the blow, snaps back. The smug look is gone from his face. "That's not how it was. We were upset when we found out, but we only found out after she died."

"What about the thumb drive then? How did you know I had it?"

"My guys, the two guys from the bridge. They were at Chell's apartment the night you took it. They saw you come out and get in a car, and they figured you had it. After we figured out who Chell was, we thought she swiped it, which she did. It's paperwork. Financial records. But that's all. We did not kill her for it."

"Liar." I slam my boot into his crotch, and unlucky for him, I decided to put on the steel toes this morning. He doubles over in pain and dry-heaves, his eyes crossed. Fanny screams, "Stop! Of course I wanted this job, but we didn't kill her!"

"Shut up," I tell her over my shoulder. I take Rick's chin in my hand, pull his eyes up to mine. "You're a sexual deviant. People like you don't change. They never do."

"That wasn't how it went."

"Then how did it go?"

He's almost crying now. "It was my ex. She was trying to get back at me for something and she accused me, but it wasn't true. That's why I'm not in jail. I'd never do that to a woman."

"I feel like you're lying. Should I kick you in the nuts again?"

Fear blooms across his face like ink in a tank of water. I take the vial out of my pocket and put it to my nose, but it's not the coke, it's the lavender oil. The smell of it floods my head. Chokes me. I pull the vial away and the smell lingers along with Chell's voice.

Asking me what I'm doing.

That voice makes the room look different.

Like the pieces suddenly don't fit together so well.

"If you didn't kill Chell," I ask Paulsen, "then who did?"

"I don't know. I don't know. She said something about a guy. A guy she knew. He grabbed her wrist. It was sprained. It happened right before she came into work."

"Who?"

"It wasn't my place to ask."

"Not your place?"

"It's not like that. You know Chell. She liked to handle her own shit. She didn't tell me who did it. But it was definitely someone she knew. The way she talked about it, it sounded like a guy she was involved with."

I reach the gun back over my shoulder like I'm going to hit him. He arches away from me. "I swear that's all I know." His body is shaking.

The room is filled with the scent of lavender.

The room is filled with the scent of Chell, forcing me back into a well of doubt.

It's in his eyes, and it's in his voice. And no matter how

badly I want it to be him so I can put this to bed, it's not.

He's telling the truth.

But I'm pretty sure I know who wrenched her wrist.

Quinn, when she refused to marry him.

Maybe I was wrong about him. Maybe he's enough of a monster to kill a woman. Maybe after she refused his proposal he hurt her, then followed her and finished the job later that night.

And Chell didn't say his name on the phone because she knew how much it would upset me.

That's got to be it.

Rick is still hiding his eyes from me when I pull his cell phone out of his pocket and smash it against the wall. Rick asks, "You're just going to leave us here?"

"You'll get out eventually. I don't need your friends getting in my way right now. When you do get out, you tell your king I think your plan is fucking stupid. A couple of muggings aren't going to make this place better. And tell him to clear his appointment book, because I am going to find him and beat his goofy ass into the fucking dirt."

They're still protesting as I close the door and head out through the darkened hallway, holding my hand against the wall as a guide. I eventually stumble onto a staircase, and a grate leading to the sidewalk. I throw it open and scare the shit out of a group of smokers assembled outside a hookah restaurant.

Rick was texting during his monologue. He probably sent someone to go search Bombay's apartment for the drive. I break into a run, pray I can beat them to it.

BOMBAY'S APARTMENT IS trashed worse than mine was before I abandoned it.

His laptops are smashed. The bookcases in the living room have been torn down. The coffee table is upended against the wall, and the lamp that was next to the couch is now in pieces, scattered around the room.

Looking at it, I can't even be angry. How am I even supposed to react to this? It's my life in microcosm.

I'm about to turn around and walk back out when I come across my dad's scanner. Someone put a boot into the top. The faux-wood metal casing is bent, and the black plastic on the bottom is cracked.

I plug it in to see if it still works. It doesn't.

All the inside pieces are smashed.

I'm sorry dad. I'm so sorry.

There's movement behind me. I expect to find Bombay ready to tear my head off, but it's not. It's the hipsters from the bridge. They must have been in the kitchen or the bedroom when I came in.

The redhead is holding a long silver knife with a black plastic blade. He moves to my left, the blond flanking me on the other side. The redhead says, "The drive. Now"

The blond is closer so I drive my fist into his stomach. He doubles over and I grab the back of his jacket, smash him into the wall. He doesn't get up. The redhead holds up the knife in front of him. His voice is vibrating in a spot somewhere between fear and rage. "Don't think I won't use this. And you don't have a fucking bridge to jump off of this time, asshole. This time you answer to me. No more games."

He doesn't die when I throw him out the window into the alley below. We're only two floors up. But it does shut him the fuck up.

I text Bombay: *I am so sorry.*

I turn off my phone before he can write back.

A S I WANDER through the West Village, I text everyone in my phone: *Where's Quinn?*

Finally Mikey writes back: *Speakeasy.*

Speakeasy doesn't have a name. That's just what people call it. And even that is a little misleading, considering there are people lined up around the block to get in. And anyway, a speak makes me think of hard liquor. This place specializes in crappy beer and mixed drinks.

The line is at least forty people deep but Jimmy is working the door, so he waves me in as a collective groan erupts from the crowd. As I'm stepping past him he puts his hand on my chest. "You're bleeding."

"From where?"

"Ear. Head. Couple of places."

"I'll take that under advisement."

"Clean yourself up when you get down there." He takes my hand and stamps it with a black star, then picks up the rope and lets me go downstairs.

The club is at the bottom of a staircase, in a room that reeks of beer and bodily fluids. Everyone is glowing. The entire place is outfitted with black lights. With all the blood I'm covered in I must look like a crime scene. The club is laid out like a square, with some hallways and alcoves and side-rooms, centered around a sunken dance floor.

From the DJ booth stuffed in the corner, someone yells into

a microphone, "Prophetnoise!" A guy in a silver and orange mesh outfit with a shock of tangled hair that makes him look like a homeless clown appears at the controls. He flips open a laptop, hunches over, and drives enough bass into the crowd to make everyone sterile.

I push through the crowds looking for Quinn. It's hard to see more than a few people in front of me.

After fifteen minutes I'm getting frustrated and antsy from a lack of cocaine in my bloodstream, so I find the bathroom, and there he is, standing at a urinal with his back to me, wearing a white polo shirt, a Heineken perched on the ledge in front of him.

There are two guys at the sink. I get their attention and point to the door. They leave, clearly unnerved by my appearance. Quinn hears the door and looks over his shoulder, then jumps. "Ash."

"Quinn."

He finishes peeing and heads to the sink, says, "You're bleeding."

"I am aware."

He stares at me like he's waiting for me explode. "Look man, I was hoping I'd catch you. After everything that's happened, I don't want this stuff coming between us, you know? It sucks that Chell's gone now, but that doesn't mean we can't make things right between us."

He finishes washing his hands, dries them, offers me his hand.

I slam my fist across his jaw. He hits the floor like a car dropped from a plane, scrambles to get up, but I kick him in the ribs and put my foot onto his back. He coughs and sputters and asks, "What are you doing?"

"You hurt Chell, this is what happens."

He tries to get out from under my foot. "I didn't kill her, Ash!"

"Stop lying and just admit it." I pull him to his feet and throw my knee into his stomach. He lands in a pile at my feet. If he doesn't want to tell me, that's fine. There are plenty of hard surfaces in this bathroom that could convince him to tell the truth.

And then he starts crying.

"Ash please. I didn't hurt Chell. I would never hurt Chell. Stop hitting me. Please."

"Bullshit."

"Ash, I'm not that kind of guy."

I pull him to his feet. There's a line of blood trickling out of his mouth. My heart is racing so fast I fear it might burst. I tell him, "I have known you nearly my whole life. Don't you dare lie to me."

His body is wracked by sobs and he pulls away from me. Snot pours down his face as he chokes on his words. "I would never Ash. I would never."

I throw my fist into his stomach, hard, and he doubles over. All I see is red.

I tell him, "You don't hit women."

Reach back to hit him again.

Then something heavy cracks across the back of my skull.

SIXTEEN

FADE IN, FADE out.

Things happen but I feel disconnected from them. Like watching a movie while doing something else. After a little while I regain enough cognitive ability to realize there's a hood over my head. I try to pull it off but my hands are zip-tied behind my back. The plastic digs into the skin of my wrists. It hurts.

I push myself up until I'm sitting. The hood comes off and the lights are so bright it stings. Someone grabs my arm to steady me, then cuts the ties. A door slams behind me.

There's a carpet underneath me. Shag, pink. The walls are faux-wood paneled. To my left is a small table with a Burger King crown on it. Stomped on and bloodied.

In the middle of the room is a green easy chair. Sitting crossed-legged, regarding a book in her lap, is Ginny. Wearing a polka dot dress and an apron, a red wig tied back under a handkerchief. Thick red lipstick and rouge on her cheeks.

She doesn't look up at me, just turns the page in her book and says, "Good morning, darling." She checks her watch. "Well, evening. It's a few minutes to midnight."

"What the fuck am I doing here?"

"I'm saving you from yourself."

"Where's Quinn?"

"On his way to the hospital. My people convinced him to blame his attack on a random mugger whom he could not accurately identify. He'll be paid, of course. You are welcome."

I reach up and touch my head. My hat is gone. When did I lose it? Did Ginny take it? Doesn't matter. I reach into my pocket and pull out the coke. I'm going to need more soon. I take a bump and Ginny looks at me from the chair, a condescending look on her face. I pull the vial away and it's rimmed in blood.

We sit there for a little while like that. Me on the floor, Ginny with her book. Finally I tell her, "You sold me out."

"Do you know what kind of mess you've caused me?"

"I don't give a shit. It's true, isn't it?"

Ginny closes her book and sighs like she's on a stage. "Yes. I sold you out. There were politics involved. It's hard to explain, but I really had no choice."

"You sent me to get killed by T-Rex."

Ginny looks hurt by this. "I didn't think they would kill a messenger. I just figured it would give you something to take your mind off this whole thing. As for the guy I sent to your apartment…"

"Wait, the guy I chased? He was yours?"

"Babe, I know the USB drive is practically impenetrable,

but that doesn't mean I shouldn't give it a shot. Your apartment was already trashed anyway."

"And the hipsters?"

"They're not as powerful as I thought."

"But you still told them where to find me?"

"I did."

"Why?"

She lights a cigarette. She still hasn't looked me in the eye. "It was a business decision."

"Business?"

"I deal in information Ash. It's the most precious thing in the world. No one can take it from you and it never loses its value. You need to understand that what you did put me in a bad position."

"So this is your standard of friendship?"

"Don't be so foolish."

"And Chell?"

"I still don't know what happened to Chell. I tried my damndest to find out, because I wanted to give you that. I would have handed that information over to you and you would have been out of my hair. Instead, you've been doing nothing but causing problems." She pauses. "I'm sorry, but it needs to be said. Chell didn't love you like you loved her, Ash."

The back of my throat is hot. I choke back tears, vomit. "It wasn't about that. She was my friend. Who are you?"

"I'm your friend, Ash. I am. Chell is dead. And I am sorry. But people die. Why, why, why are you doing this to yourself? She wouldn't even fuck you."

I climb to my feet. "I was a fucking shoulder to cry on. I was a sounding board every time she fucked someone and it went south. I gave everything to her and never asked for anything back. What was so wrong with me?"

Ginny's face goes slack. The words hang in the air between us. I feel like I'm standing naked in front of her.

"Ash," she says. "You sound like a child who had a toy taken away. Is that all you thought of Chell? That she was an object for conquest?"

"I don't mean... it just... it can't all be so random. There needs to be a reason that she died. Somebody needs to pay for it."

"Ah." Ginny relaxes. Then she laughs, a modest giggle, like she just understood a mildly clever joke. "There it is. I can't believe it. Cannot believe I didn't put that one together. It was obvious that this was about your father."

"This has nothing to do with my dad."

"Doesn't it?"

I walk over to her and stand in front of her, and since she's biologically a man, I don't feel bad about this. "Ginny, get up."

She sighs again and climbs to her feet. "What are you going to do?"

I don't answer, I just swing at her, but all my fist feels is air. The next thing I feel is the carpet crammed into my face and my arm twisted behind me, ready to pop out. Ginny keeps a hold on my arm but manages to crouch down next to me. "Ash, I love you. Despite everything, I do, and that's why this is so hard."

I try and twist away. Ginny pulls harder and lights explode behind eyes. She's not even breathing hard.

Under my breath I mutter, "Fucking cunt."

She twists harder. "So you can't hurt me with your hands, you're going to hurt me with words? Is that it? You know me, Ash." She leans close into my ear and yells, "I don't have feelings."

Bone scrapes against bone.

"Darling, going around and knocking people out isn't going to bring her back. And it's not going to bring your father back. I can see how establishing some sort of narrative might work to assuage your pain, but all you're doing is chasing ghosts. And ghosts do not exist."

I stop struggling but she doesn't let up. "I know what happened is terrible. It's unfathomable. These things are bigger than us. They are devoid of meaning. And yet, you are no one's dark rider of vengeance. You will find no answers. I am telling you this as your soon-to-be-former friend."

Ginny lets my arm go and I collapse into a pile on the floor, dive for her legs.

She twists around me, puts her knee in my back, right between two vertebrae, and pins me to the floor. She says, "Here's the truth. You are young and foolish. You do not know nearly as much about the world as you'd like to think you do. And you will not grow as a person until you realize that."

She gets close to my ear and drops her voice to a whisper. "No one knows anything. The first step toward recovery is admitting to that."

She gets off my back and I pull myself to my feet.

"Go, while I'm still in a good mood, darling," she says. "Or the next thing you'll see is a ceiling. Of a hospital room or a pine box, it makes no difference to me at this point. Don't expect a Christmas card this year, either."

WALK A FEW blocks and people give me a wide berth. I stand on a quiet corner and stare up and the sky like I'm going to find an answer there. My body is a sea of pain, waves crashing against my head and ribs and leg. Things move inside me that shouldn't be moving.

I need a drink.

I need to be numb.

Apocalypse will save me.

The bar is so crowded I can barely get through the door. Dave isn't bartending, which is good, because he probably doesn't want to see me. Tony hands me my bottle of Jay without waiting, without asking. I considering poking around to see if there's anyone I know, but the noise overwhelms me so I figure I'll head down to the office. At least it'll be quiet down there.

The 'out of order' sign is already up on the bathroom. I wait until I think no one is looking and slip inside. The bookshelf is ajar. It's not supposed to be. Against the rules. Otherwise anyone could find the back room.

I step through the dark hallway and into the office and Margo is sitting on the leg of a couch, her friends from last night scattered around the room. But there's no one from the old guard with them. No Lunette, no Bombay, no Dave. No one who is supposed to be down here.

Everyone stops talking and looks up at me. I ask Margo, "What the fuck is this?"

Her face twists in shock. "What?"

"Why the fuck are these people in here?"

"Lunette showed it to me. I thought it was cool."

"It's not fucking cool." I kick the coffee table so the wine glasses and beer bottles fall over. "Everyone get the fuck out."

The asshole, Eye-Anne, looks up at me and shrugs. "Do

you own the building or something? Because if not, I don't think you can tell us where we can be."

I reach down and grab his collar, pull him to his feet. A pair of arms wrap around me from behind. I throw whoever it is off. I shove Eye-Anne back down on the couch and turn to Margo. "You know what? Fuck you." She freezes. "It's your fucking fault. You brought all these dumb fucking gents here and now the neighbors want us out. And that's fucking bullshit."

"Ash…"

"No, just, fuck off. This space doesn't belong to them. It belongs to us. We fucking earned it. And these fucking kids just showed up and took it from us." I tell the crowd, "Get the fuck out, all of you, or there's going to be a big fucking problem."

Eye-Anne gets bold. He stands up and gets in my face, says, "Don't talk to a lady like that."

I nearly pick him up off his feet before I toss him into the wall. He falls to the floor and the room holds its collective breath. I tell them, "You know what? Fuck this."

As I'm leaving someone mutters, "Fucking hipster asshole."

I turn, make a noise that sounds like something ancient and angry, and dive at the door. Someone swings it closed and locks it. I bang on it until my fist hurts.

Fine. Fuck it. It doesn't matter. This place will be gone soon anyway. This whole place will be gone from us and it doesn't matter. Let it sink below the sea. I crash through the hallway, out to the grate in the sidewalk, leave through there so I don't have to go back through the bar. Light a cigarette.

Considering kicking in the window.

Considering burning down the building.

Here's the thing about living in New York City: Fuck this place.

Someone calls my name. I turn and it's Bombay. He's looking at me like he's never seen me before.

I should apologize.

And I try to, but the wrong words come out.

"It's because she's gone," I tell him. "It's not my fault."

He drops his shoulder, rears back. Broadcasts the punch in high-definition.

I don't bother to stop it, and let his fist connect with my jaw.

I REMEMBER WHAT HAPPENED the night you died.
I wish I didn't.

Maybe a chunk of my brain finally bit the dust after years of abuse and it's hard to process memories. Maybe Bombay knocked it loose. Maybe I've been actively trying to block this.

Doesn't matter. Because now I remember.

I finished up my shift at the office, sent the decoy and bodyguard out to try and catch that groper. I should have gone home, but I couldn't sleep and I couldn't stay inside so I wandered, smoking cigarettes and ducking into phone booths to blow lines of coke, and then I saw you and Quinn coming out of KGB.

You were arguing. It was intense enough you wouldn't look him in the eye, which for you meant that you were wrong about something but were too proud to admit it. I watched from across the street, peeking around a parked van, wondering what I should do, when I saw him shake his head. Then you kissed each other. A knife twisted in my gut, and he got in a cab and left.

When a fight like that ends with a kiss it means there's something there worth saving.

You know what it was, Chell? I had convinced myself that you had made a promise that you wouldn't see him. I know that's not true, but it's what I made myself believe. And I know now it was wrong of me to ask that, but I didn't know it then.

You were walking to the subway. I stopped you at the mouth of the station and asked you why you were with him. We argued. I don't remember what we were saying. We were yelling and people were watching and you made me angry.

And when you tried to get away from me, I grabbed you by the wrist, hard.

Hard enough you twisted your face in pain.

The kind of pain you never expected to feel from me. I held you there and yelled at you, right in the middle of the sidewalk, and some guy stopped to see if you were okay, and I pushed him and turned around and you were gone.

The train pulled into the station as we were running down the stairs and you managed to get on just as the doors were closing. I was a few seconds too late, tried to pry the doors open, but it didn't work. I watched through the window as you held your wrist, a red mark around it from where I squeezed.

And I cried, in front of all these people pressing their faces up against the window.

The subway began to glide out of the station. I pulled a pen out of my pocket.

And I wrote the wrong thing on my hand.

It should have been: *I'm sorry.* That's what I should have written. But I was stupid and angry and drunk and I wasn't thinking.

I wrote: *You promised.*

Even as I was doing it, I felt like it was a mistake, but once I pressed my hand to the window it was too late. I held it there, walking alongside the train, picking up my pace as it went faster. You pulled a pen out of your pocket and you wrote something on your hand.

I was running alongside the train at that point, trying to keep up, and just as you put your hand to the window, before I could read it, the train whisked into the tunnel and I ran full force into the wall.

That was the last time I saw you.

That's why I made a half-hearted attempt to stop with the booze and the drugs. I didn't like the person I was when I pumped myself full of poison. The way I grabbed your wrist, the way your face looked, it stayed with me, even though I didn't realize it, and that's the only way I can see you now.

Twisted in pain, angry.

You used the train to get away from me, and then you went to work and I went out and drank more until I went home and passed out on the floor. If I had been awake, maybe I wouldn't have gotten to you in time, but anything would be better than this.

I could sit here all day and come up with a million reasons for what this means and why I did it and why I'm after the person who did this to you, but no matter what I say it wouldn't be the truth.

The only truth is that I wanted you to know I was sorry and I don't know how to say it without hurting someone.

What would you say to me if you could see me right now?

SEVENTEEN

I WAKE STARING INTO the sun. It intensifies the hangover stomping around my brain. My body feels heavy, like I'm being pulled into the ground. The thought of moving terrifies me. I'm not sure I'll stay together.

Buildings. There are buildings whipping by, like I'm being carried, and I figure maybe I'm dead and this is what it looks like. Maybe this city has decided that it's done with me, that I don't deserve it. And it's sent someone to carry me away, far from here, to make a life somewhere else.

I wonder if that's a bad thing.

Then the buildings stop moving. I hear horns honking and smell exhaust.

I push myself up and I'm in a boat.

My hat is back. It's sitting on top of the cooler next to me. I reach into the cooler and come out with a beer and a bottle of water. I put back the beer and chug the water, then retch it over the side, into the street.

It would be nice to know where the hell I am, but I'm too tired. I curl up into a ball, roll onto my side and go back to sleep.

PALE BLUE SKY, and the boat is listing back and forth on water. Tibo is half-naked, pulling on a full-body diving suit.

He sees me stir and says, "Good morning."

"Where are we?"

"On a boat."

"Why?"

"You don't remember last night at all, do you?" He gets the suit zipped up and pushes his dreads under the hood. "The boat was parked on the street. I let you sleep in it because you said you couldn't go home. When I said I had to leave early, you said to just bring you with me."

I climb onto the bench and look out across the water. Mammoth cargo ships drift past us. I pray they can see us down here. "Are we even allowed to be out here?"

"Until someone tells me we can't be."

"This is the Hudson. You are going to go into that water and come out with syphilis."

He tosses me a bottle of bleach. "For when I get out."

"Can we sign a waiver or something to say I'm not liable for when you die?"

Tibo isn't listening to me, just fits a huge pair of goggles to his face. He flicks a switch on the side and a lamp pops on.

He lowers himself into the water and his body goes rigid from the cold. He hangs on the side of the boat, takes the breathing device out of his mouth and says, "Let's say if I'm down there for more than a half-hour, want to call the Coast Guard? There's a radio at the front of the boat. I don't know how to work it, but I'm sure it can't be terribly hard to figure out."

"I will, as long as you understand I'm not coming in after you. Is it even warm enough to be swimming in?"

He pats his cowl. "Dry suit. Rated for cold-water diving."

"Do you know how to scuba dive?"

"Learn by doing."

He slides under the water. I check my phone and wedge myself into the bottom of the boat until I'm comfortable, take a beer out of the cooler. It's warm. But between that, the smell of salt and the sun on me, the cold air forcing my skin tight, it helps a little.

And it's quiet. So quiet. All I can hear is the slap of water against the side of the boat and the distant call of ship horns. There's also a faint sucking sound, and it takes a bit to realize that's just the quiet.

From here, the city looks like a painted backdrop. The buildings are sharp and crisp. I've always loved the cold weather in the city. The air is dry, so there's no humidity to hold on to water vapor, pollution, whatever crap makes the views hazy on hot days. Starting in October, you can see for miles. Go outside on a cold night, and you can see every lit window in every building.

Any other day, I would be more wistful about this view, but right now the city looks like pictures from someone else's story.

I take out my phone. Still getting service. I text Good Kelly: *How's Austin?*

Within moments she writes back: *Good! Already feels like home.*

Miss you here.

Come visit.

Maybe.

Nothing from Bombay or Margo or Lunette. Probably for the better.

As I'm getting close to sleep again, Tibo's hand appears on the side of the boat. He pulls himself up, dripping wet, and I move away from him so he doesn't get any water on me. I know it's getting cleaner, but the sewer system still flushes into the harbor when it rains.

He pulls off the mask. The look of dejection of his face says it. He puts his hands on his hips and shakes his head from side to side. "I found a car and a shopping cart. Not very useful."

"What's it like down there?"

"Like swimming through oil. You can't see very far in front of you, and every now and again a fish darts out at you and it sort of comes out of nowhere. It's like being in a horror movie I can't turn off. I think I peed myself a little."

"You're basically swimming in it."

I uncork the bleach, and we sanitize him, taking care to keep it out of his face. He strips down to his t-shirt and boxers but doesn't bother getting the rest of the way dressed even though it's pretty cold out here, just piles his gear in the corner of the boat, puts his feet up and cracks a beer.

Finally he says, "Do you think we can try again tomorrow?"

"Tell me again, about what it's going to pay for."

"Construction costs, supplies. I'm thinking geodesic domes and farming. Treehouses. Chickens and goats. It needs to be a sustainable community that could support up to a few hundred people if necessary."

"How soon do you want to start construction?"

"Six months ago."

"Where?"

"Somewhere south. It's easier to deal with the heat than the cold, at least when it comes to crops."

"You really want to leave all this?"

"I love living here, but sooner or later, either you outgrow it, or it outgrows you. If you don't recognize when that happens, you're just going to end up being miserable."

"This is our home."

"Home is any place you want it to be."

"How do you even know the silver is down there?"

Tibo shrugs. "Because I already found eight bars."

"No shit."

He laughs. "My bank account is pretty damn flush, brother."

"So this whole thing might actually work."

"You should come."

"I'm thinking about it."

He laughs.

I ask him, "What?"

"Every other time I've asked you to come and you've agreed, I knew you were humoring me. Except this time. This time you're really thinking about it."

Tibo finishes his beer, takes another out of the cooler. He says, "But you're not ready to go yet."

"Actually, I think I may have one foot out the door."

We don't say anything after that. Just float, and after a little while I have Tibo drop me off at a dock on Staten Island.

THE HOUSE IS cemetery quiet. I walk through the living room, directly to the mantle above the fireplace. The memorial to my father.

Pictures of the family. Me, my dad, and my mom, out at Lido Beach for the annual firehouse picnic. My dad, decked out in his bunker gear, surrounded by the rest of the guys assigned to his firehouse. In the middle of the mantle is his helmet, wiped free of dust and still warm whenever I touch it. The only piece of him they could find.

After dad died and I left, my mom settled into a routine of working as much as she could. She never had the heart to date again, and I'm glad she didn't. I'd never be able to accept that, because I'm selfish.

Footsteps shuffle on the basement steps. Mom comes out of the doorway hauling a basket of laundry. She's in her bathrobe and pajamas, her blonde-to-white hair poking out from underneath a handkerchief wrapped tight around her head. She looks a little more frail than she did the last time. She always looks a little more frail, like without my father around, she's getting smaller.

As she stares at me I try to imagine what I look like. Bruised and broken. Nothing hurts as much as the shame. She bursts into tears and drops the basket, clean clothes spilling across the floor.

She wraps her arms around me and her grip is tight despite her size. She asks, "Ashley, what happened?"

I don't say anything. She leads me into the kitchen, says, "Ashley, talk to me."

"I messed up, Ma."

"What did you mess up?"

"I got caught up in something bad."

"Ashley."

"The girl who died. The one in the papers. I loved her. I

wanted to hurt the person who did it to her. And this..." I look away from her.

"Ashley. Please. Just, please." She puts her hand on my cheek. "Oh god, we should go down to the hospital."

"I think if I'm still alive at this point I'm not in any real danger."

Her mouth drops open and she can't speak. She shakes her head back and forth, trying to find a thought to latch on to. "Please Ashley. Not after your father. Please."

The kettle whistles but we ignore it.

"I think it's time to leave, Ma," I tell her.

The change of subject composes her. "Where?"

"The city. This place is bad for me."

She nods, pushes me toward the table so I can sit, and turns to the stove. She busies herself making the tea, adding sugar to hers and not mine, being careful to not look at me. When the mugs are ready, she places one in front of me and says, "Do you want to leave because you feel like it's right, or because you're running away from something?"

"I don't know how to answer that. I just... the whole way over I just knew. This is the thing I need. You know how sometimes you get an idea and it just fits? But I'm worried. I think Dad wouldn't want me to go. If he had a say in it."

She smiles, and her eyes well up at the thought of him. "He would want you to be happy. I'm a tough girl, I can take care of myself. I'm not alone. Your friends aren't alone. No one is alone as long as they don't want to be." She pauses, and adds, "You're not alone either, even if it feels that way."

"I know Ma, I just... I don't want to make the wrong decision."

"You won't know if it's right unless you do it."

"I don't know."

"Just stop. Stop it. If you think it's the right thing to do, then you should do it. Ashley, you have a big heart, and you care about people, and that's a wonderful thing. But you have to care about yourself first. You can't be there for everyone. No one can." She looks away from me. "Your father needed to protect everyone. And look what happened."

"That was different."

For the briefest moment, anger flashes across her face. She asks, "Is it?"

"It's different."

She sits next to me and wraps her arms around my shoulders, says, "If you need to go, I'll support you. I'll miss you like crazy, but a change of scenery can be a very good thing. You can always come back, and then you can stay here as long as you need. Just promise me you will answer your phone when I call you? Please? Can you promise me that?"

"Yeah Ma. I promise."

She smiles, and points to the hat on the kitchen table.

"That's a nice hat."

"I always wanted a fedora."

"That's not a fedora, honey. The brim of a fedora is wider. That's a trilby."

"Really?"

"Yes honey." She runs her hand through my hair and says, "You look so much like him, you know that? More and more every day."

"Should I get a haircut? Grow a beard? Would that help?"

"No, I love that you look like him. He would be so proud of you."

I wish that were true.

MY MOTHER'S WORDS follow me the rest of the way back into the city.

All I wanted was to be like my dad. And I succeeded at making a mess of that. The only silver lining in him being dead is at least he can't see me like this. What I've become.

I'm there before I realize that's where I'm even headed. The street corner in Alphabet City where Chell disappeared, the last place she stood that I can place her. I drop to my knee and run my fingertips over the ground. The warmth has been sucked out of it. I can't smell lavender.

Another unmarked grave in a city full of them.

I take the vial of lavender oil out of my pocket and pour it onto the concrete. Close my eyes. Pretend she's standing here, just for a second.

She called me. Even after what I did, how I acted, she called me. She didn't write me off. Maybe she even would have listened to me apologize.

I can hold on to that.

And that's the end of this. Let the cops handle it.

The door of the bar across the street opens and closes. The bouncer, a big black guy nearly seven feet tall, takes his position at the front.

I should get up and leave. Go find a place to sleep tonight and figure things out. The cops are probably still looking for me. I've still probably got some fallout to deal with from T-Rex and The Hipster King, if he's still alive. There are an awful lot of people with silly names who want to kill me.

But I cross the street toward the bar. I never got to follow up with that other bouncer, and the thread is dangling in my face, irritating me.

As I approach the guy, he takes off his sunglasses and

surveys my face, raises an eyebrow. "Rough night?"

"Rough lifetime. Are you Steve?"

"That's me."

"Great, listen." I point across the street. "Couple of nights ago a girl got killed, right? She was taken from over there, on that corner. The muscle-head covering the door the day after said you were the one working that night."

"I remember that. She was the girl in the papers. But I wasn't working that night. Who did you talk to?"

"I didn't get the guy's name. Body builder. Personality of a chainsaw."

Steve purses his lips and nods. "That's Bret. I was supposed to work that night but called out sick. He covered my shift."

"Wait. That guy was working? Is he working now, or tonight?"

"Nah, boss let him go. Some bullshit with the girls here, they didn't feel comfortable working with him. I think he made a grab at one of them."

He keeps talking, but I don't hear it.

The sidewalk drops out from under me.

How did I not see it?

I spoke to the guy. I spoke to the guy a few hours after he dropped Chell's dead body in an empty lot in Queens. He probably still had blood under his fingernails.

I pull out my wallet, fish out a hundred bucks of T-Rex's money and hold it up to Steve. "Can you get me his address?"

He pulls out his phone and scrolls through. "Whatever. Dude was an asshole."

EiGhTeEn

GETTING TO LONG Island under the radar is not an easy feat.

Can't rent a car, there'll be a record. Plus the tollbooths have cameras. The trains have cameras, too.

It's hard to get things done without Ginny's pull, but it's not impossible. It took a little work, but Tibo knew a guy with a car, and that guy was willing to not ask questions. I handed the driver a pile of money and he agreed to the plan.

I filled the trunk of his car with blankets. Told him to stick with the speed limit and obey every traffic rule. Just to be safe. I don't know how long the ride took because I fell asleep.

After he dropped me off, he went to a pool hall where he could meet up with a friend and establish an alibi. Better to have it and not need it. While he was doing that, I was cutting through side streets, climbing through bushes and shrubs.

NEW YORKED

Getting things done without Bombay is also not an easy thing, but he's taught me enough that I could pop into an Internet café and do a little research and cover my tracks. I found out that Bret Carte lives with his parents, and he's been popped twice for sexual assault. Somehow he got a job guarding drunk women. The politicians will work themselves into frenzy over this.

It's dark and the houses are spread out so far that even if his neighbors looked outside, they wouldn't see me crouching in the bushes behind his house, watching him through the kitchen window.

The ski mask and the black clothing help.

The gun I borrowed will also help.

I check the clip for the twentieth time, just to be sure, my hands shaking a little as I push it back into place. I watch Carte for a little while, puttering around his kitchen. The child inside me expected fire and brimstone. That there'd be some outward sign of rot.

But he just looks like a guy with a bad attitude.

Still, I don't know why I didn't see it. He was right there in front of me. I could have reached out my hand and touched him.

Funny thing is, trapped in that trunk for the ride out here, in the dark with the roar of the engine and my own solitary thoughts, I didn't falter.

I am ready to end this.

THINGS WERE NEVER easy between us Chell, but do you want to know my favorite memory of you? The one that comes back to me right now, so easily?

It was the night of the blackout. Remember that? The entire metro area, dark.

It was so hot that day. It was even worse inside my apartment, which is why I left to go for a walk. I went outside and I ran into Good Kelly and she told me there was a party on Tibo's roof that night.

The last time the city went dark like that was back in the seventies. I wasn't alive for that but I heard stories. My dad told me working that night was chaos. Every stereotype and scary story you've ever heard about New York City came true. Riots in the streets, looting, people attacking each other. It was his first week with the FDNY and he nearly quit. But of course he didn't.

So this blackout was making me think of him, and whenever I thought of him it was kind of rough. I didn't really want to go to the party, but I'd been sequestered in my apartment, ignoring the phone, sitting on my fire escape, chain-smoking cigarettes and drinking the cheapest, ugliest beer I could find at the bodega.

But that night, finally, with the power out, there would be no light pollution, and we'd be able to see some stars. More than the twelve strong enough to fight through the haze. The thing that had been deprived of us for so many years.

I thought that maybe it was the kind of experience that shouldn't be taken in alone on a fire escape.

I left my apartment and found grills lining the sidewalks, carried down from roofs so frozen food could be cooked before it thawed and spoiled. Stoops were jammed with people drinking and playing acoustic instruments. Many of them barefoot, like a blackout turned the city into a provincial back-road town. Civilians mingled with police officers, standing at intersections, directing traffic through the clogged streets. I ate a cheeseburger cooked by a stranger, and when I thanked him he tossed me a beer.

When I got to Tibo's building I was having second thoughts, thinking maybe it wasn't the best time to be around people. No one needed me sulking in a corner, because then everyone would hover over me and want to know if I was all right and that would just make it worse for all of us.

But lingering by the staircase that led to the roof, I heard your voice though the open door, and that was enough to get me to the top.

The sky was orange on one end, fading to dark blue on the other.

There were a few dozen people cooking, putting yellow tape and construction cones by the edges of the roof. There was a band setting up on a wooden deck. People were hauling around coolers and passing out drinks.

I found Lunette sitting on the lip of the roof, one leg dangling over the chasm, her plaid shirt buttoned down just enough to make me feel bad for looking. She was struggling to get an empty Zippo to light. I offered her mine. She took two drags and said, *I thought you were dead.*

Yes, well, those rumors were exaggerated.

Two buildings over there was a ruffle of red. Even in the fading light, those legs looked like the same poison darts I saw on that burlesque stage in Coney Island. I couldn't see your face because it was buried in some gent's beard. Lunette saw it, too.

That's messed up if Chell knows you're here, she said.

It's fine.

Right. Listen, why do you keep doing this to yourself? And by this I mean Chell. And by Chell I mean her breaking your heart on a weekly basis. Why don't you just find yourself a nice girl and settle down.

It's complicated. And what do you mean 'settle down'?

You know what I mean. You need something stable.

Stable how? Stable like horse?

I regretted the words before I said them but I said them anyway. Lunette took a long drag of her cigarette and poured the smoke out of her lungs. She said, *I'll let you take that one. But just know I do so under great duress.*

Look...

Don't say anything. I'll tell you this much, at least I've accepted that it's never going to be good for me.

Chell gives me something no one else can.

Right.

Lunette got up and walked away. I went in the opposite direction, toward the last building at the end of the row, where no one else had set up camp. I leaned against a dormant steam pipe.

If I was still a kid, I would have laid on my back and stared at the sky, and I would imagine my dad up there somewhere, in heaven maybe, and he would be watching down on me. I would find the brightest star and say that it was him. And every time I saw it I would find solace.

But the sun was gone and laying on my back, all I could find, filling every inch of my vision, was an overcast sky.

I lit a cigarette and slid myself to the corner of the roof and looked over the edge. I thought about my dad being gone and the anger that threatened to push me over. I wondered if the fall would be enough to stop it.

Ashley?

No matter how many times you've seen me cry, I never wanted you to see me cry again but I couldn't seem to stop when you were around.

You sat down on the roof next to me and said, *Why didn't you tell me you were here?*

I didn't answer, so you lit your own cigarette. I listened to you inhale and exhale, the smell of cigarette smoke lingering with the perfume of lavender.

You said, *You're thinking about him, aren't you?*

I couldn't hide it. The muscles in my stomach convulsed. You pulled my head close to your chest and stroked my hair. You said, *You're thinking about whether the fall would be enough, weren't you?*

... Yes.

Honey, I promise you, it's never going to be okay, but it's going to get better.

I don't believe you.

You know how I get along with my dad. We're okay, but we've never been close. When my mom died, you know how hard it was? And you've got a great mom. I wish I could have had a relationship with my dad like you had with yours.

You kissed me on the cheek, and I asked, *Who's the gent?*

You laughed and said, *Some guy. He left already.*

Where is he from?

Connecticut.

Of course. No one who lives here is actually from here anymore.

He's not a gent.

He had on a sweater in the middle of June. I'm sorry, he's a gent. Anyway, forget him, I hope wherever he's going he has better luck than we're having here.

With what?

I pointed up and said, *No stars.*

Ashley.

I was hoping we could see them. That's why I came. That's the only reason I'm here.

Ashley.

I thought, maybe if I go out and try to be social and I saw the stars, I don't know. It would remind me how small I was. That my problems are small in comparison. Does that even make any sense?

Ashley Florian Fucking McKenna. Will you please stop talking?

You placed your hands on either side of my face and turned my head, and all that light I expected to see in the sky was scattered across the city.

The roofs were webbed with long strands of white Christmas lights. Miles of them, stretched around the corners of the buildings and cutting patterns over the deck. There were lanterns, and candles with covers to block the wind. All across the city there were dots of light, the golden glow of candles in windows and the blue tint of flashlights shooting through the streets.

With all the darkness, that light reached out forever.

No remnants of my father's blackout.

The words you whispered to me right then, I didn't hear them. Not really.

You said, *We found the angels of our better nature, Ashley.*

The music started. A couple of acoustic guitars, then a violin and an accordion. Bongos and a xylophone. A banjo. The music swelled in waves, slow and relaxed, and then someone plugged an amplifier into a generator and the music crashed into us.

You pulled me to my feet and into the crowd. There were more people than could possibly be safe up there, but no one was worried about that. No one was worried about anything. We raised our hands to the sky, stomping our feet and singing the words to songs we didn't know.

In the weeks and months and even years after my dad died, my life was full of people who would ask me if I was okay. And I hated that question. He was murdered by the mistakes of our past. Mistakes none of us were responsible for making.

You never asked me if I was okay. You just held my hand and let me cry.

No matter how things broke down between us, I will always have that.

You and me on that roof, floating amongst the stars.

CARTE IS STANDING by the refrigerator, putting something away, his back to the sliding door that isn't locked. I push it open and lead with the gun. It's the first thing he sees. He looks at it, frozen, like he doesn't know what it is. Then the realization hits and his body goes rigid.

I climb the rest of the way into the kitchen and put my finger up to my lips, so he knows to be quiet. I don't like that he lives with his parents and I'd like to keep them out of this.

I wave the gun at the table, indicating that he should sit. He obeys. I slide out a chair across from him. I give him a minute to let the gravity of it sink in. Make sure he gets a good look at the gun. I put it on the table, resting it on the butt, but I don't take my hand off it. Then I ask him, "Why?"

"Why what?"

"Why did you kill her?"

He pauses. "Who?"

"Do not fuck with me right now."

He brings his hands to his face and rubs the skin around his temples, contorting his face. "I don't know."

"Yes you do. Or else you wouldn't have done it."

He looks away from me. "I'm sick."

"Who else did you attack? There was someone else, wasn't there? A second woman."

He peeks at me through his fingers, like a child. "How did you know that?"

"Because you're sloppy. There were two sets of DNA."

He speaks so low I can barely hear him. "She wouldn't report me to the cops. She loves me."

My hand tightens around the gun. There is so much bad about him. So easy to believe the world would be better without him in it. I fight to keep my voice steady. "The girl you dumped in Queens. Tell me what happened."

"Why?"

"Consider this your last rites."

"You can't kill me."

"You killed her. Why can't I kill you?"

His voice catches, thick in his throat. "I'm sorry. I'm so, so sorry."

He cries. A trickle at first, then gushing. Tears streaming down his flushed face. He wraps him arms around himself, hugging himself, and leans forward.

He's a blight. A big broken thing.

The sight of him bawling, that's not what does it. What

holds me still is the kitchen. The way it looks. The faux-wood surfaces and the stainless steel appliances. The boomerang pattern on the countertops. The cuckoo clock over the stove's exhaust fan. It looks like a kitchen anybody could have grown up in.

My parent's house has the same boomerang pattern on the countertops.

"Listen," I tell him. "I'm not your mother. I'm not your priest. I'm not your lawyer. I'm not even your conscience. So don't fucking rationalize what you did. Just tell me why. Tell me why you would do that to somebody. Somebody who never hurt you."

"I wasn't myself."

"Stop it. I want a real answer."

He looks at the floor. "She had no right to talk to me like she did."

"Like what?"

"She was pretty and I tried to talk to her. And she blew me off like I was a joke. And I'm not. I'm not a joke."

"No. You're not a joke. You're a man, right?"

"It's not like that. But I was angry."

"Why were you angry?"

"Because. Sometimes I get angry. I can't control myself."

"Why do you get angry?"

"People not respecting me."

"Why?"

His eyes flash red. "Because I'm not smart. I'm not handsome. I'm big. That's all. My whole life people laughed at me. Told me I was stupid. And I'm not stupid. It's not right. It's not fair."

"You showed her, I guess."

I look down at the gun, sitting on the table. His shoulders slump, like the air has been let out of him. His face is blank.

Those last few moments of Chell's life must have been so scary. So painful.

The worst part, the very worst part, is that I see him for what he is.

Someone who's been hurt, and the only way he knows how to cope is to hurt other people. What Tibo said, about humans just being animals. We are, but with one major difference: We're the only animals who need to share pain.

He looks at me with eyes huge and pleading, but for mercy or death, I can't tell. I'm not even sure he knows.

The kitchen is silent, save for the sound of us breathing and the hum of the dishwasher. The gun is heavy and cold and hard.

Violence is a learned trait. If it's learned than you can choose to unlearn it. I stand up from the table, a little dizzy, the oxygen in here too thin. The gun is still trained between Carte's eyes.

He sits back, waiting for the shot.

My rage is a white hot point in my stomach, burning like a sun. Begging to be given life in a terrible fucking explosion that will obliterate him, and me with it.

Inhale, exhale. Unlearn it.

He asks, "Are you going to kill me now?"

I chew on my words for a minute, trying to put them in the right order. "I needed there to be some kind of explanation. Like a reason she died. A conspiracy or a vendetta. Something I could contextualize and understand. I fought so hard to put a story on her death because I didn't want to accept the reality that sometimes terrible fucking things happen, and you can't control them. All you can do is learn from them and try to be better. I don't know. I don't know if this even makes sense." I grip the gun so hard it hurts. Deep breath. "No. I am not going to kill you."

"Why?"

"I'm breaking the cycle."

And I leave.

Down the patio stairs and across the backyard, to the next street over. I leave Bret Carte and everything he did in that kitchen. Hopefully along with a part of myself that I never have to see again.

When I'm a few blocks away and out of the shadows I ditch the mask, pull out the burn phone I bought earlier in the night, and call the 9th Precinct, ask for Detective Grabowski.

As the phone rings I hold it against my face in the crook of my shoulder, and check the gun with shaking hands, just to make sure it's still empty. I don't know why I need to check, but I do.

NiNeTeEn

THE LAST NIGHT of Apocalypse and I can't bring myself to go inside. It's my last night too, but I'm not telling anyone. Goodbyes are easier when you don't have to make them.

Tibo knows I'm leaving. Plus everyone I visited on my apology tour. Bombay might forgive me one day. Lunette isn't too burned up, but she's still worried about me. Bad Kelly slammed the door in my face, but I'm glad I at least got to tell her I was sorry.

Ginny, I don't know. I feel like I owe her something. Whether it's a handshake or a kick in the shin. I sent her a text: *Thank you. I'm sorry. Pick whichever one fits.*

Never heard back. I hope she read it.

And Margo, I practically prostrated myself before her. It wasn't right, the way I treated her. She's a better person than me. She saw that I was loaded and going through some shit and cut me some slack.

Let her have this place. She deserves it more than I do.

She's inside. So are a lot of other people with whom I share broken memories of wild nights. They're just stories now. I don't need them anymore.

I watch the façade of the bar for a little while and wonder how it'll look as a Starbucks. Like a fucking nightmare, probably. I'll miss a lot of things but this place will be high up on the list. I'm just turning to leave when the door opens. Tibo walks toward me, lighting a cigarette. "Saw you lurking. Forgot something."

He hands me an envelope. It's thick. I open it up and it's filled with cash.

"What is this?"

"Your cut."

"What do you mean, my cut?"

"From the silver. You told me Kuffner's dad had a boat. You said to cut you in."

"Dude, I was kidding." I hold the envelope back toward him. "I can't take this."

"Too bad. It's yours."

He pulls me into a hug and disappears back into the bar.

A snowflake smacks my jacket, dissolves into water. I look up and there are a few stray flakes, floating down between the buildings, lit by the streetlights.

Footsteps behind me, coming down the block. I turn and it's Bombay. We stand and stare at each other for a few moments. I ask, "Are you going to hit me again? You should, but a little warning just so I could brace myself would be nice."

He shakes his head. "Not this time."

"Good."

He nods. Looks up the street, back down the other way. Asks, "One last drink?"

"I'm living clean. For a little while, at least."

"Not what I was thinking."

ESPERANTO IS MOSTLY empty. Usually it would be packed with kids from the NYU dorms up the block, but winter break sent most of them home.

It used to be that before me and Bombay were old enough to get into bars, we would come here. That was back before the smoking ban, and there was this little alcove in the back with books and easy chairs and a little table right between us. He would order coffee and I would order green tea and we would sit and smoke cigarettes until the sun came up.

The easy chairs are gone. There are small wooden tables crammed in, a way for them to fit more people. Bombay shakes his head. "Nothing is sacred."

We slip into a table. The disinterested waitress comes over. Bombay orders a coffee and I get a green tea.

He says, "So this is it?"

"My flight leaves in the morning. I guess as long as the snow isn't so bad."

"Texas?"

"Yes."

"Seems dumb," he says.

"I may not stay there, but it seems like a good place to start. I can crash on Kelly's couch while I'm getting settled. After that, I don't know. It's a big country."

The waitress gives us our drinks and I put my hands

around the glass to warm them up. I tell him, "I have a million things to say to you. Thank you. Apologies. Everything. I was a really shitty friend and you were a great friend and I wish I had recognized that."

"I knew what I was getting into with you. You've always been a pain in the ass."

"No, really. I needed to hear what you were saying, even if it seemed like I wasn't listening. I appreciate that."

"I'm glad. And it all worked out in the end." He pauses, says, "And it's over. They caught the guy. He'll go to jail and he won't be able to hurt anyone ever again. Some bad man is going to make him his boyfriend, and if there's any kind of justice in the world, that'll be it."

"Maybe. I don't know."

"So how's your mom with all of this?"

"She's more supportive that I would have guessed. Gave me the money for the ticket and everything. I think she knows I need a change of scenery."

"Will you be back?"

"Eventually, I figure."

"I'm asking this as your friend, and I don't want you to get upset, but is it just that you're running away from this? From what happened here? I mean, we can help."

"It's not that. At first it was. The day after you punched me I was like, 'Fuck this place, I'm going where people don't want to hit me.' But I spent some more time thinking about it, and you know what? I've never lived anywhere else. This is going to sound kind of cliché, but I need to grow up. And if I'm going to do that, I need to go out and do it, not wait around for it to happen."

"I know why you need to do it, but I wish you weren't

going."

"I love you too. You'll still be here when I get back."

"Technically. I'm moving to a place in Brooklyn. Lunette is thinking about it, too. A little cheaper there."

"Well. The great migration begins, I guess."

We lose track of the night, the two of us sitting there, trading stories about the city, about how things used to be and how they're going to turn out. We talk about the first time we came into Esperanto, and Apocalypse, and all the places that belonged to us in fleeting moments. Outside the window the snow swirls in circles under the streetlights, accumulating on the sidewalk and store awnings and cars.

Before we leave I ask him, "Can you do me a favor?"

"Of course."

"Keep an eye on Margo. And Lunette and my mom."

"I would have done that without you asking me."

I push in my chair, pull out the envelope from Tibo, hand it to Bombay. "I'll never be able to make amends for what happened to your apartment, but I hope this helps."

Bombay flips through the money, raises an eyebrow. "I can't take this."

"You're going to have to. Otherwise the waitress is getting a huge tip."

"What'll you do for money?"

"This place couldn't break me. I'm sure I'll be fine."

IT'S PAST FOUR, maybe not yet five. MacDougal is quiet and covered under a blanket of snow that glows amber in the streetlights.

There isn't a soul in the street. The windows are dark and the wind whips around the buildings and over parked cars that are disappearing under piles of white. I walk to the middle of the street and the only sound is the crunch under my feet. I look for fresh footprints besides the one I leave behind me, but there aren't any.

There have been nights when I've been on this street and there have been so many people spilling out of the bars that traffic stops. And now it's deserted. Untouched by a city of more than eight million people. Everything is covered with a white blanket that's been thrown over the grime and the dirt, the trash on the street.

The quiet saturates me, my clothes soaked from the snow that won't stay snow on my body. It's not cold, though. The way it doesn't get cold sometimes when it's snowing, like the flakes are sucking it up and you can stand outside in a t-shirt and feel okay about it.

I put my canvas bag down in the middle of the street and sit on top and watch. Pull my hat down closer to my eyes. Any second I expect a wave of people to come thundering around the corner, like everyone ran off to watch something real quick but they'll be right back.

It's like the whole city took a deep breath, exhaled, and finally agreed to a long-needed nap.

Pretty soon it'll wake up. The snow will be crushed and trampled underfoot. It'll turn black from discarded trash and car exhaust. It'll melt into giant piles of slush that pool at the corners of the sidewalks and people will have to jump over for fear of drowning. The cabs will be back out and the revelers will be here again.

But right now it's the most beautiful thing I've ever seen in a city full of beautiful things.

Here's the thing about living in New York City: There are people stretched around the block, ready to tell you what the thing is about living in New York City. But those people don't live here. They live in an idea of what they want the city to be. It ends up defining them before they have the chance to define their own experience.

Instead of defining this moment, I let it happen. Watch the snow sparkle in the streetlights as it drifts to the ground. Listen to the wind breathing around the buildings like a lover on the next pillow.

I put in my earbuds for the walk to the subway, set my iPod to pick a random song. Iggy Pop comes on. "The Passenger".

Ha.

That works.

I touch my hand to the snow and pull in the moment, one that will never exist again outside the glass bottle of my memory.

Then a cab comes rolling around from West 3rd Street.

Ash McKenna will return in
City of Rose

Coming Soon from
Polis Books

ABOUT THE AUTHOR

Rob Hart is the associate publisher at MysteriousPress.com and the class director at LitReactor. Previously, he has been a political reporter, the communications director for a politician, and a commissioner for the city of New York. Rob is the author of *The Last Safe Place: A Zombie Novella*, and his short stories have appeared in publications like *Thuglit, Needle, Shotgun Honey, All Due Respect*, and *Helix Literary Magazine*. He lives in New York City.

Find more on the web at www.robwhart.com and on Twitter at @robwhart.

ACKNOWLEDGMENTS

Cheers to Josh Bazell and Craig Clevenger, both of whom contributed blood and sweat to the DNA of this book.

Thanks to Tony Tallon, Todd Robinson, Matt McBride, Chuck Palahniuk, Steve Weddle, Joshua Mohr, Jenny Milchman, Suzy Vitello, Ed Kurtz, Nik Korpon, Jon Gingerich, David Corbett, Chris Holm, Patrick Wensink, Johnny Shaw, Bryon Quertermous, Tom Pitts, Joe Clifford, and Otto Penzler. Writers and editors who gave me a kind word or counsel (and in the case of Tom and Joe, a killer burrito) through the process of getting this thing live.

To the teams at Shotgun Honey, All Due Respect, Crime Factory, Thuglit, Needle, and Helix, thank you for publishing my stories so I'd have a shot in the arm when I needed it.

To all the people who are going to call me out on inconsistencies with locations and historical timelines: Thanks for reading so closely, but also, shut up. I took some liberties.

Thanks to Tom Spanbauer and Michael Sage Ricci and Kevin Meyer and everyone in my Dangerous Writing workshop. You all left a thumbprint on this, and on me.

Cheers to Renee Pickup and Jessica Leonard at Books & Booze, who hosted the first interview about this book.

Huge thanks to Dennis Widmyer, Kirk Clawes, Josh Chaplinsky, Cath Murphy, and everyone at The Cult and

LitReactor. I would not be here without the support and sanctuary of those communities.

Bigger thanks to my parents, for doing right by me and understanding this is a work of fiction (please stop making plans for an intervention, Ma).

Humongous thanks to my agent, Bree Ogden, who is a rock star superhero. And to my editor and publisher, Jason Pinter, for his unwavering enthusiasm for this book.

To everyone I should have thanked who I forgot to include: Fuck. I am so sorry.

Finally, and mostly, thank you to my wife Amanda. For *everything*. I don't even know where to start.